Carol,
Great to meet
you in E. Lyme
Best wishes,
Ron Jansen

What is HERS

Ron Janson

SterlingHouse Publisher, Inc. Pittsburgh, PA

ISBN-10: 1-56315-451-X
ISBN-13: 978-1-56-315451-5
Trade Paperback

Library of Congress #2009922482

Requests for information should be addressed to:
SterlingHouse Publisher, Inc.
3468 Babcock Boulevard
Pittsburgh, PA 15237
info@sterlinghousepublisher.com
www.sterlinghousepublisher.com

Pero Thrillers
is an imprint of SterlingHouse Publisher, Inc.

Cover Design: Brandon M. Bittner
Interior Design: Kathleen M. Gall

Printed in U.S.A.

Dedication

To Marie,
the love of my life,
who enjoys the shoreline as much as I do.

Acknowledgments

A number of people have helped to make this novel possible.

First, my appreciation to Christopher J. Molyneaux, an attorney and friend, who provided valuable insight and information regarding criminal court proceedings, along with how cases are prosecuted and defended.

Next, my sincere thanks to my agent, Suzanne T. Isaacs, who continues to immerse herself in my work and helps to make it better.

Finally, now that two of my novels (this one plus *Red Money*) have been published by SterlingHouse, my gratitude goes out to an outstanding support team—Editor Megan Davidson, Production Manager Brandon Bittner, Graphic Artist Nicole Tibbitt, Operations Chief Jennifer Piemme, Promotional Director Lisa Keller, and CEO Cynthia Sterling.

Chapter 1

"I'm exhausted, but what a wonderful day this has been," Katherine Hunter-Kent said to her daughter, Anita, while finishing a cup of green tea on the verandah of her waterfront home as the sun was starting to set. Earlier that day, the first Friday in June, her only grandson, Jon, had received his high school diploma from a private school in Rhode Island. The elderly lady's son Tony (Jon's father) had barbecued steaks for a family dinner at Katherine's house, after they had all traveled back to Hunter's Point—the family compound on the eastern Connecticut shoreline of Long Island Sound. Over dinner, the four family members had chatted about the commencement ceremony and a graduation party tomorrow which the "family", many close adult friends, and some of Jon's friends from his prep school would be attending. Jon had left a half-hour ago with Michael Hunter, his only youthful relative, who had recently finished his second year of college and had returned to the family residence to spend the summer. The two boys, who hadn't been together since last Christmas, had gone out to visit some friends at a neighboring beach community.

Entering the verandah after he had cleaned up the outside grill area, Tony Kent joined his mother and sister, settling into one of the chairs and lighting a pipe. A pipe smoker for many years, Tony kept a pipe, pouch of tobacco, and one of his initialed lighters at his mother's home (known within the family as the "main house") in a drawer in one of the verandah tables.

Katherine, approaching eighty years of age, smiled at her two "children" (now in their late forties) as she gazed out at the water glistening from the rays of the setting sun. "Jon's graduation from high school, along with Michael's two years ago, means that three family generations have now spent a good portion of their childhood here," she exclaimed. "Except for my mother and father, all of us in the Hunter and Kent families have enjoyed our youth and grown into adults here. Jon and Michael join my brother David—may his soul rest in peace, your cousin Jerry, the two of you and me. You probably don't know what this means to me."

Reflecting on what his mother had just said, Tony replied, "You're right, Mom, I'm not sure that I do." He looked at his sister, seeking out her thoughts.

"I think I understand, Mother," Anita said, casting a wry smile at her brother. "There's a lot of history here at Hunter's Point, and we love when you talk about it and your deep feelings for our family's home and how it's followed us through the generations."

That was all the prodding that Katherine needed. "Let me *again* remind both of you, especially you, Tony, that I consider this place to be my only true home. I understand that with what happened to you here and your job in Hartford you need to have your space and your permanent home in that area." Chuckling softly, she said, "You don't get subjected to the indoctrination that Anita gets from being here every day with me." Then, looking lovingly at him, she continued. "I do cherish the summers you spend in your cottage here and look forward to seeing more of you now than I do during the rest of the year. My hope is to spend the rest of my life here. Should I ever get very old and feeble and unable to care for myself, I think I would rather be shot than wind up in some nursing home."

"Come on, Mom, you don't really mean that...do you?" Tony asked. "I've never heard you talk quite like this before."

"Well, maybe that thought is a bit extreme, but think about this, Son. How many people are blessed with a pristine five acre wooded shoreline property with two winterized homes protected by a high rocky embankment and two summer cottages adjacent to a private beach? We are truly one of the luckiest families anywhere, thanks to my father having the vision for a family retreat when I was just a baby, and then the tenacity to build this home when I was a young child and complete the compound in the late fifties when I was a young woman, married and getting ready to have your sister and you. And to imagine the paltry sum he paid for the land, even considering values in those days, especially when you think of what it's worth today. As I get older, I realize his wisdom in building an additional winterized house close to this one and the cottages along the beach with working fireplaces so they could be used for much of the year, except when it's really cold. Can you believe it? Our family has inhabited this incredible place for most of the past fifty years! With your grandfather naming it after himself, his legacy lives on. Even though your father was a Kent, he liked the fact that Daddy chose his own surname rather than some descriptive name, and always said it was the best one."

"And, let's not forget, Tony, that your son is named after Grandpa Jonathan, so he's connected," Anita chimed in, looking wistfully out at the water that was now starting to darken under the evening sky, and fully understanding the feelings of her mother.

"Speaking of young Jon," Katherine said, "I'm so proud of him for curing that youthful temper of his and taking it to the prep school's hockey rink, improving his grades and earning that college scholarship."

Tony smiled at his mother and mused as he puffed his pipe. He was thinking of his son's accomplishments over the past two years, culminating in his acceptance at a college in southern New Hampshire. Soon his thoughts drifted to wondering why, when away, he tended to distance himself from Hunter's Point and his mother's affection for the place. He realized that it was at least partly due to the sadness he felt over his wife, Rebecca, dying in this very house after a battle with cancer when she was only thirty-eight, just before their son's tenth birthday. Apart from wanting to have his own place as an adult, this was the main reason he and Jon lived in one of the cottages when they spent the summers here, and why he had Anita drive his mother to his home outside Hartford for occasional weekend visits during the winter when the cottages were shut down. He did not like to sleep in the main house any more. He reminded himself, though, how grateful he was that his mother and sister collaborated to be a surrogate mother for his young boy who was severely traumatized by his mother's death.

Tony brought himself back to the present. "Okay, but I never fully understood why, after Grandpa Jonathan passed away, you took this house instead of the one built later that Uncle David and Aunt Martha lived in, and that Jerry inherited after they died. Didn't the two of you alternate staying in the other house when you visited Grandpa and Grandma when they were still alive and before you had Anita and me?

Did you and Uncle David come to some sort of agreement after Grandpa died?"

"Well, sort of," Katherine answered. "Actually, the choice wasn't mine. Since David was older, it was his choice as to which house he wanted. He had gotten used to the newer one and liked it, so he chose it. He did ask me, though, if I was agreeable."

"I know the answer to that one," Anita said.

Katherine smiled at her daughter. "I suppose that some things are just meant to be. I always preferred this house, even though the other one is lovely…and newer. Even when I stayed in the other house, I knew that this was the one I wanted for myself when that time would come. Maybe it's because this one was the original house and there's so much history in it for me. I don't exactly know all my reasons, but I do know that I was delighted with David's decision. It's made all the years that I've been here so pleasant."

"I think it's been good for all of us," Anita interjected. "Jerry and Miriam seemed to be happy here during the warmer seasons and Susan seems to adore living here on a full-time basis. She said it's like a dream come true for her to live in a place like this. I get the feeling it's an achievement for her."

"Yes, I think you're right about that," Katherine replied. "I know that Miriam loved it here and regretted not being able to return after the divorce. Miriam cherished her summers here, and also the spring and fall weekends. She told me that more than once. Jerry doesn't talk about her much anymore, but Michael does and said his mother will miss being here this summer, even though she was left with a very nice home with access to a beach in Fairfield County as part of the settlement. I'll miss her."

"Me, too," Anita said quietly. "But, we have to deal with reality. Miriam is gone and Susan is now part of our family. I'm starting to make the adjustment, although it has taken several months to do so."

Katherine sighed. "I agree with what you just said. During the times I've spent with Susan since she's been here, I also get the feeling that she really likes it here, and didn't seem to mind moving into a house where her predecessor lived."

"I guess it goes with being a Hunter, or a Kent," Tony said softly, reflecting again on his deceased wife.

"I wouldn't know," Anita said, snickering. "I never brought anyone into the family."

"Touché," Tony replied.

Katherine sensed that her daughter was feeling discomfort. "Even though it's been strange having someone so young replace Miriam, with whom I had bonded, I'm glad Jerry kept his house and that Susan likes it here. It would be lonely with only Anita and me here, especially during the off-season. Anita's library job leaves me alone most of the day, but that I can handle. The nights and weekends during the winter get lonely without people around."

"I agree," Anita said.

"So, you don't mind it that Jerry travels a lot during the week and Susan has her nursing job at the outpatient clinic?" Tony asked.

"Not at all," his mother replied. "Remember that, before the divorce, Jerry and Miriam were like you—only here full-time in the summer and then weekends in the spring and fall. Now, with Jerry giving up their other home to Miriam, he's here most weekends, except for when he and Susan spend a weekend at his apartment in New York, and occasionally during the week. When Jerry travels, Susan usually joins us one night during the week for dinner. She's been very sweet to me and tries hard to bridge the age gap. I enjoy sitting out here and reading during the day, and you know that I have my noontime soap opera that I've watched for as long as I can remember. With my walks along the beach and occasional afternoon tea sessions with an old friend and now, Dan Davies, a new friend whom I've grown to really like, I have just about all I need during the day. And with you and Jon moving in for the summer, my life is complete. Did I hear you correctly when you said that my grandson is working as a life guard again?"

"Yes, you did. He'll be at the same beach as he was last year. It's a good summer job for him, and will give him the spending money he'll need next year for college. Mom, you mentioned Dan Davies. Isn't he the retired cop from New York City who moved to Condor's Nest Beach last year?"

"Yes. Actually, he was a plain clothes detective for many years before retiring."

"That's an interesting kind of person to have as a new friend. Perhaps I should get to know him, now that I'll be here for the summer."

"Yes, indeed you should. He is such a nice man. What a wonderful surprise when I first met him at Rocky Bar last year. The stories he has about his days as a detective are fascinating. Crime is something we're not much exposed to here, and it's a subject I've never given much thought to. Sometimes, when I sit out here with him in the afternoon sipping tea, I feel spellbound by his tales and wish I could visit some of the locations where they took place. Whenever I say that, though, he reminds me that many of those neighborhoods are not so nice and not the best place for an elderly lady like me."

Katherine leaned back and closed her eyes. She was getting tired and slowly got up out of the verandah chair. Bidding good night to Anita and Tony, she picked up her china and walked out of the verandah on her way to her bedroom.

Tony was at the end of his pipe smoke and beginning to clean out the bowl. After his mother had left, Tony turned to his older sister and said, "I'm going back to the cottage to watch a movie, but before I go, you said earlier that you wanted to talk to me about something."

Anita rose from her cushioned rattan chair, walked slowly to the edge of the verandah that overlooked the water, and then turned to face her brother. Choking a bit as she began to speak, she blurted…"I know about the affair between you and Susan, and I think it could be a very bad situation for this family. Jerry and Susan have only been married for six months. What in the world are you doing?"

Tony gazed out toward the ocean, rose from the sofa and said softly, "I'm not sure that I know. She's so young and beautiful and reminds me of what I've been missing during all these years without Rebecca." He winced as the guilt he'd repressed since that eventful night started to re-emerge.

"I can understand that. As I alluded to before, I've *never* been married and there are many nights when I long for the touch and feel of a man in my bed. But, while I have had a few affairs, I try to do so discreetly and outside the family and Hunter's Point. Would you like for me to go to bed with Jerry—say, in the cottage that's vacant?"

"Okay, you're right. I probably should end it, but…but, it's just so hard. Susan is a physical magnet. In case you haven't noticed, she is absolutely drop dead gorgeous and seems to be looking for an outlet when Jerry's in New York. I've never really thought of her as being in the immediate family. That was Miriam. She was the typical relative. Susan is his second wife, but I don't think of her as a blood relative. She's more like a young girlfriend. And the way she looks at me sometimes...."

"Well, maybe Susan has an excess appetite for sex, and maybe she doesn't care about the repercussions, but you're running a risk of setting off an explosion that could really rock this family. Jerry's and Miriam's divorce was hard enough to deal with, and this affair would be especially devastating for Mother. At this point, I don't think she knows anything about you and Susan."

"I certainly hope not. Do you think anyone else knows? What about Jerry? And how did you find out?"

"I don't know about Jerry. He's never said anything. As for me, I found out when I was strolling outside the house and going toward the beach one night a couple of weeks ago. It was Thursday before Memorial Day weekend. Mother had just gone to bed. I heard some sounds and thought I saw the outline of something moving in the sand, perhaps an animal of some sort on the beach. When I got closer, I ducked behind the cottage closest to the beach. What I saw was two human bodies—the two of you. You must have come up for a breath of air from underneath a blanket."

Tony winced again, realizing that his recent nocturnal rendezvous was no longer a secret. "Yeah, that was quite a night. I had come a day early for the long weekend to spend some extra time with Mom, and Jerry wasn't returning until Friday afternoon from a business trip. Susan wanted to go swimming in the nude and then make love on the beach. The water was very cold, so we warmed up under the blanket on the beach."

"I guess you did, judging from the moans and groans I heard. Swimming around here in May during the day is almost unheard of, much less at night."

"Yeah, I agree with that. It was the first time swimming so early in the season for me. Now, I'm embarrassed at getting caught by my big sister. I hope no one else was roaming the beach that night."

"Hmmm," Anita mused. After a moment of silence, she said, "You know, Tony, my reflection is a bit fuzzy, but I think I did see the outline of a person down near Rocky Bar. But that's far away from where you and Susan were, and nobody could see that far unless they had a pair of binoculars and were looking right at you. There was no moonlight that night as I recall, so you were probably not seen—except by me."

Tony, now totally chagrined, looked away from his sister and shook his head slowly. "Okay…I get the message. Now, I'm going to go back to the cottage for *another* Friday night alone. That much I can promise you."

Chapter 2

The early Saturday morning sun glistened over the waves of Long Island Sound and awakened Katherine. She rubbed her eyes and silently said a prayer of thanks for the beautiful day they would have for young Jon's graduation party.

Katherine, an early riser, loved the quiet beginnings of the days along the shoreline. She never tired of the sound of the waves gently crashing into the stone cliff and adjoining beach. She awakened to it and went to sleep with it, and prayed that she would never have to be in a place where she would not be able to hear this beloved rhythm that had been with her for so long.

After dousing her face with water, she showered, ran a brush through her medium length hair that was now all white, and got dressed. Her sunglasses and visor were in their customary place on one of the end tables on the screened verandah overlooking the ocean.

A large sandy beach extended north to the end of the family's property, where it ended at a rocky barrier called Rocky Bar, which extended out into the Sound for about sixty yards and bordered Condor's Nest—a private beach community. There was a path through a wooded area leading to this neighboring beach, and Katherine had gotten to know several of the residents while thoroughly enjoying her walks along the beach. She was getting too old to venture out on the rocky barrier, but liked to sit on one of the large rocks at the water's edge and gaze toward the far end of Long Island's north shore. She was about to return to get started on her contribution to the day's festivities—baking some of her famous pies—when she heard a soft whistle.

"Good morning, Katherine," a male voice called out.

Katherine turned and smiled. Recognizing her friend, she waved and said, "Good morning to you, Dan, and a beautiful one it is."

"What a great day for Jon's graduation party."

"Oh, isn't it divine? I couldn't be more pleased. I'm so glad you decided to come. I feel like I had to twist both of your arms to make an appearance. That's quite a stressful effort for an old lady like me."

"Well, I am honored that you've included me in your circle of family and friends, being that we got to know each other last year by accident at this very spot."

"Well, Mr. Davies, my feeling is that anyone who likes this beach and Rocky Bar in the early morning, and tea on my verandah in the late afternoon as much as I do—which you seem to—ought to be someone that I'm friendly with." She held out her hand to him and, trying to keep a straight face, said, "I do like having a big, strong law enforcement officer here to protect me from any evil creatures. Especially one that's so nice."

"*Retired detective*, with the emphasis on *retired*," he chuckled. "This is a long way from New York City, and I certainly am grateful to have found such a great place, away from the *real* evil creatures of the world. After a year here, my former life seems so distant. I just wish that my Sarah could have been with me to enjoy this."

"I know how you feel, and can see in your eyes when you talk about her that you miss her. I had my Walter for a long time…a *good long time*, but it still gets lonely and it's never the same without them."

"Well, I guess we should be thankful for this beautiful place and this lovely day."

"Indeed, Dan, we need to be thankful for each day, since we never know what the next one will bring. And this place…there's a mystique about it that you can't put into words. You have to be here to feel it. But it's very real. God has given us a bit of paradise here."

"You're right about that," Dan said with a smile. "You do get a special feeling just being here."

"Well, that's enough melancholy," Katherine sighed. "I must get back and start my baking."

"I think your pies may have been what induced me to come today…just kidding! By the way, how are you feeling? And how's your energy?"

"I'm still tired a lot…can't seem to get through the day without my afternoon nap. I'd probably fall asleep sipping tea with you, Susan and Anita if I didn't take my nap. I get nauseated every once in a while when I'm sitting around and sometimes get cramps in my legs. Other than that, I'm just dandy! Anita hasn't been feeling that well, either. She's been having the same bouts with nausea that I've been having and sometimes gets leg cramps when she sits for a long time. Fortunately, at the library, she gets to be on her feet for at least part of the day, which helps to keep her circulation going. Both of us have lost some energy. Mine is understandable at my age, but Anita's condition bothers me."

"Hasn't this nausea, tiredness and energy loss been going on for two or three months now?" Dan asked. "Have you thought about seeing a doctor?"

"Oh, I've seen enough doctors over the years. I guess this is just part of getting old."

"If you say so," Dan said, shaking his head. "You mentioned the name Susan. Isn't she Jerry's new wife?"

"Yes. I thought you'd met her."

"No, I don't think so. You've mentioned her name a few times, but I've never seen her. She's never been at your house when I've been there for tea. What's she like?"

"Well, for one thing, she doesn't like tea like you and I do. She drinks coffee when we're together—hot when it's cold and iced when it's hot. Are you sure you haven't met her?"

"Not yet," he replied.

"Well, you will this afternoon at the party. And, when you do, you won't forget her. She's quite young and very pretty. I think Jerry's going through a mid-life crisis—divorcing Miriam for Susan. I can't understand it for the life of me. Miriam is so nice and such a good mother and devoted wife. I really like her. She was devastated when Jerry told her. And it seemed to happen so suddenly, although I suspect that Jerry had been seeing Susan secretly for a while before anyone knew. I just hope this divorce isn't going to affect my great nephew, Michael, too much. He's very devoted to his mother and has been splitting his time between his parents, so I don't see him as much as I used to. I must say, though, that Susan is very nice to me and is pleasant to be with."

"Yeah, you never know how those things are going to work out. I take it that Miriam won't be at the party today."

"No, that would be uncomfortable," Katherine said, lamenting the divorce. "It's very sad, because I know that Miriam misses this place and may never get back here again. That was part of the settlement. Miriam got their home in Fairfield County and some money. I've actually thought of inviting her here if Jerry and Susan ever take a trip far away, but I'd have to do it on the sneak." Katherine winked at Dan as she uttered the last sentence.

Dan winked back. "That's too bad. I had just met Miriam last fall and then heard that she and Jerry were splitting. My first impression was that she seems nice and is attractive. Divorces can be nasty and both sides usually lose. Well, I'll let you go now and see you later." Dan turned and ventured out toward the end of Rocky Bar.

"Three o'clock, in case you forgot," Katherine called out, as she began walking along the beach back toward the compound.

At the appointed time, the guests started to arrive at Jon's graduation party. Forty or so had been invited and all came. Some just wanted a chance to spend a glorious early June afternoon at Hunter's Point. A gentle breeze was blowing, just enough to cause some whitecaps on the waves of the clear blue Long Island Sound. The gracious lawns on the property had been cut two days before and the setting was magnificent. Within half an hour, the guests were mingling, sipping their initial round of drinks and nibbling the food that was spread around on the tables. Looking out the kitchen window and noticing that the party was in full swing, Katherine turned off the oven, covered her pies and placed them on the counter for the catering people to bring out later, after dinner was served. After closing the oven door, she walked out her kitchen door and toward the large grassy area to greet and mingle with the guests.

Jerry Hunter had just returned from a walk on the beach and spotted the young man he thought of as his nephew. "Let me be one of the first to congratulate you, Jon. I wish I could have been at the graduation ceremony yesterday, but I had to do some schmoozing with one of our most important customers. My boss would have gone ballistic if I hadn't been there."

"I understand, Uncle Jerry," Jon replied. "Hey, a graduation ceremony is kind of boring. Today's a lot more fun."

"I'll second that," Jerry shot back, giving Jon a bear hug. He then strolled over to the outdoor bar set up on the sloping lawn between the two main houses. "Gin and tonic, please, and make it a double," he cracked to the bartender. "It's been a long week and now it's time to unwind. So, bring me up-to-date, Jon. I can't believe I haven't seen you since Christmas."

"Well, let's see. I got my grades up during the past year, which Dad, Grandma and Aunt Anita are all happy about."

"You should be happy about that, also."

"Yeah, I am," Jon said, feeling his chest expanding a bit.

"Michael told me that you were accepted by a good college. I know he's happy for you, especially since you won't be that far from Boston. I hope you two can see each other more often."

"For sure," Jon replied. "Don't see any reason why not. So, how are you doing?"

"I'm fine…getting adjusted to a new life and a new wife."

"Yeah, that was quite a surprise! I hope I can get to know Susan this summer. I only met her for the first time at Christmas."

"I guess a lot of people were surprised—shocked might be a better word—that I was attracted to another woman. I got smitten. I don't know how else to say it. I didn't plan for this to happen, but it did. I know my son is not pleased, but I hope he can adjust as time goes on."

Jon gazed past "Uncle Jerry" and out at the water. "Well, your mother is very special and really can't be replaced…by anyone." Tears started to appear in his eyes as he finished the sentence.

Jerry wrapped his left arm around the young man and held him tightly. "I know and, for what it's worth, I'm thankful that this didn't happen when Michael was younger. I know what you went through losing your mother at such a young age and how we all tried to pitch in to do what we could. But, as you say, you can't replace your mother. I know that Susan will not replace Miriam for Michael, but I also hope he'll accept her and be able understand my feelings."

Jon wanted get away from this subject and focus on his graduating and today's festivities. He wiped his moist eyes with the back of his right hand. "Come on," he said, easing away from Jerry's grip, "I've been waiting a long time for this day. We need to party!"

"You're right," Jerry said. "We've got to celebrate what you've done and move on. It *is* time to party!" He motioned to the bartender for a refill.

Katherine noticed Dan Davies standing by himself as she got to the large lawn where the party was taking place. She went over to him and leaned her head into his chest, as he gently put his arms on her shoulders. She then grabbed Dan's hand and escorted him toward where Jon was standing, as Jerry patted Jon on the shoulder and then walked over to meet a friend who had waved to him—his second drink in hand.

"Jon, I want you to meet Dan Davies, my friend from Condor's Nest," she said.

"Congratulations, young man," Dan said, "both for graduation and getting accepted to college, which your grandmother told me about over tea recently."

"Thank you, Mr. Davies. Grandma says you're from New York City?"

"Yep. I was. But, now I'm from over there," Dan said, pointing toward the woods and Condor's Nest Beach. "Sold my co-op in Riverdale, New York, bought a place near the beach next to this beautiful location, and retired just over a year ago."

"Cool. What did you do before you retired?"

"I was a detective with the New York City Police Department, for more years than I care to remember. It's nice to be here and able to relax just about every day."

"That sounds exciting. How many bad guys did you put away?"

"At least as many as the number of years that I worked on the force. But now I'd like to forget about it."

"Got it," the lad replied.

"I hear you're a hockey player. Are you going to play in college?" Dan asked, changing the subject.

"You bet. I got a partial scholarship and hope to get a full one after next year."

"Terrific. I love hockey. I'm still an avid Rangers fan, but the team hasn't been that good since winning the Cup back in the nineties."

"I like the Bruins, so we can have a little rivalry."

"Just as long as it's friendly," Dan retorted, as the two shook hands.

Katherine, who had been talking to a couple of friends nearby, saw that Dan and Jon were ending their conversation and motioned to Dan to join her again.

Dan rejoined Katherine and she introduced him to her friends. Tony had ended a brief conversation with a small group and was walking toward the bar. Susan was standing alone, directly in his path. Tony smiled as he approached her, momentarily mesmerized. *Damn it, she's so good looking,* he thought.

"Hey there, big boy," Susan whispered into Tony's ear.

"And hey to you, beautiful! Great day, huh?"

"Glorious…I wish we had the place to ourselves and could go to 'you know where' and do 'you know what'!"

Tony shuddered, thinking of last night's encounter with Anita. "You'd better not let Jerry hear you talk like that. He'd probably be mighty upset if he found out. By the way, do you think he suspects anything?"

"I don't know. Why don't we ask him?"

"Very funny."

Just then, Jerry approached them, on his way to the bar for another drink, with Michael walking next to him.

Susan noticed them out of the corner of her eye. "Hi, Honey," Susan said sensually to Jerry. "Enjoying the party?" She smiled at Michael, who feigned a smile back.

"Hi, my love…and congratulations to you, Tony. I just saw Jon and said the same to him. So, now we'll both have our little guys in college—drinking beer, causing havoc, chasing girls…."

Michael couldn't resist, retorting with, "Yeah, I'm going to take after my old man!"

"Touché," Tony interjected. "Jerry, you asked for that one!"

"This family is getting tough," Jerry chuckled. "Your little boy grows up and starts busting your chops!"

Susan was not amused and started to walk away, glancing furtively at Tony, who looked away—wanting to avoid any risk of their "secret" going beyond Anita.

"Okay, enough of the wisecracks," Jerry then said. "Let's enjoy this party." He gently grabbed Susan by the arm and motioned for her to escort him to the bar for another drink.

Tony stayed with Michael but cast a quick glance at Susan as she strolled away. He hoped no one had noticed and gazed at the Sound, his mind racing with thoughts about what Susan had just said and Anita's comments of last night. *I've got to get away from this fascination with her,* he thought. Placing his hand on the young man's shoulder, he spoke. "Michael, it really is good to see you again. We haven't had much time together since your mom and dad split, and with you being away at college. It was difficult to talk about it at Christmas. Are things going all right for you?"

"Yeah, I'm okay, Uncle Tony. I had a good year in college and I see Mom every chance I get. She came to Boston a few times during the school year and I spent part of the winter recess with her. I came here once a month last semester and am trying to get along with Susan, but to me she's just someone living under our roof."

"I understand," Tony said, nodding. "I kind of view her as Jerry's girlfriend, not a close relative like your mother. I guess you can only have one of those. She is quite a looker, though."

"I see you've noticed. I guess everyone has. My second mom—the beautiful babe! It's more like having an older sister, except this one sleeps with my dad."

Tony thought he should move the conversation in another direction. "On a lighter note, Jon pointed out the hideaway you guys found in Rhode Island near Wappinger Pond as we drove back yesterday along Route 1. If the ladies hadn't been with us, I would have taken a detour off the highway to see it. I probably should have, since they slept through most of the trip."

Michael smiled. "Oh, yeah, the abandoned cottage next to the YMCA camp...what a place! It's become a love nest for some guys. The rumor is that it was abandoned a couple of years ago when two elderly owners with no heirs went into a nursing home and the place went into a trust. One of Jon's friends at prep school, who's from the area, took him there last fall and Jon then told me about it. After I figured out where it was, I went out there on a weekend toward the end of the semester when the weather started to warm up with a college friend who has a car. We had a couple of girls with us. What a great place! Before Memorial Day and after Labor Day, you can really have privacy...if you know what I mean."

Tony winked at him and smiled back. "Hey, fella, you're approaching twenty-one, so I guess it's alright if the girl goes along with what you want to do. Come on, lover boy, let me buy you a drink. I hear we've got a well-stocked bar, being that I stocked it." Then, noticing Jerry saunter away from the bar with another drink, Tony said, "I just hope your dad leaves some for the rest of us."

By eight-thirty in the evening, all of the guests had left after enjoying a delicious barbecue, followed by a scrumptious dessert table. Michael, a gin and tonic in hand, was sitting at the edge of the rocky embankment between the two main houses, gazing out into the Sound as one of the coastal region's beautiful sunsets was starting to unfold. Susan had helped Katherine and Anita carry some things back to the main house and saw him. She called out, "Michael, have you seen your father?"

"He looked pretty smashed about half an hour ago. I saw him walking toward our house, so maybe he went to sleep it off."

"Well, that's just great," Susan countered, disdain evident in her tone. "Just when I'm looking for companionship."

"Well, maybe Dad is a bit old and worn out for a young, vibrant lady like you," Michael said with a snicker.

"Oh, your dad is all right—most of the time. He just hits the sauce too heavy sometimes. I hope this isn't one of those occasions."

Michael had planned on stretching his legs a bit before going out for the night. "I'm going to take a walk on the beach before I go out tonight. Jon and I are going to see a friend who has a place at Condor's Nest. See you later," he said as he walked away.

Susan stayed to watch what was left of the magnificent sunset. After staring out into the blue waters and watching the sun slowly drop below the western horizon, she strolled home, her mind consumed with lovemaking. She had hoped to find Jerry in their home intoxicated and wanting a sexual encounter. What she found, though, confirmed what Michael had suggested. Jerry was sound asleep on the living room couch. She tried to wake him, but to no avail.

Feeling frustrated, Susan then walked out of the back door toward Tony's cottage. Out of the corner of her eye, she saw him approaching from the outdoor bar, which was being shut down by the hired bartenders. She whistled softly, just loud enough so he could hear, and motioned toward the beach with her right arm.

Ten minutes later, Susan was at the rendezvous location. "I'm here, in the thicket," she said softly, as Tony got close and could hear her.

About thirty yards from Rocky Bar and away from the ocean on the fringe of a three-acre forest, there was a large thicket. The thick brush in front and woods on the other three sides formed a natural barrier. It was a perfect place for a nighttime interlude—virtually impossible to see inside. Tony had migrated from romancing girls during his youth to an occasional tryst with Rebecca and now lovemaking with Susan at a place he thought of as his private little domain. They were soon in each other's arms and then naked. Pine needles covered the sandy soil and made for a comfortable, bedlike setting for making love.

Susan, aided by a number of drinks, wanted to have sex and was extremely passionate. She assured him that Jerry was passed out and then began seducing him. Tony became excited. He looked at and then caressed her nude body.

Susan rolled over and gazed up at the sky after the act had been consummated. Tony was still caressing her. She looked at him and spoke softly. "Can you imagine what it would be like to have Hunter's Point all for yourself? I wonder what your grandfather must have felt as he walked along the beach in his early years here—knowing that this place was all his...his alone."

Tony looked at her with a puzzled expression. "That's something I've never thought of. Mom, Anita, Jon and I—and, I assume Jerry and Michael—have always considered ourselves very lucky to have this place as a family residence. I've never heard anyone in the family ask a question like this. What makes you wonder about that?"

"Oh, I don't know. Just a random thought I've had from time to time...what it must feel like to find a place like this and then be able to have it...all for yourself. Imagine what it must be like to say to yourself, 'this is mine...all mine.'"

After another couple minutes of intense kissing, they got dressed and emerged from the thicket. At Tony's direction, they began to walk back toward the houses separately, about two minutes apart—just in case anyone was walking on the beach from the other direction. Tony left first and walked at the water's edge. Susan followed, walking away from the water and close to the forest. She smiled to herself as she thought about how easy it was for her to seduce a man.

Michael had taken his walk to the end of Rocky Bar and was returning along the water's edge when he thought he heard a sound coming from somewhere close by. He saw Tony emerge from the thicket, followed by Susan. He ducked behind a large rock so he wouldn't be seen, and craned his neck around the rock to get a clear view. He was so startled that he started talking to himself. *Holy shit…Susan and Tony! Is this what goes on when Dad is away or when he gets drunk? He must be passed out at home! Maybe Tony was making more than idle chatter when he was talking about Susan this afternoon. And the way she was so close to him when Dad and I came over to see them. This is amazing! I can't imagine how pissed off Dad will be if he ever finds out. I've got to tell Mom that her replacement may be two-timing Dad. She'll love it! What a freakin' loser my old man is turning out to be. Trading in Mom for this sexy broad who looks like she's getting banged by his cousin—the man I think of as my uncle. You can't make this stuff up. No one would believe it!*

Chapter 3

The following day, Sunday, Michael was having a late morning breakfast when Jerry sauntered in, holding his head, which was throbbing.

"Had a little too much to drink yesterday, Dad?"

"Yeah…I suppose I did. Man, that was a blowout party. Guess I wanted to forget about the week on the road too much. Did I do anything I need to be aware of?"

"Maybe it's what you didn't do that you ought to be concerned about."

"What do you mean by that?"

"Oh, nothing much."

"Come on, Michael. I lost track of things just after eight o'clock. Did anything happen?"

"Nah, nothing Dad. I think all you did was come back here and fall asleep," Michael said, a wry smile appearing on his face. "So, where's your 'bride' this morning?"

"Still sleeping. Guess we both had a lot to drink."

Michael turned away and looked out the kitchen window toward the ocean, reflecting on what he had observed last evening. He had to keep from laughing out loud as he thought, *Oh, she may have had a lot of something all right—just not booze!*

"So, Son, what are you doing today?"

"Have you forgotten? I'm driving to see Mom today. I guess with you, Mom is outta sight outta mind. But she's still my mother and I love her deeply. I've got a few days before I start my job at the marina at Devil's Cove on Thursday. I'll be back Wednesday night."

"Yeah, yeah…I remember now. I'm leaving tomorrow for New York and then to Chicago. I'll be back Thursday night, so I hope we can talk about your first day on the job when I return."

"That should be exciting. Can't wait. Don't be surprised, though, if I'm not here."

"Say hello to your mother for me."

"Sure. Should I tell her you miss her?"

"Don't try to be so funny. Just keep it to a 'hello and hope you're well' message."

Michael smiled at him on the way to his car, but was thinking... *Loser!*

The drive to the home at the other end of the state took just about an hour and a half, as the traffic was light on Sunday morning. As Michael pulled into the driveway, Miriam Hunter came out of the front door. They hugged each other and Michael put his arm around her as they walked into the house.

As she prodded him for details, Michael gave his mother a run-down of the highlights of the party for Jon at Hunter's Point. She asked about certain people, and he would recall as best he could whether or not they were there and if he had spoken with them and what they talked about. She said that Katherine had called her a few weeks ago, one of the few times she had spoken to the matriarch of the shoreline property since the divorce. A tear appeared in her eye as Michael described the setting and then how the day had ended for him—sitting near the rocky embankment where she used to spend a lot of time as the sun went down.

They spent the afternoon sitting around the pool in the backyard of Miriam's comfortable and spacious house. Miriam was relishing the experience of her son being with her and directed the conversation. They talked about a number of things: his past semester at college, his monthly visits to Hunter's Point to give the impression he was trying to accept his father's new wife, his scheduled courses of study for the upcoming fall semester along with a thought about giving varsity soccer a try, his summer job at the marina that would start soon, her adjustment to life without a husband, plus her daily and weekend activities now that she would not be back at Hunter's Point for the summer. As the dinner hour approached, Miriam spoke about a couple of other matters related to the divorce, which weighed heavily on her mind. She was pleased about her son's attentiveness when she talked about things that were important to her.

Michael helped with dinner by grilling chicken that his mother had marinated in barbecue sauce. As they were clearing the dishes off the outdoor patio table, she asked him if there was anything else she should know about. Michael looked at his mother intently and said, "You won't believe what I saw near Rocky Bar last night. I thought I'd save the most bizarre aspect of the day and night for last."

"What? Was there some type of unique sea creature in the water?"

"No, the creatures I saw there last night were of the human variety. And they were on land. In a thicket near the woods. My guess is what they were doing was unique."

"What's that supposed to mean?" she asked, a puzzled look on her face.

"How about two creatures who are now related—Susan and Tony—doing some lovemaking? Or, certainly giving that impression to a casual observer."

"Come on, Son. You've got to be kidding. That's not possible, is it?"

"It's not only possible, but may be happening, based on what I saw!"

Miriam shook her head and gave her son a crooked smile. "Now, that's some development. You're right, this is bizarre! Well, maybe it serves your father right. Do you think he knows about it?"

"I don't know, but my guess is that he doesn't."

"I wonder what he'd do if he found out!" she said, musing.

"Good question. I think he'd be really pissed off."

"I think you're right. After all, she is his 'trophy' wife. He tossed me aside for her and I never thought of myself as ugly or unattractive. I'd love to be there to see his expression and reaction if and when he ever does find out. He can have quite a temper when he's angry."

"If Tony and Susan are 'doing it' on the property, don't you think that Dad almost has to find out?"

"You would think so, wouldn't you?"

Tony took the first three days of the next week off to be with Jon before he started his lifeguard job on Thursday. They hadn't had a lot of quality time together since Jon had been away at prep school and were going to drive to Newport, Rhode Island to spend a few days together there. The timing was good. It was the last week before the start of the summer season, and accommodations were available at reasonable rates. Fortunately, the weather forecast was looking favorable.

Monday evening, as they sat across the table from each other at an outdoor café overlooking the harbor at Newport, Tony said, "I'm real proud of you, Son. You got good grades, did well on the hockey team and will be college-bound in less than three months. How I wish your mother could have lived to witness your accomplishments, especially when I think of how lost you were after she passed on." He wiped a tear from his eye as he spoke. He still longed for his beloved Rebecca.

Jon choked up. "I miss her more than anyone can know. I'd do almost anything to have her back here. I just hope she's looking down and is proud of me."

"I'm sure she is, my boy. I feel as though your mother has been silently guiding you along and is happy with the way you're turning out. Now that you're a high school grad and she's not here to reprimand me, let me ask you another question."

"Okay, what's that?"

"Are you dating any girls?"

"No one steadily. A weekend movie once in a while, but that's about it. I did have to study a lot to get those grades up. There's a girl I met here last summer. Her name is Nicole. It'll be interesting to see if she's back this summer. We sent a couple of emails last fall, but I haven't heard from her since then. I probably should have contacted her and tried to see her, but...well, I just didn't get around to it."

"Alright, I understand. So, what else is going on?"

"Not a lot. I'm glad to be out of high school. I think I'm ready for college. But I do want to enjoy the summer and goof off."

"I don't blame you. That's about all I wanted to do when I was eighteen." Tony shuddered. The guilt feelings were surfacing again. *Who am I kidding? I'm well into my forties. I'll be 50 before long and I'm still goofing off with Susan. Maybe I have the same genes as Jerry. I don't know if I can end it just yet, but I can't let Jon, or anyone else for that matter, find out about it. Having Anita know is bad enough.*

Noticing that his father was engrossed in something, Jon said,

"Dad, this is really special for me, being with you. It's nice being alone like this and together."

"It's special for me too, Jon...very special." Tony shuddered silently again as he spoke.

Tony and Jon returned to Hunter's Point Wednesday evening around nine o'clock.

At ten o'clock the verandah lights in Jerry and Susan's house flickered three times; it was a signal to Tony that Susan would be at the thicket in fifteen minutes. Tony's flickering of his cottage porch lights indicated that he was back, had received her signal and would be there. *This may be crazy,* he thought, *but I want her tonight. One more night and then I'll try to end it.*

He felt passionate as they embraced. Last night, just before going to sleep, he had longed for her naked body. Unlike last Saturday night, when she was on the attack, tonight Tony was the aggressor. He suppressed his guilt feelings, placed his son and deceased wife into the background for the moment, and let his physical cravings take over. She didn't resist him. He sensed that she had missed the touch of a man. Jerry was away this week, and Tony felt that he was a good substitute. *Right now I don't care about what others think,* he thought. As they were ending their lovemaking and getting ready to walk back to the compound, Tony thought he heard a sound coming from Rocky Bar. Then Susan heard it too. "Listen!" she said. Tony nodded. He could clearly hear the sound of a man whistling a tune to himself.

"What should we do?" Susan asked.

"We can't walk back toward the compound. If someone is down by the water, he'll see us. You walk along the woods to where Rocky Bar comes into the beach. Then go to the edge of the water and start back toward the Point. If someone is there, distract him...start a conversation...anything...and make sure he's not looking over here at the thicket. I'll dart down to the water as though I'm taking a walk toward Rocky Bar."

Susan tiptoed silently along the edge of the woods for about sixty feet and then made her way to where Rocky Bar and the beach came together. "Ouch," she cried softly, just loud enough so that Dan Davies could hear her.

Dan bolted up from the rock he was sitting on and moved toward her. "Who's there?" The cop's instinct had not totally left him, even in this tranquil environment.

"It's me, Susan."

"Are you all right?"

"I think so. I slipped and stubbed my toe, but I'm okay. Aren't you Dan, and weren't you at the party last weekend?"

"Yes and yes! With the light from a full moon glistening over the Sound, I decided to take a walk over here and gaze at one of nature's truly beautiful sights. And you're Susan, Jerry's wife."

As Susan and Dan were bantering back and forth, Tony approached them. "Who's there?" he asked.

"It's Susan…and Dan," Susan said.

As he approached them, Tony held out his hand toward Dan. "Hey, neighbor, how ya' doing?" Tony grimaced as he spoke.

"I'm fine, Tony. Out for a walk on this beautiful evening before I turn in. In fact, it's getting near my bedtime. How are you doing?"

"I'm great. Took three days off to be with Jon and just got back from Newport. We wanted to spend some time together, just the two of us. After the ride back, I thought I'd take a walk before turning in for the night. You know, stretch the legs a little!"

"That leaves you, Susan?" Dan said, looking toward her inquisitively.

"Oh, *me*…I guess I had the same idea. Jerry's away on business and I got tired of sitting alone in the house, so I decided to venture out onto Rocky Bar."

"That's strange," Dan shot back. "I was all the way out to the end of the Bar and didn't see or hear you."

Susan thought for a moment and said, "I was on the other side and went toward Condor's Nest before turning back. I like to wander on a night like this. I'm going to head back now. I've got to get up early tomorrow."

Tony decided to stay so as not to cause any suspicion with Dan. After they said goodnight to Susan and she had walked beyond earshot, Dan turned to Tony and blurted, "Has Katherine talked to you about her being tired a lot and having bouts of nausea? Anita hasn't been feeling so well lately either and apparently has had some problems with nausea and cramps."

Tony sighed, grateful for what he believed was a successful deception. "Mom's mentioned it a couple of times. Last Friday night, after we'd had a long day and returned from Jon's graduation, she said she was really exhausted, but I just figured that was from all the day's activities and the trip back and forth to Jon's school. She's said a couple of times during the past month or so that she's often tired and has nausea, but every time I try to question her or suggest seeing a doctor, she shrugs me off and says it's just old age setting in and nothing we should spend time worrying about."

"Yeah, she's basically said the same thing to me," Dan shot back. "I'm a little worried, though. I just hope she's all right."

"Well, let me tell you something about my mother. She doesn't like doctors or hospitals and will do just about anything to stay away from them. This lady's got to be seriously ill before she'll go anywhere near a doctor or a hospital."

Dan groaned. "Okay, at least we know what we're dealing with. But keep an eye on her as best as you can. And keep one on Anita, too."

"As for Anita not feeling well...that *is* news to me," Tony said. "Guess I miss this sort of thing by not living in the same house with them and not being here year-round. I really haven't noticed anything unusual with Anita, except...well, now that I think about it, she slept almost the entire trip back here from the academy. Mom did also, but she sleeps in the car a lot. Anita is usually talkative on car trips, so that was unusual for her."

"Well, Tony, please keep an eye on them. I'm going to head back now."

"Okay, Dan. Goodnight."

As Dan walked away, Tony sat on a rock, placed his head in his hands, and started talking to himself. *That was a close call. This affair has got to end. Anita's right. It's too damn dangerous. I have to cut it off!*

Friday night there was a barbecue at Tony's cottage. The whole family was there: Tony, Jon, Katherine, Anita, Jerry, Susan and Michael.

As they were sitting on the deck overlooking the water, Katherine went over to Michael, who was getting a soda out of a cooler. "Michael, can I talk to you for a minute or two?"

"Sure, Aunt Katherine. What's up?"

The elderly woman grabbed his arm gently and pulled him away. "Let's take a short walk." As they walked toward the beach, she stopped. "This will do. I just wanted to speak to you alone for a moment. How's your mother? I miss Miriam and you're the only one who can tell me anything about her."

"In spite of what's happened to her, which has been humiliating and traumatic, she's actually doing very well, and I know she would appreciate your asking about her. No one else around here except for you and Anita seems to care much about how she is."

"Divorce is an ugly thing, Michael. Everyone gets hurt in some way. I hope she can recover from the hurt she's suffered."

"I hope so, too. She's doing some volunteer work, which she likes very much, and it's keeping her busy. I had a nice time this past week and enjoy being with her, which kind of surprises me. I told her all about Jon's party."

"Well, that makes me happy, even though it was strange and not as nice as it could have been if she had been here. I'm glad that you had a good time visiting with her and that you two enjoy being together."

"Is it normal for a twenty year-old college guy to like being with his mother? I don't want to be known as a mama's boy."

"I wouldn't worry about that, and I believe it's all right. . .flattering for her, I would think, that you want to spend time with her."

"That's what she said when I left—that it was quite a flattering experience to have me there, doting on her and helping with dinner and cleaning up the yard. Do all you woman think alike?"

"Not about everything, but about our children I think we do. Come on, let's go back. I found out what I wanted to know. Now, let's enjoy Tony's barbecue."

"Man, that was good," Jerry exclaimed—putting both hands on his stomach and patting it gently. "Better than most of the restaurant food I eat almost every week. I've got to make a trip to the bathroom before I have another of your libations, Tony."

"Let me go first, Dad," Michael said. "The sodas are hitting me hard in the bladder. I'll be fast, I promise."

"All right, Son, I can wait. It's not an emergency…yet," Jerry chuckled.

Michael returned in a couple of minutes and Jerry headed for the cottage's first floor bathroom. Once inside, he closed the door and relieved himself. After washing and drying his hands, he noticed a pair of women's panties hanging on the hook hear the top of the inside of the door. He was puzzled. *What the hell is this doing in the bathroom of a summer place where two guys live? I wonder if one of them has a girlfriend. If it's Jon, why wouldn't it be in the upstairs bathroom since he sleeps up there? Tony's bedroom is the only one on the first floor.* He was smiling as he pondered which one of them, Tony or Jon, might have a lady friend that no one else in the family seemed to know about. He was about to open the door when he noticed a familiar pattern on the small garment. He took it off the hook, looked closer and saw a label that he had seen a number of times. He read the label and the size. *For Christ's sake, these are either Susan's, or the lady that one of these guys is seeing wears exactly the same brand, the same color and the same size as she does. That's a hell of a coincidence!* he thought. He rolled the garment into a small ball and thrust it into a back pocket of his trousers. When he returned to the deck, his smile turned to a scowl as he noticed a glance from Tony to Susan and then back.

He was starting to burn inside, but Jerry joined in the family's conversation and tried to focus on a story that Katherine was telling about enduring one of the major hurricanes of the 1950s, named Carol, which did a significant amount of damage to the area. He was born during the year following the devastating storm, and a picture of his mother and father in the aftermath of the hurricane hung in the living room of his home.

At around nine-thirty, Katherine said she was feeling tired and was going back to her house to read a novel that she had just started. Anita also got up, thanked Tony, and said she would walk her mother home and then go for a stroll on the beach. Michael had left ten minutes earlier. He had gone home to get his wallet and put on a clean shirt. Michael got back to the cottage just as Katherine and Anita were leaving. He and Jon waved good-bye and walked toward Michael's car. Jerry winked at Susan and they got up to leave.

"Thanks again, Tony," Jerry and Susan said in unison, as they walked together toward the steps at the end of the deck. Jerry was silent as they walked to their home.

"I need to go to the bathroom," Susan said as she and Jerry entered their house. "There's a good movie on tonight. Want to watch it? Afterwards, maybe we can find a way to entertain each other."

"Sounds good to me." Although still burning from the discovery at Tony's cottage, Jerry was hoping that it *was* just a coincidence, and was feeling a need for lovemaking with his young wife, who aroused him almost every time he looked at her for any length of time. His sex drive had not diminished with age. In fact, he sometimes thought it was increasing, which he attributed to Susan. Miriam was attractive, but during the past couple of years he had tired of her appearance, felt a loss of physical attraction, and had become annoyed when she gained a few pounds along with a redistribution of weight, even though he knew this was normal for a woman entering middle age.

As Jerry sat on the couch and clicked the remote control to turn on the TV set, he felt the panties he had placed in a rear pocket. As he got up to bring it to the bedroom and put in his dresser drawer, figuring he would ask her about it later, he noticed something shiny on the end table next to the couch. It was an initialed lighter. He picked it up and read the initials 'TK'. *These are Tony's initials and this is one of Tony's lighters. I'd recognize it anywhere. God knows, I've seen him light up his pipe hundreds of times with this lighter or another just like it. What the hell is this lighter doing here?* He felt his face reddening as he held the panties in his right hand and the lighter in his left.

As Jerry pondered his recent discoveries and the implications, Susan came back into the room, walking sensually toward him. He glared at her and held out the items he was holding. She put her hand to her mouth in a gesture of surprise. He remained silent, waiting for her to say something. The silence continued for another fifteen seconds or so, as he glared at her and she looked puzzled. She finally broke the silence. "That looks like one of my panties. Why are you holding it? And what's in your other hand?"

"I just happened to find the panties hanging on a hook on the bathroom door in Tony's cottage—the one on the first floor which I believe he uses. The lighter is Tony's and I just found it next to the lamp on the end table as I sat down to turn on the TV. Would you like to offer an explanation?"

"I...I don't have one. Maybe the panties aren't mine, and I don't know what Tony's lighter is doing here. He hasn't been here in a while."

"Are you sure he hasn't been here in a while? How about when I'm away? Think hard, Susan," he said, walking toward her and holding the items out to her. "The panties are exactly the same brand, color and size as yours. I'd say that's more than a coincidence. You want to tell me what's going on between you and Tony?"

"Nothing...nothing," she stammered nervously.

"Are you sure?" Jerry had now placed both of the items in his right hand and was grabbing at Susan's right arm with his left hand. Born left handed, Jerry had undergone rotor cuff surgery in his right shoulder three years ago, weakening his right arm and causing him to become even more left hand dominant, especially if he needed or wanted to do anything requiring strength. Squeezing her right bicep tighter, he said nastily, "Are you sure there's nothing going on?"

"You're hurting me!" she cried out.

"I can squeeze a lot tighter than this and make it hurt a lot more."

Susan was trying to back away, but Jerry's grip was vise-like. She started to cry. "All right, we've had a couple of trysts, but it was just a physical thing. Two people—one without a woman to make love to and one whose man was away—succumbed to temptation."

Jerry loosened his grip on her arm. "I guess you *have* succumbed to temptation. I just wonder who tempted whom? Do you have any idea of the opportunities that I have when I'm on the road, with the kind of expense money we have to throw around? But I haven't succumbed, at least not yet. Maybe my attitude will change in the future."

"I'm sorry. What we did was wrong, but I was lonely and so was he."

"You said a 'couple' of trysts. So, this affair is more than a one-time fling. Are you sure it's just been a couple of times?"

"Three times, to be precise."

"Three times...three fucking times my cousin has been inside my wife! If I didn't know it was medically impossible, I'd have to worry about you maybe bearing Tony's child. That would be cute—a man approaching fifty, with an eighteen year-old son, having a baby by a relative through marriage!"

"Well, Jerry, as you said...you know that's not possible."

"Well, you may not be fertile, but you certainly can be sensual." He reached down and locked his left arm around her waist, hoisted her small, slim body onto his shoulder and walked quickly up the stairs and to their bedroom. He slung her onto their queen-sized bed and jumped on top of her.

"What are you going to do me?" she cried out.

"I'm not sure, but whatever it is, I'm not going to wait for the end of the movie. How about a beating to get started?" he yelled, raising his left arm toward the ceiling.

"No…please, no!"

"Then, take your clothes off. It's my turn!"

He pulled her sweater up over her shoulders as she unbuttoned her shorts. He was mad. He took his anger out by pushing her shoulders hard into the mattress and then engaging in rough sex—something he had never done before. She didn't try to stop him, even when it hurt. After fifteen minutes, they collapsed into each other's arms, she now on top of him. Exhausted and panting, they fell asleep.

Thirty minutes later, Jerry woke up and roused Susan. He rolled her over so that he was now on top. Still agitated, he pointed a finger at her and began talking. "If you ever hook up with Tony again, or any other man for that matter, I may just kill both of you."

"You don't have to worry," she whispered.

Jerry got out of the bed and grabbed a pair of shorts and a tee shirt. Looking down at her with a sinister expression on his face, he said, "I'm going to take a quick shower and then I have something else to do."

"What's that?"

"Tell Tony to keep his itchy hands off you."

"Do you have to do that?"

"Yeah, I have to do that."

Jerry stormed into the shower as Susan remained in their bed and shuddered. Ten minutes later he ran down the stairs, grabbed the small yet heavy shovel from the set of fireplace tools, and bounded out of the house toward Tony's cottage.

Earlier, as Jerry and Susan had started to doze, Michael and Jon were making the rounds at a party at Ocean's View, one of the neighboring beaches. Having separated, Michael was yelling at his "cousin", trying to get his attention over the sound of rock music coming from a compact disc player. "Hey, Jon, look who's here!"

Jon saw Nicole, the girl he had dated last summer, walked toward her and embraced her. She responded by wrapping her arms around his waist and hugging him. Jon liked her and hoped she would be back at the beach for the summer. One of his few regrets of the past school year was that he had not kept in contact with her. *Maybe it won't matter and this summer will be a good one,* he thought as they held each other. Neither said anything, as their embrace transmitted their feelings.

A girl that Michael had dated last summer, Amy, was also at the beach party. Michael spotted her just after he had seen Nicole and they soon embraced.

"Wow, what good fortune," Michael exclaimed to Amy. "I was really hoping you'd be back this year. I missed you during the school year."

"Oh, sure you did, big-city college man," she said, snickering. Amy was a student at a small college in Rhode Island. "I'll bet you stayed awake thinking about me at night after all the Beantown frat parties. We're not that far apart, you know. You could have called, at least once or twice."

"Yeah, I know," Michael replied sullenly. "Chalk it up to a stupid ego or immaturity. How about an enjoyable summer together? I promise you that this year will be different."

"Sounds like a plan to me," Amy replied with a smile.

As Michael and Amy were reuniting, so were Jon and Nicole. They had walked outside to the deck of the cottage and were having an animated conversation. Nicole was cute and had an outgoing personality. They acted as if it was last summer all over again, and the school year was a non-event. Jon felt exhilarated. He had graduated from prep school, earned a partial hockey scholarship to college, had his summer lifeguard job lined up, and was now with a girl that he really liked.

Jon walked over to Michael. "Hey, Michael, can you believe it—Amy and Nicole both being here! Why don't we go back to Hunter's Point with the girls. We can take a walk on the beach and maybe go out onto Rocky Bar. There's a full moon tonight and it should be beautiful."

"Sounds good to me," Michael said, grinning.

"Would you and Amy like to come with us to Hunter's Point?" Jon asked Nicole.

"Are you kidding! I love it there! You've probably got the absolute greatest place on the whole shoreline." Nicole walked over to Amy and whispered in her ear. Amy nodded in approval. "Let's go," Nicole said enthusiastically.

Ten minutes later they drove into the family compound. They decided to go to the vacant cottage, the one next to the one that Tony and Jon lived in. As they got out of the car, they heard a loud conversation coming from the outside deck of Tony's cottage. Michael looked at Jon inquisitively. Then, he said to the girls, "Why don't you two go inside and make yourself at home. We'll be right back."

Michael and Jon ran the short distance to the other cottage and dropped down behind a group of rhododendron bushes.

They heard Jerry screaming at Tony. "What the hell kind of a relative are you, anyway? I'm not fooling around with you. I mean it! Keep your God-damn hands off my wife…unless you want your head bashed in with this shovel!"

"Okay, calm down, damn it. You know, Jerry, it takes two to tango. Maybe you need to be around more and stay sober when you're here."

"Hey, just because I travel and may get loaded once in a while, doesn't give you the right to mess with Susan. Got it?"

"Yeah. I think Susan and I both knew this would cause a problem, but that sexy babe you're living with is a tease…and a damn good one!"

"I'll deal with my end of it with her. You just keep your distance."

"Alright…now put that God-damn shovel down and go back to your woman. I'm going inside to have a beer and watch a movie."

Michael and Jon were shocked and speechless. They stayed hidden behind the rhododendrons and listened to their fathers going at each other, remaining silent until Jerry had almost made his way back to his house and Tony had gone inside his.

"Jesus," Jon finally exclaimed. "What the hell was *that* all about?"

"Sounds like your old man is dippin' into my old man's personal property."

"Are you shittin' me?"

"What the hell else would have provoked my dad to come over here with what looked like the shovel from our fireplace and yell and curse at your dad…and threaten him?"

"Dad? Screwing Susan? You gotta be kidding. I thought it's supposed to be the kids that are messed up!"

"Yeah, well, don't think the old folks are perfect," Michael replied. "Man, this is a freakin' beaut! We better keep this to ourselves."

"You ain't shittin', man. Can you imagine if Grandma found out? She'd probably have a heart attack and freakin' die. This might just kill her! Holy shit, Michael. This is crazy!"

"Yeah, but listen. We've got two pretty girls that we really like sitting in the other cottage. At least, I hope they're still there. Let's go." The two boys then ran back to the cottage where they had left the girls.

As they entered, the cottage, they heard the girls on the screened back porch and went out there. "We heard something like two people yelling at each other," Amy said to Michael, a puzzled look distorting her pretty features.

Jon looked strangely at Michael, who quickly said…"Yeah…it was our dads. They were arguing over some work that may need to be done to the place. I think my dad wants to do it, but Jon's doesn't. They sometimes get carried away with certain things around here. They'll work it out."

Jon sighed in relief, walked over to Nicole, put his arm around her and gave her a gentle kiss. "Anyone for a walk to the end of the beach?"

Chapter 4

"Oh my, Dan, you really do have some spine tingling stories," Katherine said with a sigh. "Your former life certainly was dangerous and scary, at least for a little old lady like me who's never spent much time in a big city."

It was Monday following a quiet weekend. Dan and Katherine were having afternoon tea on the verandah of Katherine's house. The retired detective felt connected to the lady sitting across from him. He had never met anyone quite like her and had come to enjoy her outlook and view on life, which he found to be very wholesome. Dan had never dreamed that he would be spending significant time with anyone, much less a woman approaching eighty years of age. With too many nights of investigative duty that kept him away from his own son, now grown and living in New York, and the death of his wife of thirty years, he felt a longing for the type of family environment that Katherine fostered.

After spending a number of afternoons with her, he had come to realize that this woman had a peaceful and pleasant influence if you listened to her and observed her mannerisms. He would often lean back in one of her verandah chairs, look out at the water, close his eyes and say a short prayer of thanks that he had found the Connecticut shoreline—a radical departure from the big city life he had known for his entire existence up until a year or so ago—to retire to.

Dan had just concluded a story about a raid in the East Village of New York ten years ago that broke up a major narcotics ring, where he had just missed being killed or seriously injured. A bullet had grazed his left shoulder and, if he had been leaning the other way, might have hit him close to the heart. They had each finished a cup of green tea and Dan was preparing to pour another cup for each of them as he concluded the tale. "So, what's new at Hunter's Point?" Dan asked as he poured the tea.

"Oh, not a lot since the party. We had a barbecue at Tony's Friday night and the weekend was very quiet, a big change from the previous weekend. The only peculiar thing was loud voices coming from the direction of Tony's cottage after I had returned here and was getting ready for bed. My hearing's not so good any more, so it must have been shouting. It sounded like Jerry and Tony arguing about something, which seemed strange since we had enjoyed such a nice time earlier in the evening. Nothing has happened, so maybe it was someone else. Maybe it was the two boys shouting about something. I guess I just don't know exactly what it was. Oh, my, I'm rambling like an old fogy. Anyhow, it didn't last long and the rest of the weekend was quiet. I like it that way—quiet. I especially love the silence of the night when I can hear the waves breaking into the rocks. It's my favorite way to fall asleep."

"I know what you mean. I've come to enjoy it also, which is why I take walks out to the end of Rocky Bar in the morning and at night. I call it 'the sound of the Sound' and I never get tired of it. I've also come to enjoy your company...and your pies."

Dan had just finished a piece of key lime pie, one of his favorites, and Katherine was rising from her chair to return to the kitchen and cut another small slice for each of them, when the phone rang.

"Hello," she said, answering the phone. A strange voice on the other end of the line asked her if she was Mrs. Kent. "Yes, I am."

"This is the emergency room at Shoreline Hospital. We need to inform you that your daughter, Anita, was admitted here thirty minutes ago."

"Anita? What's the matter with her?" Katherine almost fell into the kitchen counter.

"She had an episode of dizziness and vomiting, and then collapsed at the library. They called an ambulance, and then we picked her up and brought her here. She just regained consciousness a few minutes ago and asked us to contact you."

"Well, thank you for calling. Tell Anita that I'm on my way."

"Yes, ma'am."

Katherine walked quickly to the verandah where Dan was standing and looking out at the water. He turned and noticed there were no plates with slices of pie in her hands and her face had taken on an ashen appearance. "Is something wrong?" he asked.

"Yes, Dan, there is. Something's happened to Anita. She's become ill and was taken to the hospital. Can you drive me there? We can take my car."

"Of course. Let's go! What happened?"

Katherine briefly related what she had just heard as they started to leave the house.

"How long has she been at the hospital?" he asked.

"I think the woman said…let's see now…what did she say? Oh, yes, she said thirty minutes."

The hospital was a twenty minute drive along the main shore road.

Anita was dozing when Dan and Katherine arrived at her room. She opened her eyes as her mother bent down to give her a kiss on the cheek. "What…what on earth happened to me?" Anita stammered. "I remember feeling sick and dizzy, and then things went blank."

"Well, my darling daughter, it seems as though you passed out and were brought here by ambulance."

Anita looked past her mother to Dan who was standing behind her. She smiled at him and he smiled back.

"I wonder what could have caused this." Anita sighed. "I haven't been feeling that well recently, but I didn't think I was going to wind up in the hospital."

"We don't know exactly what happened," Dan interjected, "but the doctor who treated you said they're going to do some tests as soon as you're a bit stronger."

"Tell them to do the tests now. I feel all right and want to know."

"We'll stop by and see him again on our way out," Dan replied, smiling at her.

Katherine and Dan spent another ten minutes with Anita. During those minutes, Dan thought about the times when he had been in hospitals to observe people who had passed out for any number of reasons and tried to recollect the circumstances. Nothing clicked as a quick explanation for him. After they had been in the hospital room for fifteen minutes, the time limit imposed by the doctor and nurse on duty, Dan and Katherine left.

They drove to Stan's Steamers, a popular seafood restaurant on the waterfront, not far from the hospital. "This is a mystery," Katherine said, looking across the table at Dan.

"Well, you said she wasn't feeling well, didn't you?"

"I guess I did say that. That was the morning of Jon's party when you asked me how I was feeling."

"And what about you?" Dan asked.

"I'm still tired and don't have much energy. Thank goodness I took a nap before you came over this afternoon, or I might be falling asleep now. My legs hurt a little, but it's nothing I can't live with."

Even though he felt he knew what the answer was going to be, Dan asked, "Are you sure you don't want to check yourself in to the hospital or at least get some tests done by your doctor?"

"I'm sure." Changing the subject, she said, "Oh, my goodness, Dan, we need to call Tony and tell him what happened. He's traveling this week, and in all the commotion I forgot to call him."

Dan pulled his cell phone out of its holder on his belt. "Give me his number."

After Dan had punched in the number, Katherine took the phone and began speaking the moment Tony answered. Dan looked intently at the elderly lady sitting across from him as she recounted the details of their visit with Anita in the hospital. He was concerned and more than a little frustrated that he could not convince a woman approaching eighty years of age to seek medical help when she was not feeling well. *This isn't normal where I come from,* he thought, as memories surfaced of all the medical treatment his wife had undergone before dying. *She is one stubborn and feisty little lady. I just hope she doesn't get seriously ill and regret it.*

After they finished their dinner, Dan drove Katherine home and said he would take her back to the hospital tomorrow.

It was now Wednesday afternoon. Anita's doctor had called Katherine with the results of blood tests that had been run on her daughter. After ending the conversation, Katherine immediately called a number at Condor's Nest Beach. "Dan, it's Katherine. They found methanol in Anita's blood."

"Methanol—are you kidding? That's a poison! How in the world could methanol get in her system?"

"I wish I knew. The doctor was totally puzzled. It's not exactly something we eat."

"Or drink," Dan added, feeling perplexed himself.

"Well, the lab is going to run additional tests on her. Fortunately, she's feeling much better and regaining her strength."

"I figured she'd be a lot better today. She made good improvement yesterday." Determined to get his elderly friend to a doctor or a medical clinic, he said, "You know, Katherine, maybe you should have some lab work done, also. Just to be on the safe side. Would you do it for me? I'll drive you back and forth to wherever you have to go."

"I thought I've already answered that question," she said curtly.

Dan could detect the tone of defiance in the elderly lady's response, and decided not to press the issue any further. "Alright, have it your way for now. Is there anything else I can do for you?"

Softening her voice, Katherine replied, "Can you come over here? We can have a cup of tea and then go to see Anita. They're going to release her tomorrow. Tony cut his trip short by a day and is on his way back as we speak, and we'll meet him at the hospital. He'll be here to help me with her tomorrow."

"Sure, I'll get going and be over there shortly." Dan sighed and shook his head as he hung up the phone. *Maybe I can work on Tony to try and get her to a doctor,* he thought.

About a half-hour later, as they were sitting on the verandah and pondering what had happened to Anita, Dan Davies was scratching his head as he spoke to Katherine. "What do you think it could be? How could she have ingested a toxic substance found in paint thinners and removers? Anita isn't using methanol! There probably isn't even a can of it on the property. And, why have you had bouts of nausea and cramps?"

Deflecting the question, Katherine replied, "Is it possible, Dan, that it's in something Anita ate or drank, either here or someplace else?"

"Well, I suppose anything's possible, but it doesn't compute, at least not in my mind. Tomorrow night, let's all sit down and go through everything in the kitchen—the cupboard and refrigerator. Maybe there is something that she ate or drank that contained this substance. If it's here, then there's a chance that you also ingested it. Maybe that's why you haven't been feeling well."

"But I haven't been feeling well and have had these various things happening for a few months now. Could she…we…have been taking in something for that long? What about what she eats at work? They do go out for lunch almost every day, and to different places."

"That's a possibility," Dan said. "Do you know how hard it would be to track down all the meals she's eaten in the area? Jeez, that would make finding a needle in a haystack seem easy. This is a complex puzzle, with so many pieces that it's hard to know where to start. But we have to start somewhere, so tomorrow night let's list everything in this house and try to discover anything suspicious. Then we can talk about her eating out at lunch. Come on, Mrs. Kent, let's go to the hospital."

Tony met his mother and Dan at the hospital and visited with Anita. After leaving Dan, Tony and Katherine drove back to Hunter's Point for dinner at the main house. They had invited Dan, but he had a prior commitment. As they ate, Tony and Katherine wracked their brains about how methanol could have gotten into Anita's blood stream. Katherine traced their eating and drinking habits and what they might have consumed over the past three months, but could not come up with anything. She also wrote down names of restaurants where she and Anita had eaten recently. After dinner, Tony walked to Jerry and Susan's house to give Susan an update on Anita's condition. Susan had told Jerry that she would call and inform him of what Tony or Katherine had communicated to her. Tony had planned to call Susan on the phone, but since her house was on the way back to his cottage, he decided to stop in and deliver the message in person. He also wanted to tell Susan that their affair should come to an end, and felt he should do this in person.

Tony knocked on the front door. He had decided to first give a recap of Anita's condition and then talk about ending their affair. He gulped as the door opened. Susan was barefoot, dressed in a pair of tight-fitting short shorts and a low cut sleeveless tank shirt with no bra underneath. She smiled seductively at him, put her hand on his chin and gave him a gentle peck on the cheek. She motioned for him to join her on the living room couch, where she leaned into him as they sat down.

He told her about what had happened to Anita and that she seemed to be recovering and would be home tomorrow.

She listened as he spoke. When he had finished, she turned to face him and asked, "Is that everything?"

"Well, there is one more thing we need to talk about."

Susan put her finger to his lips and moved closer, her breasts now touching his chest and one of her legs on top of his. "Before you say anything more, Tony, let's have a quickie." Susan now had her arms around his neck and wouldn't let go. "Jerry won't be home 'til tomorrow night and Michael is out."

"For Christ's sake, Susan, my sister's lying in a hospital bed and you want to have sex? Are you freakin' nuts?"

"Look, I'm concerned about Anita and wouldn't act like this if she was in real danger or wasn't making progress, which you just said she is. This affair of ours is going to have to end…I think we both know that. But I'd like one last time with you…Please?" She took her hands from around his neck and pulled the strips of the tank shirt over her shoulders and down to her elbows. She then started stroking his thighs.

He gulped for a second time. He couldn't resist her. He started kissing her—first gently, then passionately.

"Not here…the bedroom," she whispered in his ear.

It was over in ten minutes.

"Susan, we have to end this…but how? You drive me insane!" Tony rose from her bed and started getting dressed. "I don't quite know how to stay away from you, in spite of the consequences now that Jerry has found out, and Anita already knew about us."

"Anita…how did she find out? You never told me about this!"

"Remember that night in May when you insisted on going swimming nude and then having sex on the beach under the big blanket? Well, Anita saw us. She was taking a walk toward the beach, heard a noise and then spotted us."

"Oh, my god…I can't believe it! Does Katherine know?"

"I don't think so."

She grabbed him and kissed passionately, even though he was now almost dressed and she was still naked. "I'm afraid, my illicit love, that maybe this is it. It's just too risky to continue, and I do love Jerry, even though I have feelings for you. I've never been in this type of situation."

"Me neither," Tony replied, his head shaking and his voice trembling. "Now the question is how do we co-exist, living so close together?"

"I don't exactly know how, but we'll have to figure out a way, since neither of us wants to leave this place, and we can't run off together. For you, it's your summer home and for me it's a dream come true to be here. Are you seeing anyone else?"

"No, but maybe I should start looking. I need to preoccupy myself with something, or someone else, for the summer. Then, Jon will be off to college and I'll be away from this place except for weekends."

Tony walked quickly out of the house and toward the beach. He needed a walk to clear his mind and, hopefully, to find a solution to the dilemma he was in with Susan. He promised himself that, despite the temptation and seemingly uncontrollable desire, he would not have another romantic encounter with her.

Chapter 5

Susan had come to the realization that she was risking her marriage and the opportunity to live at Hunter's Point by having the affair with Tony Kent. Early the next morning before leaving for work, she placed a note stating that their affair was over on the driver's seat of Tony's car, which was always left unlocked on the property.

Dan had a dentist appointment and Katherine was bothered by a bout of nausea and leg cramps, so Susan took the afternoon off to drive to the hospital and bring Anita back to Hunter's Point. She struggled with knowing that Anita was aware of her sexual relationship with Tony, and dealt with it by asking Anita several questions about how she got sick and what she thought the cause of the poisoning might be.

Susan was at the front door to greet Jerry with an affectionate hug and kiss when he returned late in the afternoon. Just before dinner, Jerry visited with Anita at the main house to check on her condition. Michael joined Jerry and Susan for dinner after returning home from his job at the marina and changing into his bathing suit.

"Delicious...absolutely superb," Jerry exclaimed, after digesting the last morsel of his meal. He complemented Susan on her marinating of the chicken he had grilled on the barbecue. She smiled sensually at him.

Michael, noticing the gesture, got up, brought his plate to the sink, and rinsed the food off. "I'm going for a walk down to Rocky Bar and out to the end for a swim. Then I'll come back and take a shower. I'll be going out in about an hour."

"Okay, Son, see you later."

After Michael was fifty or so yards away from the house, Susan came over to Jerry and sat on his lap. She started kissing him. "Let's go upstairs and have dessert," she said seductively.

"That's what I had in mind."

Anita, Tony and Dan were in the kitchen of Katherine's house, getting ready to inspect its contents. Katherine was lying down on a sofa in the living room, feeling tired and sapped of energy. Anita was in a wheelchair. She didn't really need it to get around, but the doctor had ordered her to use it for one more day to rest her legs. He had told her that tomorrow she could be up and walking about a little, but to take it slowly for the next three days, so she could go back to work again on Monday.

Anita and Tony looked at Dan for instructions. "Let's begin with the cupboard and then go to the refrigerator," Dan said.

"You two pull the things out and I'll write the list," Anita suggested.

Tony pulled items out of the cupboard and handed them to Dan, who told Anita what to write down. "Kosher salt, salad dressing, canned tuna, tomatoes and corn, baking potatoes, pasta, rice, walnuts, cake and pie mixes, frosting mix, olive oil, vinegar, garlic, spices, coffee, tea, pepper, salt. . . ." They went through the remainder of the cupboard and then the refrigerator, jotting down all the contents.

"If this is from ingesting, which it's got to be to show up in your bloodstream," Dan said, scratching his head, "then it's got to be a series of small doses of something you've ingested on a regular basis, or a large dose recently. What I'm wondering is if there's something that both you and Katherine have eaten or drunk, or if it's something that you alone, Anita, have taken into your system. With Katherine not feeling well, it could be that there's also something nasty inside her. So maybe we need to keep an eye on her now, especially since she refuses to get any lab tests."

"Well, we both like almost all of the same things," Anita sighed. "We eat the same meals and drink basically the same liquids. I guess you could say 'like mother, like daughter.' Oh, God, I hope it's something from eating lunch out somewhere and there's nothing in mother's system. She's older than me and not as strong."

Anita then looked at her brother. "I know that you don't like sleeping here, Tony, but could you spend the nights through the weekend in the guest room? I may need a little help and can't be of much use if Mother doesn't feel well and needs someone."

"Of course. I was thinking about doing that. Jon can take care of our place at night. I'll start spending as much time here as I can."

Dan sighed and said, "That's a great idea. Now, why don't we all sleep on what we did tonight, have dinner again here tomorrow evening, and see if we can narrow this list."

"Sounds like a plan," Tony shot back. "Hey, Dan, how about stopping at my place for a quick beer on your way home? I'll come back here later and spend the night. I'll tell Jon, who should still be home, that I'll be here tonight and for the weekend."

They all nodded. Tony went over to Katherine, who had dozed off, and kissed her gently on the cheek, before he and Dan left the main house.

Twenty minutes after they had strolled arm-in-arm up the stairs toward the bedroom, Jerry and Susan rolled over and apart from each other in their bed. The comforter had been cast to the floor during their lovemaking, revealing a stain on the bed sheet. "What's this?" Jerry asked.

"What's what?" Susan responded.

"This stain. It looks like semen, and the sheets were clean when I left here on Monday."

Susan shook convulsively as she tried to remain calm.

"Was *he* here?"

"No!"

"Bullshit—this stuff isn't mine! We put clean sheets on the bed after we made love last weekend, and this is the first time I've been in bed with you since then, except for sleeping Sunday night. And my stuff is inside you tonight. So, what the hell is up, Lady? Has Tony been shooting his gun…in my bed…with you?"

"I told him it was over, but he insisted on one last time. He was forceful, kind of the way you were last Friday night." Susan, fearful that Jerry would hurt her in a fit of rage, decided to lie and place the blame on Tony, putting aside any potential consequences.

"That son-of-a-bitch…that god-damn son-of-a-bitch. After we had it out, he still comes over here to bang you. I ought to kill him! And, maybe you, too!" He vaulted on top of her, sitting on his bare knees, and grabbed her arms. His left hand squeezed her hard and she let out a scream. He was about to hit her when he heard footsteps on the first floor. "It must be Michael coming back from the beach. My son may have saved you from a beating."

Jerry jumped out of bed, went to the bathroom, relieved himself and came back. Susan was still naked in bed, shaking all over, a look of absolute fear on her face. Jerry shot her a look of disdain and then put on a pair of shorts and a sweatshirt. His sandals were in their customary place by the nightstand, and he slipped his feet into them. Then he was off to Tony's cottage.

"Where's your father?" Jerry shouted at Jon as he saw the youngster sitting on the deck.

"He just went inside to get a beer for Dan and himself. Why?"

"You'll find out." Jerry raced through the screen door into the cottage as he was yelling.

Dan and Tony were walking toward the deck from the kitchen, each with an unopened bottle of beer in hand. Jerry bounded toward them and, without saying anything, lunged at Tony. "You bastard, I told you to stay away from her. I ought to kill you!"

Dan, bigger than both Jerry and Tony and still strong despite his age, jumped in to separate the two men. "What the hell is going on?"

"Tony can't control what's inside his pants, that's what's going on!"

Tony shuddered. His fear of a fiasco within the family was now becoming a reality. "Look, Jerry, she said it was the last time. I wasn't going there to do anything, but then something just started, and...." Tony couldn't finish the sentence.

Jerry lunged at Tony again, leading with his left side as a boxer would do, and Dan almost fell onto a dining chair as he separated them.

"Get out of here, Jerry," Tony finally stammered. "We'll deal with this privately."

"You bet your ass we will, and be prepared for the worst," Jerry shouted, extricating himself from Dan's grasp and storming out of the cottage and back toward his home.

"Jeez, is this the way relatives get along at Hunter's Point?" Dan exclaimed, falling back toward the dining area's table and rubbing his sore arms. "This isn't exactly the image I have of this place. Maybe I should have been more suspicious, Tony, when I ran into you and Susan down at Rocky Bar that night. Maybe retirement has dulled the old detective instincts."

Tony looked at Dan and then hung his head, saying nothing for a moment. Then he mumbled, barely above a whisper, "This is my fault. Jerry's right. I haven't been able to control myself, at least not with her. Oh, Christ, we've got to keep this from Mother. She'll flip out if this gets back to her."

Jon had heard just about everything and now walked into the cottage. He noticed the look of consternation on his father's face. He and Michael were going out in about ten minutes and he was on the way to his room to put on a clean pair of shorts and a sweatshirt. "Something the matter, Dad?"

"I guess you could say that."

"Anything to do with Uncle Jerry storming in here?"

"Oh, shit, did he tell you?"

"Well, not exactly. What's going on?"

"Can I tell you at another time? I've got a lot on my mind, with Anita getting sick in the hospital, Mom not feeling well, and this Goddamn thing with Susan."

"Susan?"

"Oh, Christ, I guess you'll find out, so I might as well tell you. I've been lonely a lot lately. Susan and I…oh, shit, this is hard to say…we've had an affair."

Jon stood silently, looking first at the floor, then at Dan and then at his father. He knew about it, since he had witnessed his dad's first encounter with Jerry, but didn't know what to say.

Dan placed his beer bottle on the dining table and said, "Hey fellas, why don't I go home and give you two some space together?"

Tony nodded at Dan, who had already started to walk toward the deck and out of the cottage. Tony put a hand on Jon's shoulder and sobbed. "I made a mistake, Son, and I've got to keep this from blowing up into a huge firestorm for the family."

"That's heavy stuff, Dad. I don't know what to say."

"Maybe it's best not to say anything. I'll reconcile somehow with Jerry. I don't want to ruin his marriage. I…I just got too carried away with her. God damn it! This is really screwed up." Tony put his head in his hands and headed for the living room and the couch. He didn't want to talk about the affair any more tonight. "Are you going out, Son?"

"Yeah, I was planning to go out," Jon answered. "Michael and I are seeing Amy and Nicole. Michael said he's going to Charlestown tomorrow night for the weekend, so we thought we'd double date tonight. Is that okay?"

"Of course it is. You go out and have a good time. Don't worry about me. And, by the way, I'll be staying with Mom and Anita at their house tonight and through the weekend." Tony sighed and sank into the couch.

As Michael and Jon were driving out of Hunter's Point to pick up the girls, Jon turned to Michael and said, "Well, I guess it's out."

"What's out?"

"You know, the 'thing' between my dad and Susan."

"It is? Since when?"

"Since earlier this evening," Jon said. "We just had a donnybrook at our cottage. Grandma's friend—the retired detective guy—was there to see it, so now it's gone beyond the family."

"Jeez, now I get it. That's why my dad had a look on his face like he was going to kill someone, and Susan looked like she'd seen a ghost. Man, was he pissed off, but I thought it was because of something at his business. Susan was cowering like a freakin' dog that chewed a pair of good shoes and had just gotten the shit kicked out of it by its master." He shook his head after he had spoken.

"Well, for what it's worth, my dad seems really sorry and says he's going to reconcile with your dad," Jon said.

"We'll see about that. I doubt my dad is going to reconcile with anyone about this. I heard him muttering something just before I left but couldn't make out exactly what it was."

"Michael, we've got to keep quiet, especially around my grandma. Like I said the other night, something like this might just kill her."

"Just so you know, Jon, I don't plan on saying anything. Let the old folks work this one out. Hey, they created it!"

"Okay...let's forget about this and go get those pretty girls."

Chapter 6

Anita was finally able to enjoy a complete meal at dinner Friday night. Sitting around the dining room table were Tony, Jon, Anita, Katherine and Dan.

"Oh, does this taste good," Anita exclaimed. "I haven't eaten much since going to the hospital, although I did have a decent breakfast this morning. It's so nice to have my family here…and you, too, Dan. It's too bad that Jerry, Susan and Michael couldn't join us, but maybe that would be too much for me tonight."

Dan and Tony cast wary glances at each other, checking that the two ladies didn't notice.

"Yes," Katherine jumped in, "we thought that would be a bit too much, Anita. Let's have a quiet weekend, get you back on your feet, and then see what happens."

"Alright. When she brought me home from the hospital yesterday, Susan told me that Jerry had a one-day trip today…I think she said to Boston…and might not be home until later tonight. If so, she's going out with a couple of people from the clinic tonight."

After they had eaten, Tony and Jon started to clear the dishes.

Dan then said, "Why don't we go to the verandah and talk about this list of items that we wrote down last night and see if we can narrow it down and figure out where the methanol came from. Anita, will you be all right if you lie on the large sofa?"

"I should be fine. I'm feeling much better, and can sit on the sofa or in a chair. What about you, Mother? Maybe you want to lie down."

"I think I will do that. Wine has a mellowing effect on me and I only took a short nap today, so maybe lying down will feel good."

After they were all seated on the verandah, Tony said, "Dan, you're the detective, so why don't you get us started."

"I thought I was getting away from this sort of stuff, but this is serious and I'll do what I can to help. Let's start with the list we put together last night. Next to each item, we'll write down the store or stores where you buy these items."

Anita jumped in with, "I'll be the scribe again, since I do most of the shopping. Here's what we started with last night." She took the pad they used last night and began writing and speaking at the same time.

"Kosher salt—Shopper's Delight...salad dressing—same...canned tuna—same...canned tomatoes—same...canned corn—that must be old, from Shopper's Delight, since we usually buy fresh corn at Roland's Outdoor Market...baking potatoes—Roland's...pasta, rice and walnuts—Shopper's...cake and pie mixes and frosting—same...now, we get our olive oil, vinegar, garlic, and spices from Greta's Gourmet Foods...and, we also buy our coffee there, since they have so many good blends. Let's see, the tea is from...where's the tea from, Mother?"

"Well, the regular tea is from Greta's and Susan brings the green tea—the herbal blend that you and I like. She gets it at a place like Greta's near the clinic where she works. I think it's called Natalie's Naturals. Greta's doesn't carry the green tea brand she buys, and I've asked her to get it for me ever since the first time she brought it here, just after she and Jerry were married."

"Oh, yes, now I remember. She seems to know our tea consumption and always has a new box just before we run out."

"Sometimes she asks me," Katherine added.

"Hmmm, so you buy everything, Anita, except the herbal tea?" Dan said inquisitively.

"Well, let's see. Pepper and salt are from Shopper's. Now, let me think," she said, eying the rest of the list from the cupboard and the list of items from the refrigerator. "Yes, I guess I do. The only other stores are the bakery for our breads, Scruppy's for seafood, and Supreme Creamery for the ice cream. We do go a bit overboard with the ice cream; it's so rich and creamy."

"And fattening," Katherine chimed in, a wry smile on her face. Ice cream was one of her great loves. Fortunately, she had never had a weight problem, much to Anita's consternation.

"Are either of you aware of any recent product recalls?" Dan continued.

The two women looked at each other and then at Tony, who had been silent so far. Jon had left, since Tony didn't think he could add anything to what the adults would be thinking about, and Nicole wanted him to drop off something at her cottage before Michael picked her up to drive her to a friend's summer home, about 45 minutes away, where she was going to spend the weekend. Katherine also didn't want Jon to be involved in what the adults were talking about tonight.

Tony shook his head and said, "I'm not aware of anything, but I don't do as much shopping as you ladies do."

"Neither am I," Dan added, responding to his own question.

"I can't say that I've seen or heard anything since the canned tuna scare over mercury food poisoning, but that was at least a couple of years ago." Anita sighed, putting the pad on an end table next to the couch where Katherine was sitting.

"Is there anything that you eat more than anything else?" Dan then asked.

Katherine and Anita pondered this question for a couple of minutes, looking at each other and then at Tony. Katherine then spoke. "Well, I have a bowl of cereal every morning and usually a piece of toast, a small glass of orange or grapefruit juice and a cup of tea."

"What kind or kinds of tea?" Dan asked.

"I like regular in the morning and then, as you know from being here with me, a type of herbal called 'green' tea in the afternoon and again after dinner. I don't drink much coffee any more. I used to drink coffee, but that was long ago."

"What about you, Anita?"

"I'm not a big breakfast eater, so it's usually dry toast or a low-fat muffin—which Mother won't touch—a small glass of juice and regular tea. I like herbal tea after dinner and will join Mother if I'm here for afternoon green tea on the weekend. I don't drink coffee either."

"What about lunch?" Dan probed.

Katherine thought and then spoke. "Mostly salads and an occasional sandwich."

Anita nodded, indicating that was her standard. She then blurted out, "And, before you ask, dinner is varied. You name it...just about anything you can think of."

"What about alcohol?" Dan asked, wanting to complete his questioning.

"Well, you know," Katherine replied with a twinkle in her eye, "I do like a glass of red or dry white wine with dinner on occasion, but that's it for me. I don't drink any hard liquor and detest beer."

"Ditto, here," Anita chimed in. "As I said before, 'like mother, like daughter.'"

Darkness was descending on the shoreline and Dan rubbed his eyes. They had been at this for a while and he couldn't think of anything else to ask them. He was starting to feel drowsy. He wanted to take a walk to Rocky Bar and reflect on what everyone had said this evening. "May I be excused? I'm feeling a bit tired and want to clear my head. Maybe a walk out to the end of Rocky Bar and a long gaze up at the stars would do me good, before I head home. We all need to think about what was said tonight and see if anything stands out or could be a source of poisoning. Anita, maybe you could think of the places where you eat lunch and try to remember if any would be suspicious regarding the quality of the food. I can come back tomorrow at almost any time if you want to talk about this. Just give me a call." He shook his head as he got up to leave, since nothing was jumping out at him at the moment.

"Of course, you can go, Dan...and you don't need to ask permission." Katherine cast a fond look at Dan as she spoke. "I think that my son, daughter and I can manage by ourselves for the remainder of the evening. Maybe it's a good idea to get back together again tomorrow." She looked at Anita, who nodded in agreement.

Katherine, Tony and Anita sat on the verandah for another thirty minutes, chatting about a variety of things, including a review of the places where Anita and her co-workers at the library ate lunch. Katherine and Anita were sipping green tea and Tony was nursing a brandy.

"There are about a dozen or so places we go back and forth to on a regular basis and, as far as I know, none has ever been cited for violating health codes or have been in the news for food poisoning," Anita stated, as she ran over the list in her mind. "There was one kind of dumpy joint that we went to once, but that was a couple of months ago and it closed down after a series of citations by the Board of Health."

"Well, I've just about had enough for one day and I'm tired," Katherine said, yawning as she spoke. "So, I'm going to bed to listen to the waves and then off to sleep."

After Katherine had left the room, Anita turned to Tony. "We haven't talked about the situation with Susan for a while and I've been preoccupied with something else this week. So, has this thing ended?"

"Yeah, it's probably over, but it's not ending quietly."

"What do you mean?"

"Jerry found out."

"Oh, my God," Anita gasped. "Say it isn't so!"

"I'm afraid it is…and it's ugly."

"How did he find out?"

"I don't have all the details, but he found a pair of panties that belong to Susan at my place. They were hanging in the first floor bathroom last Friday night when we had the barbecue at my cottage and he saw them. About the only time Susan was here was the night that you saw us on the beach, but I don't ever remember seeing her panties hanging in the bathroom. They must have been behind a towel and I didn't notice them. Then, that same night, when they returned to their house, Jerry found one of my lighters on one of the end tables in their living room. I don't remember smoking there since we started coming here this year, so this is kind of a mystery. But he found these things and, when he confronted Susan, she admitted to our affair. He came storming over to my place later that night, carrying the shovel from their fireplace and waving it at me as though he were going to attack me with it. He made a threatening comment. I don't know if he was serious."

"Oh, my little brother, what have you done?"

"A bit more, I'm afraid."

"What do you mean, a bit more?"

"Well, there's been another incident—in fact, it was last night."

"Last night! What are you talking about? We were here!"

"It happened after we were here, when Dan and I walked back to my place."

"You were with Dan? So, now he knows?"

"Yeah…he knows." Tony was close to tears as he spoke.

"What was this incident about?"

"Well, Susan and I had a brief encounter Wednesday evening when I went over there to tell her about your condition."

"You have got to be kidding! You go to Susan's house to report on me and then have sex with her?"

"Damn it, Sis, I haven't been able to keep my hands off her. She comes on to me and I go nuts. Maybe I'm sex-crazed or have a problem I don't know about, but this woman drives me insane and has made me do things I've never done in my life."

"How did Jerry find out about this encounter?"

"That I don't know. Maybe Susan said something, but he knew about it...he knew...and, he was angry—really angry. He came storming into the cottage just as Dan and I were going to crack open a couple of beers. Jon was on the deck and Jerry came running through the front door and lunged at me. Dan got in between us and held him off. I told him to get out of the cottage and that I would deal with him privately. So, he left."

"You say Jon was there. So, now your son also knows?" Tony could only hang his head. He was distraught as he thought about the implications that could result from his impropriety with another family member. Anita stared at him, a look of disgust consuming her face. "So, now everyone in the family except Mother knows. Even Dan, an outsider, even though a close friend, knows. What about Michael? Does he know?"

Tony shook his head. "I don't know if Jon has said anything. I hope not."

Anita held her stomach. She was feeling anxious and started to double over.

"Are you all right?"

"I don't know. I didn't really need this on top of what I've been through this week. Let me say this, Tony, either you end this affair and reconcile with Jerry, or you're going to have to make some excuse—maybe a special assignment at work—and get away from here for a while. We simply can't have Mother finding about this, and I don't have any reason to trust you and Susan when you're near each other, especially when Jerry is away."

Tony nodded, feeling weak and humiliated, and wanting to assuage his sister. "It *is* over. We agreed to end it after our last encounter. She even wrote me a note and left it in my car the morning after. I promise you it's over! Now, I'm going outside and wander around for a while. Maybe the night air will clear my head."

"I hope so," Anita shot back disdainfully. "It certainly hasn't been functioning very well lately. I'm totally drained by this and am going to check on Mother and then I'll go to bed—by myself! You are staying here, in the first floor guest room, aren't you?"

"Yes," he said softly, moving away from her, toward the outside of the main house at Hunter's Point.

Tony walked slowly along the edge of the rocky embankment, which was on his left, to the end of the family's property. As he walked, he thought about his married life with Rebecca and how he enjoyed not only their romance, but also just being with her. *We'd probably be taking a walk along the beach together after having dinner.* His thoughts came back to the present. *Am I that lonely? Have I just not realized it all these years that she's been gone? Is it the companionship I'm missing that led me to pursue Susan sexually? I've got to get a grip on my life and what I'm looking for in a woman. Maybe I'm still young enough to have a relationship and there can be life after Rebecca. Perhaps I should stop feeling guilty about getting involved with another woman in a meaningful way.* He reached the far end of the property and sat down on a large a large rock at the edge of the lawn and the steep cliff. After sitting and staring out at the water for about five minutes, he swore to himself that the affair with Susan was over and he would stay clear of her for a while. Tony then started walking back toward the main house. He was about thirty feet from the verandah when a dark-clad figure jumped out from the bushes that bordered the house and shouted, "I told you to keep your hands off her!" A vicious overhand blow from a dark metal object caught him on the left temple and sent him careening onto the embankment, his right shoulder crashing into one of the thousands of rocks on the cliff and breaking his fall. In great pain and unable to move, he felt blood from the head wound running down his cheek, trickling over his lips and into his mouth. Then, everything went blank.

After washing the teacups and brandy glass by hand, Anita went upstairs, undressed and put on a nightgown. As she was brushing her teeth, she heard a loud groaning sound coming from her mother's bedroom, which was next to hers. She dropped the toothbrush and ran into her mother's room. Katherine was vomiting and falling out of bed.

Anita, not thinking of her own condition, dove toward her mother. Her chin, chest and stomach hit the carpeted floor as Katherine landed on top of her. Anita's arms were pinned beneath her and she lacked the strength to move. She lay there for a full two minutes, not able to lift Katherine, who was lying on her back, unresponsive.

"Mother, are you all right?" Anita screamed. "Tony, where are you? Help me!"

There was no answer. Anita became delirious and gathered enough strength to push her arms upward, uttering a soft scream as she saw her mother's limp body roll over onto its back on the carpet, the vomit flowing out of the side of her mouth. She was getting hysterical, but had the composure to roll her fingers inside Katherine's mouth and place her head on its side, so that the elderly lady would not choke on her own vomit. Anita remembered her co-worker saying that this was done for her when she got sick at the library.

Anita then groped for the lamp on Katherine's night table and turned it on. She grabbed the telephone and dialed 911. "Can you send an ambulance to the main house at Hunter's Point," she whispered into the phone, her voice barely audible.

"Could you repeat that, madam?" the operator asked.

"Hunter's Point...off the shore road in Lyme...the main house. My mother, an elderly lady, has collapsed and I think she's unconscious. Please get an ambulance here."

"We'll send one right away."

Anita replaced the phone. "Tony...Tony...where are you?" she cried out. There was no response. She took the telephone receiver off the hook again and dialed Tony's cottage. There was no answer. "Damn him...where is he?" she muttered. She walked quickly down the stairs to the first floor guest room to see if her brother was there. He was not. "Tony," she called out again, as she gazed toward the living room and the verandah. As before, there was no response. She walked back up the stairs to Katherine's bedroom and to the phone on the night table. She depressed the hook and dialed Jerry and Susan's house. There was no answer. "Oh, God, neither of them is back home yet," she moaned. Anita went back to where her mother was laying on the floor and cleared some more residue from Katherine's mouth. Then she then went to the bathroom and got a washcloth, moistened it with lukewarm water and hurried back to her stricken mother. She kneeled down, gently placed the washcloth on Katherine's face, and wiped it clean. Feeling desperate and lost, she crawled back to the night table and, grabbing the phone, dialed again. This time there was a voice at the other end of the line. "Dan, it's Anita. Something has happened here. Mother has collapsed, is vomiting and I think she's unconscious."

"I'll be right there," Dan said.

Chapter 7

Less than ten minutes later, Dan drove his car into the driveway of the main house at Hunter's Point. As he was getting out of his car, an ambulance arrived and parked behind him.

Dan raced into the main house and up the stairs, taking them two at a time. Anita was on her knees, holding her mother's head in her hands. Dan bent over Katherine's limp body and felt the pulse on her neck. It was very weak and she was beginning to turn blue. Two paramedics rushed into the bedroom with a stretcher and oxygen kit. After administering oxygen to Katherine, they motioned for Dan to step aside and gently lifted the elderly woman onto the stretcher.

"We'll take her to the emergency room at Shorehaven Hospital. Can you follow in a car?"

"Certainly," Dan shot back.

"Dan, if these men can take care of Mother, then first we've got to find Tony. I called out for him, but he's not here. Don't you remember that he was going to stay here with us? He was going for a walk and then was supposed to return. When he didn't answer my shouting, I called his cottage, but there was no answer. I went downstairs to the guest room before I called you, but he's not there either. So, where is he?"

"I don't know, but I'll take a look." Dan then ran out of the bedroom and to the edge of the stairs, calling to the paramedics. "I have to do something and then will come to the hospital. Take good care of her."

"We will," one of the paramedics called back.

Dan ran back to the bedroom and noticed that Anita was in a nightgown. "What kind of shape are you in?" he asked, speaking rapidly.

"Does it matter? I'll get by!"

"Can you put on some clothes?"

"Of course."

"Okay, I'll go to Tony's cottage and check it out. If he's not there, I'll come back."

Dan ran out of the bedroom and down the stairs and then out the rear door of the main house. He sprinted to Tony's house, forgetting about his age and that he hadn't run like this in a couple of years. There was a light on in Tony's cottage, which either Tony or Jon would always turn on when going out for an evening. The doors were hardly ever locked at the Hunter's Point homes and Dan entered the cottage. "Tony? Jon? Is anyone here?" No one was.

Dan sprinted back to the main house, out of breath when he arrived. Anita was outside, near the verandah. "Over here, Dan," she cried out, as she saw him running.

"Anita, you said that Tony was going for a walk. Do you know where he went?"

"No, but there aren't that many places here to go to...either to the edge of the property in one direction or the other direction toward the beach and Rocky Bar. Oh, I forgot to say that after dinner tonight and after mother had gone upstairs to go to bed, Tony told me about the encounters with Jerry and that you were involved in one of them."

"Oh, yeah, that was quite a scene. It was *not* a pleasant situation and I felt very awkward. I didn't want to stick around Tony's cottage after it ended."

"I can appreciate that. I wonder if something has happened to Tony. Oh God, Dan, this has been a terrible night. It's insane! I'm *so* worried about Mother and feel that I should be with her, but I'm also concerned about Tony and why he's not here. He wouldn't just go off somewhere, when he said he was only going out for a walk to clear his mind and think about the predicament he's put this family in."

"Listen, Anita, you're in no condition to go to Rocky Bar. So, let me go there. You go the other way to the edge of the property. Get your cell phone and call me if you find him and I'll do the same." Dan started jogging toward the beach, knowing that running that distance at full speed was impossible. He was half-way to the end of the beach when his cell phone rang.

"Yes, what's up, Anita?"

"Please get back here. Tony's lying on the cliff about a quarter of the way down to the ocean. He's motionless and looks dead!"

"Holy shit…sorry. Call 911 and see if they can get that ambulance back here. I'm on my way back to you." Dan's legs were starting to cramp up and his back was aching, but he knew he had to run as fast as he could. "God, I wish I was younger," he grumbled out loud.

Dan saw Anita near the edge of the rocky embankment. He ran to her and she pointed to the spot where Tony lay. Dan climbed down the rocks about twelve feet. Tony was on his back, his body limp. Blood had caked on the left side of his face and run down his neck. Dan feared the worse as he felt first Tony's neck and then his wrist. There was a weak pulse. "He's got a head wound and his shoulder may be injured, also, but I think he's still alive. Did you get the ambulance?"

"They said they couldn't guarantee coming here soon, since the one that was here and another are committed to other emergencies and they only have these two tonight. The other one is in for repairs."

"You can't be serious. No ambulance! Son-of-a-bitch, this is crazy! Nobody to help lift him up to the lawn. With a head wound, I shouldn't try to lift him by myself."

"What choice do we have? Don't we run more risk by leaving him here? Couldn't he bleed to death or die from the injuries? Who knows when an ambulance will get here?"

"I suppose you're right. Alright, then, we've got to do this by ourselves. Go into the house, Anita, and get a couple of blankets and a large pillow. Get the pillow first, bring it back here and toss it down to me. Then you can go back to the house and fetch the blankets. I'll try to keep his head as still as I can and get him up to where you are."

Anita returned within a minute with a pillow. She tossed it down to Dan, who put his arms under Tony's legs and shoulders and cradled his head in the pillow, trying to keep it still. Fortunately, Tony wasn't a large man, weighing about 165 pounds; otherwise it would have been impossible to both lift him and climb up the rocks. *Dragging him upward would kill him,* Dan thought. He now had Tony in his arms and was standing upright. He took a step onto the rock nearest to him. He felt himself slipping and fell to his right knee, his jeans tearing from the impact on a large rock. Pain shot up his leg. He steadied himself. He stood upright again, his arms aching. He reached the next rock and then another. The pain in his shoulders and arms was excruciating and he had to kneel down on a rock. About three more rocks to go, he figured as he looked upward. He stood up again and took a step upward, but misjudged the rock he was stepping onto and started to fall toward his right side. His shoulder crashed into another rock, and he almost lost his grip on Tony. He leaned against the rock and solidified his hold on the limp and lifeless man in his arms. *Damn…I hope his head didn't suffer from this*, Dan moaned to himself. *Thank God for the pillow.* He righted himself and climbed up on the next to the last rock as Anita was returning with the blankets. She gasped as she looked at Dan cradling her brother in his arms.

"We're almost there," he groaned. "Just one more rock. Lay the two blankets out flat, one on top of the other." He gathered himself, took a deep breath and carefully stepped upward with his left foot, pushing downward with his right. He had made it to the lawn, but felt himself losing his balance and leaning backward toward the cliff. Anita ran behind him and gave him a push, which prevented him and Tony from falling back onto the rocks of the embankment. He had just enough strength to gently lower Tony's body onto the blanket, keeping his arm underneath the pillow. Dan slowly removed his right arm as Anita put hers there, to prevent Tony's bloody head from moving. Dan then fell backward on the lawn. He was exhausted. But, he knew he had to get Tony to the car. "I don't know if I can do this alone, Anita. Can you help me get him to the car?"

"I'll find a way."

"I'll go to my car, drive it as close as I can to where we are and then come back here. We'll wrap the blankets around him and lay him down on his back on the rear seat."

With Tony lying unconscious on the rear seat and Anita half sitting and half kneeling on the rear floor to hold onto him and keep him from moving, Dan sped toward the shore road. After they made the turn onto the road and had gone about a mile, they saw an ambulance coming toward them, its lights blinking and siren blaring.

"Great timing," Dan said, as he pushed the accelerator to the floor and blew the horn at the Shorehaven Hospital ambulance, which had passed by him and was heading toward Hunter's Point.

Chapter 8

A medical team was waiting for them as they arrived at the entrance of the emergency ward. Dan had phoned the hospital to prepare them and also told them to contact the ambulance driver about having Tony in his car.

Tony was whisked into the hospital as Dan and Anita embraced and watched. Anita's face had a look of absolute fear and the wrinkles in Dan's temples seemed to be enlarged. "Come on, let's get inside," Dan said. "We've got to find out about your mother."

Dan went to the main desk at the emergency ward and was told that an intern, Dr. Kevin Callahan, was on duty and that he had been administering to Katherine and was now with Tony. The aid could not provide any information on Katherine's condition. She had not seen or spoken to the doctor since Katherine was admitted. Dan asked if Dr. Callahan would speak to them when he was through with Tony. The aid said she would do what she could, but didn't know when she would see or speak to him, given the extent and nature of the emergencies this evening.

Dan and Anita took a seat in the waiting area. Anita slumped down in a couch and started to sob. "Oh Dan, my mother and brother are behind that big wall, and I don't even know if they're alive."

Dan, who had started to pace the floor, walked over to her and put a hand on her shoulder. "This must be awfully difficult for you. God, it's tough for me, so I can't imagine what it must be like for you. The fact that no one has come out is good news. If one or both of them were gone, someone would be out here to tell us."

"I guess you're right. But, the waiting…and the uncertainty…it's terrible! What could have caused all this? Tony falls off the edge of the embankment and Mother collapses and is unconscious. How? Why?"

"Isn't nausea and collapsing what happened to you last week?"

"Well, yes it is. Maybe not as severely as what happened to Mother, but I did get dizzy, started to throw up and then passed out."

"Could it be the same thing—poisoning?"

"I hope not...but, I guess it could be." Anita looked up at the ceiling, as though searching for an answer or an explanation for what had happened to her and to her mother. Then she remembered something. "Dan, I've got to call Jon." She dialed his cell phone number, but got a voice mail message. "He's not answering his phone...probably with his friends at a party somewhere." Anita was shaking as she spoke.

"Okay, don't worry. We'll try him again in fifteen or twenty minutes," Dan said, trying to soothe her.

They sat in silence for another ten minutes, Dan next to Anita with his arm wrapped around her, trying to comfort her. He was struggling to think of something to say.

Suddenly, a young man in surgeon's garb approached them. He appeared to be in his late twenties. "Are you the Kents? I'm Kevin Callahan—the doctor on duty tonight."

"She's a Kent and I'm Dan Davies, a friend," Dan answered.

"Well, I admit to not being that experienced. I'm in my second year of residency, but I've never seen or heard of anything like this before—two members of the same family in critical condition for entirely different reasons."

"How are they?" Dan pleaded, casting an eye at Anita as he spoke.

"In one sense, they're not at all good. Both are barely alive, but they are still alive and we're doing all we can to keep them with us. Mrs. Kent is in a coma. We thought we had lost her after she had been here for about fifteen minutes. Her breathing had just about stopped and she had renal failure."

Dan nodded—having an understanding of what the doctor was saying, but Anita looked puzzled and said, "Excuse me, doctor, but can you clarify? Isn't renal failure related to her kidneys?"

"Yes. They weren't functioning. We put her on a dialysis machine, which we think solved that problem—at least for now. What's troubling is that we can't figure out what might have caused this condition. Can you tell us anything about her that might help? We have no record of her here."

Dan cast another glance at Anita, who said, "That's because she avoids hospitals like the plague. Sorry, doctor, please don't take it the wrong way. I don't know what I can tell you about my mother, but maybe something about *me* might be of use."

The young intern looked at her, a puzzled expression on his face. "Can you please be more specific?"

"I was admitted here on Monday after getting sick and passing out at work, and was diagnosed with methanol in my bloodstream."

"You were? You must have been treated by Dr. O'Brien…'Jack' as we call him. Monday is a day off for me, so he was on duty."

"Yes, it was Dr. O'Brien. He's a nice young man and he gave me good care."

"Glad to hear that. We try. Methanol…hmmm…interesting. That would explain a lot about your mother's condition: renal failure, breathing that stopped, general weakness and cyanosis. Maybe *that's* why her skin and lips have turned blue. But, how? How could your mother have methanol in her system?"

"That seems to be a major question for this family," Dan interjected.

"Look, you two stay here. Let me get back to Mrs. Kent and do something now that we think that methanol may be in her blood. This may just save her."

With that, he bounded back into the emergency ward, leaving Dan and Anita staring at each other.

Kevin Callahan was back in less than fifteen minutes. He looked at Anita empathetically. "I took a quick look at your record and ordered something for your mother that I hope will stabilize her for a while. I know I'm supposed to be a dispassionate physician, but I really feel for you and what you must be going through."

"Thank you…it's been quite a week. What can you tell me about my brother, Tony?"

"He was close to being clinically dead when you brought him here, but fortunately we think we have a steady pulse and heart beat now. He has a severe head wound and we're concerned with brain damage, which I think you know can be permanent. I don't want to alarm you, but it is a possibility. We just don't know yet. We'll know better tomorrow, assuming we can get him through the night. He also has broken bones and extensive damage to his right shoulder, but those injuries can heal with time. I checked on him when I was back there, and am only going to spend another minute with you now so I can get back to him. He needs my constant attention for a while. I don't know for how long, but I'll stay here all night if I have to. We have another crew coming in at eleven, but I'm not leaving given the situation."

Dan leaned forward as Anita got out of her chair, walked over to the intern and hugged him. "Thank you...and God bless you," she whispered.

"All in a doctor's day. Before I go back, do you know the cause of your brother's fall? Were you anywhere near him? Was it an accident? It looks like something beside rocks may have caused his injury. Possibly a blunt object of some sort. Falling on rocks alone should have produced more severe lacerations than he has."

Anita looked at Dan, who shook his head and whispered, "Doctor, we don't know anything. This is an insane mystery, the likes of which I haven't seen for a long time. By the way, I'm a retired New York City detective and I've seen a lot, but this is one of the weirdest nights I've ever had."

As the intern walked away, Dan and Anita returned to a sofa and lounge chair. Anita grabbed Dan's arm and fell toward him, knocking him backward. She had fainted. He cradled her and brought her to the sofa, laying her on her back and moving her head sidewise and then checking her pulse. He walked quickly to the main desk and, pointing toward Anita said, "You may have another patient tonight."

A nurse was called along with two medics, who put Anita on a stretcher and wheeled her into the emergency ward. Dan sat by himself, incredulous about what had happened tonight. Then he thought, *There's one more member of the immediate family—Jon. I've got to call him.* He reached into Anita's purse, which he had held on to as she was wheeled away, and found her cell phone. Tabbing to the phone's memory, he pushed the redial button.

"Hello...Anita?"

"No, Jon, it's not Anita. It's Dan Davies. We met at your graduation party. Can you talk?"

"Sure, what's up?"

"Where are you?"

"At Condor's Nest. In fact, we're on the next road over from your place, sitting out on the deck of a friend's cottage and shootin' the breeze. So, where are you and why are you calling me from Anita's cell phone?"

"I'm in a place where I don't want to be and a situation I don't want to be in. I'm at Shorehaven Hospital and you need to get here as soon as you can."

"Why...what's going on?"

"It's a bit complicated, Jon, but your father, grandmother and aunt are all in the hospital."

"What? Get outta here! Is this some sort of bad joke?"

"I wish it were. Oh, God, how I wish it were, Jon. But it's not a joke. More of a nightmare, but it's real. Please try to get here soon, and come alone. I'll explain when you get here. Can you drive? Do you know where the hospital is?"

"Yeah, I'm okay to drive. My friend Nicole went to Rhode Island earlier tonight with Michael, so I came over here to hang out with some guys I know. We've been here for a while and I was planning to go home around midnight. I've got my dad's car and know where the hospital is."

"Good. Then get in the car and drive here now!"

Dan gazed around the waiting room and then looked at the coffee table that was strewn with magazines. He was in no mood for reading. His mind started racing. He was in detective mode, unused since he retired. *I should write down a timeline for all that happened tonight, in case there's an investigation,* he thought. He walked over to the information desk and asked for paper and pen. He spoke silently to himself as he began to write. *Let's see...we sat down for dinner around seven o'clock. We must have been at the table for at least an hour, say until after eight. Then, we cataloged the food and drink items and talked about their eating habits for about thirty minutes or so. When I was getting ready to leave Hunter's Point it was almost dark, which would make it around eight forty-five. So, when did Anita call? The nine o'clock movie was on...had been for a while, probably in the middle of it, so that would be about ten. That's right. I recall looking at my watch as I hung up the phone. It's now eleven-thirty and I've been here for over half an hour. Tony must have taken his fall between nine, maybe nine-fifteen and ten. Katherine must have gotten sick just before ten, and I must have lifted Tony off the embankment around ten-thirty. That's about it.*

Twenty minutes after Dan had called him, Jon Kent sprinted into the waiting area where Dan was pacing the floor. "Mr. Davies, what's going on? Why is my family here?"

Dan motioned to the couch where he and Anita had been sitting. "Let's sit down and I'll try to explain this crazy night as best I can."

Dan recapped everything that he knew about the evening, starting with the list of food and drink items in the main house kitchen and trying to figure out if either of the two ladies could have ingested anything containing methanol. In response to Jon's query, Dan said that nothing stuck out. Dan then told the lad about getting a frantic call from Anita after he had returned home, driving to Hunter's Point and getting there as an ambulance arrived to take his grandmother to the hospital. After pausing for a moment to collect his thoughts, Dan explained how he went to search for Tony after Anita said that he wasn't in the house and she couldn't reach him at the phone in the cottage—ending with his running half-way to Rocky Bar and then back to the main house after Anita had found Jon's father lying unconscious on the rocky embankment.

"How did he get *there*?" Jon asked.

"I have no idea and neither does your aunt."

"So, then what happened?"

"There was no ambulance available, so I had to get him off the cliff by myself. Then, Anita and I carried him to my car and drove him here. He's been in the emergency room ever since."

"Are they all right?" Jon was now trembling.

"Not exactly. Your father and grandmother are in critical condition. They're both in comas and came very close to dying. Having to get your dad off the cliff by myself didn't help his situation. But, they're both alive and we're hoping for the best."

"You said *we*. Where's Anita?"

"She was with me, but she fainted here in the waiting room and was taken into the ward on a stretcher."

"This can't be real. It can't be! My dad, Grandma and Aunt Anita...all unconscious and behind that wall?"

"I'm sorry...so sorry. This isn't what summer at the beach is supposed to be like."

"No shit!" Jon got up and started pacing the floor. "Jesus, a half hour ago I was bullshittin' with the guys and thinking about Nicole, and now I'm wondering if I'll be a teen-age orphan. First, my mother, now, Dad." He was shaking and sobbing as he spoke.

Dan got up, went over to him, and gave him a bear hug. "Look, young man, we've got to pray for them and hope the doctor and nurses can pull them through this. Then we'll have to think about what happened and why."

Jon wanted to pursue what happened to his father. "How could Dad have fallen off the edge of the embankment in back of Grandma's house? Was he drunk? He seemed perfectly sober when I left. I don't remember if he even had anything to drink with dinner."

"I think he was sipping a brandy, but wasn't drunk, or even close to it, when I left."

"So, how could a supposedly sober man, who knows every inch of that property, fall headlong onto the rocks? It doesn't make any freakin' God-damn sense. Do you think this has anything to do with what happened between him and Uncle Jerry? Do you think Jerry could have had a fight with Dad and maybe pushed him into the rocks...or maybe hit Dad with that fireplace shovel? I heard him threaten to do that. If he did that, I'll beat the shit out of him! Maybe I'll kill him!"

"Whoa there, boy! Let's not jump to any conclusions or make a bad situation worse. Our first concern has to be with your loved ones. Then we'll get into what might have happened...and why."

"Where are they, anyhow? Uncle Jerry and Susan, I mean?"

"I don't know. I think Anita tried to call them earlier tonight, but couldn't reach them. Jerry supposedly had an out-of-town business trip today and Susan may have gone out with some people she works with."

"How convenient...they're not around when Anita has an emergency. Hey, I should call Michael and tell him what happened."

Dan looked at him and said, "Didn't you say that he drove your friend Nicole to Rhode Island when we spoke on the phone?"

"Oh, yeah. Michael dropped off Nicole in Westerly and then went to meet some friends from college and spend the weekend in Charlestown. Man, I'm really losing it! How could I forget what I just mentioned to you? I'll call him tomorrow unless Dad or Grandma doesn't make it through the night. Shit, Mr. Davies...this sucks!"

Jon started pacing again, this time faster than before. He was angry. He had a vision of a fistfight in the ninth grade, when a group of kids had cruelly teased him for having a grandmother and aunt instead of a real mother. His fist was pounding into the face of a kid, except the kid had the appearance of his Uncle Jerry. *I will beat the crap out of him! I'll really hurt him if he did this to Dad,* he thought.

The door to the ward opened and Anita walked over to them. She wrapped her arms around Jon and they held each other tightly. They were crying profusely. Anita loosened her hold on her nephew, backed away and said, "I'm all right now. I just fainted and was only out for a few minutes. They kept me in the ward until they were certain I could walk on my own and wouldn't have a repeat. Guess what? We're all staying here tonight. They have a room with three cots where we can sleep. I can't leave here. God knows if I can sleep!"

"That's good. I didn't want to leave here either," Dan sighed. "I'm so exhausted that I'm going to try to get some sleep. I won't be much use to anyone if I don't get some rest. My body is aching and I'm shot mentally." Then, looking down at his ripped jeans, he said, "My clothes aren't in such good shape, either, but I'll have to live with them for a while longer."

A moment later, an orderly came to escort them to the room. Dan looked at his watch. It was midnight.

Chapter 9

At five o'clock in the morning, an orderly knocked on the door of the room. Getting no reaction, he entered and shook Dan gently by the shoulders. "Mr. Davies, can you wake up?"

Dan turned his head and looked up at the young man dressed in a white uniform. He sat up abruptly and stared at the man. "You can't convict him! He's innocent and I can prove it, if I can have another day to gather the evidence I need," he said groggily.

"Excuse me?" the orderly replied curiously.

"Who…who are you?"

"I work here at the hospital. The doctor sent me to get you and the Kents."

"Oh, sorry, I must have been having a dream. A fitting end to a nightmarish night."

"We need to wake the others. Mr. Kent has taken a turn for the worse and the doctor thinks you should all come to the ICU…now."

"I was afraid of this. Alright, let's get them up. Anita," he said, as he put his hand on her head and moved it back and forth. "You need to get up." Dan went over to the bed where Jon was sleeping and shook him gently by the shoulders. The lad woke up.

Anita and Jon rose slowly and put their bare feet on the floor. They looked drowsily at Dan and the orderly, trying to get their bearings.

"What's happened?" Anita asked. "You must be waking us up for a reason."

"Dr. Callahan wants to see you in the ICU," the orderly replied. "Mr. Kent has taken a bad turn. That's what I was told by the nurse on duty."

"Let's go," Jon shot back, reaching for his sandals.

As they entered the ICU, they were met by the head nurse who directed them to Tony's room. Doctor Callahan was pacing outside. When he saw them, he rushed to Anita and took both of her hands. His head was shaking. Then he spoke. "He's had some internal cranial bleeding and this is not good. In fact, it can be dangerous and I'm very concerned. I've been at his bedside and Mrs. Kent's, alternating with the doctor on duty. The nurses have been monitoring both of them closely."

"What does this mean?" Anita asked, sobbing.

"He can't survive much more of this type of bleeding. We don't have much of a heartbeat and we could lose it if this continues."

"Can you do anything to stop it?" Jon inquired.

"Not too much, I'm afraid. We're giving him some medication, which is about all we can do for him. It all depends on how severe his head injuries are, but he's too weak for us to do any diagnosis. All we can do now is try to stabilize him. Also, I'm totally exhausted and am going home soon. Dr. O'Brien, whom you know, Miss Kent, has been called to come in early since he's on today, and I'll stay here until he arrives. We also have the doctor on duty for the graveyard shift here. We had another trauma case tonight—a car accident on the shore road—and he's attending to the two victims who were seriously injured."

"Oh, my God," Anita moaned. "What about Mother?"

"Actually, while weak, she's been stable for most of the night. Not any better, but not any worse either. We thought we had lost her pulse around two o'clock, but she came back and is basically in the same condition as when she arrived. We're hoping that medication we've given her will start to dilute what appears to be a lot of poison in her bloodstream. It's similar to what we did for you, Miss Kent," he said, looking at Anita.

"Can we see my grandmother?" Jon asked the doctor.

"Certainly. Let's go to her room."

They hovered over the comatose Katherine. Dan, Anita and Jon fought to hold back tears. Dr. Callahan stood silently by the bed.

Dan gazed at Anita and Jon, and then said quietly, "She's still rather blue looking."

"Yes, she is," Callahan replied. "The cyanosis will take a while to go away. Fortunately, none of her organs have failed, which can happen with methanol poisoning, and her irregular respiratory patterns have improved somewhat. They're not quite where we want them to be, but they've gotten a little better since she arrived here."

"So, you think it *is* methanol in her?" Dan continued.

"Right now, I'd bet on it. She has the symptoms of having quite a bit in her system."

"How could this happen...both to her and to Anita?" Dan said inquisitively.

"Well, they either ingested something with a high concentration of wood alcohol, or it's been building up for some period of time. Right now, I'd bet on the latter, and think that each got to a point where there was enough in their systems to trigger these reactions—Mrs. Kent much worse than Anita's probably due to having more toxins in her system and her age."

"But how?" Dan pressed on. "How could this get into their bloodstreams? They don't exactly go around drinking paint thinners or other things that contain methanol."

"I really don't know," the doctor said, his head shaking. "But they must have been ingesting something with methanol in it for some period of time. That's my best guess."

Jon, who was pacing back and forth, suddenly started to gasp, bent over and clutched his stomach. Dan went over to him. "Are you all right, Jon?"

"Not really, Mr. Davies. I'm feeling kind of sick and dizzy. I'm not good at this."

"Most of us aren't," Dan replied. "I've seen a lot of hospital wards and injured people, and it's never easy. It's worse when those hurt or sick are close to you." *Especially when you're only 18*, he added silently to himself.

Dr. Callahan, who had been talking mostly to Dan, then looked at Anita. "Miss Kent, are there any other close family members you want to contact? I just don't know how long Mr. Kent is going to hang on. While we're doing everything we can, we could lose him, and I don't want to overlook anyone you might want to be here."

Anita looked at Jon, who was shaking his head as if to say *NO*. "What about Jerry?" she blurted out.

Jon shook his head harder. "I don't want him here now. What if he caused this? He did threaten Dad, remember?" The lad looked at Dan for support as he spoke. "I'd probably call Aunt Miriam and Michael before I'd call Uncle Jerry."

"I haven't thought of Miriam, but we can certainly call her later," Anita sighed. "She would want to know about this. And, Jon, you can call Michael."

Jon nodded.

Anita turned to the intern. "I guess, Doctor, that we won't call anyone right now. Can we go back to see Tony?"

As they were standing over Tony, Dr. Callahan started to smile. He grabbed Anita's arm and pointed toward the monitor. "Look, he's coming back. The heartbeat is getting a little stronger."

Just as Callahan was speaking, a nurse burst into the room. "Dr. Callahan, come quickly. Mrs. Kent is slipping. We're losing her heartbeat and her breathing pattern is erratic."

The young intern flew out of Tony's room and toward Katherine's, with Jon in hot pursuit and Dan and Anita close behind.

"Oh, Jesus," the exhausted intern moaned. "Come on, Mrs. Kent, don't leave us now…not now." The line on the monitor was barely flickering. Then, as if by divine intervention, it started to show a slight up and down pattern. Callahan stumbled but caught himself.

Dan thought the doctor might be swooning. "Are you ill?" he asked.

"No, I'll be fine," Dr. Callahan said. "It's just been quite a night and I don't know what I would have done if Mrs. Kent had expired."

"You may have saved their lives," Anita said. "Staying here with them through the night is something for which we'll be forever grateful, whatever the outcome."

As Anita was finishing, a figure she recognized entered the room. "Dr. O'Brien…how good to see you." Anita walked over to him and extended her hand. "Thank you so much for coming in early."

"No problem," the young doctor replied. "Have the Kents of Hunter's Point made a big donation? You seem to have a monopoly on our staff and accommodations."

They all laughed, appreciating a bit of humor at the end of what had been a most stressful hour.

"I think we can let Dr. O'Brien take over," Dr. Callahan stated, "which means the rest of us can get some rest. I'm going home, and I suggest you three go back to your 'hotel suite' and get some more sleep. Today is going to be a long day for you. I hope it will be better than last night and early this morning."

"Amen," Dan sighed. "I'm ready for some more sleep. How about the rest of you?"

Anita and Jon nodded in approval, following her out of Katherine's room.

"Please wake us up no later than ten o'clock," Dan said to the orderly who had awakened them earlier, as he passed him walking down the hall.

They were awakened just before ten o'clock and went to check on Tony and Katherine. There was no change since they had last been there, which Dr. O'Brien said was a good sign. He was more concerned with Tony and Katherine deteriorating than with the timing of any improvement. The doctor suggested they get some breakfast at a nearby diner.

They returned to the hospital to find Jerry in the waiting room. Dan cast a stern look at Jon. The message was, *Don't say anything.*

Anita walked over to where Jerry was sitting on the same couch she and Dan had occupied last night.

"Anita, what's going on here? I arrived five minutes ago and thought you had taken ill and had perhaps been readmitted. I took a walk over to your house after breakfast to see how you were, but no one was there. Then, I went to Tony's house, but no one was there, either. So, I figured that everyone was here at the hospital. But you look all right. Where are Tony and Katherine?"

"Well, Jerry, you're right about one thing—we're all here at the hospital, but not for the reasons you may think. I don't know how to say this, so I'll be totally direct. Mother and Tony are in comas in the ICU. Both of them almost died last night."

"What...what are you saying? How could that have happened? Tony and Katherine almost died last night? What happened? A car accident?"

"No, not that, although we don't know the exact causes of what happened. Tony fell or was pushed off the edge of the embankment in back of our house. He has a very serious head injury. After she went to bed, Mother got sick. We think she has the same poison—methanol—that they found in me. She came here in an ambulance after I found her passing out and falling out of bed. That happened before I found Tony. That's all we know."

Jerry sat in total silence—a look of bewilderment on his face. Dan was looking very intently at Jerry, trying to pick up any hint that Jerry might already know some of what Anita was telling him. He gazed over at Jon and noticed him also staring at his "uncle."

Dan then said, "Tony's doctor was talking to us and saying that something other than falling onto the rocks of the embankment may have caused his head injury. We sat here last night thinking a lot about that, but couldn't come to any conclusions."

"What's that supposed to mean?" Jerry countered.

"I don't know," the former detective replied. "I'm just trying to tell you what we've been dealing with since about ten-thirty last night." Dan noticed a scowl creeping across Jerry's face as he spoke.

"Did the doctor say anything else?" Jerry asked, looking concerned.

"No, not much," Dan replied. "Just that his head injury appeared to be more consistent with coming into contact with a blunt object rather than the type of rocks on the embankment. That's about as far as we got."

"Hmmm…that's a puzzle." Jerry looked at Anita, whose head had dropped into her hands, and Jon, who sat expressionless. "Has anyone called Michael?"

"Not yet," Jon responded, "but I was going to do that in a little while. I assume you know he's in Rhode Island."

Jerry nodded and then said, "I should go back home and tell Susan about all this. I think it would be better to do it in person rather than on the phone. I can't do anything here, except sit around and pace the floor, which I assume you three have been doing. Why don't all of you come to our house for dinner tonight? You've got to eat, and maybe it would be a good break, assuming something tragic doesn't happen today."

Jon was about to react when Dan cut in. "Maybe that's a good idea, Jerry. Yes, I think that would be good for all of us—to get away from this place for a while." He cast a glance and a very slight nod at Anita, indicating that she should go along with what he was saying.

Anita nodded. Jon shrugged his shoulders and remained silent.

After Jerry had left the hospital, Jon turned to Dan and said, "I don't want to go to his house for dinner tonight. What if he did this to Dad and coming here is a hoax?"

"That's the point. I know something about perpetrators creating illusions of innocence. We can see if the fireplace shovel is there or if it's missing, which would implicate him. Don't you want to know that?"

Jon managed a brief smile and nodded.

Dan, Anita and Jon went back to the ICU and, for the next hour, alternated visiting the two rooms where Tony and Katherine continued to lie in comas. Both had been stabilized, and Dr. O'Brien indicated he thought they were not in any immediate danger. He warned them, however, that things could change and such changes were not predictable.

After Jack O'Brien left them, Dan turned to Anita and Jon. "I think we need to notify the state police about what happened. Why don't I go to the barracks, which is not too far away, and make a report? I'll come back here later and pick you up, and then we can all go back to Hunter's Point. I want to get cleaned up, and both of you may want to shower and freshen up before we go to Jerry and Susan's house for dinner."

"For certain," Anita said. "In fact, if Mother and Tony are stable, I would like to lie down in my own bed for a nap before we go to see Jerry and Susan. Is that all right with you, Jon?"

"Sure, Aunt Anita, you've been through a lot this week. I'll do whatever you want."

"You are a good lad." Anita sighed, smiling as she put her arms around him and gave him a tender hug.

"Okay, then," Dan interjected, "I'll leave now, go to the state police barracks and come back, say, by three o'clock and pick you two up."

Anita and Jon nodded as Dan walked away. Then they returned to Tony's room.

Thirty minutes later, Dan strolled into the state police barracks and approached the front desk, where a young trooper was sitting. "Can I help you?" the man asked.

Dan introduced himself and added that he was a retired detective from the New York City Police Department and was now living at Condor's Nest Beach.

"Wow, we're really impressed around here with anyone that served in the NYPD, especially after 9/11."

"Thanks…nice of you to say that, but I'm just an ordinary guy now, trying to enjoy my retirement in this beautiful area. Something happened last night to interrupt this new life I've embarked upon, which I think the state police should be aware of." As Dan started to describe the Friday night events at Hunter's Point, the young trooper stopped him, went to an office and came back with another, somewhat older, officer. After shaking his hand, the more senior officer, a big black man, took Dan to a small conference room where he let Dan explain the prior night's events, taking notes as Dan spoke.

"So, you think foul play may be involved, in at least one of the incidents and maybe both?" the trooper asked after Dan had finished speaking.

"It certainly is a possibility that probably should be investigated. For the sake of the family, I wish it were not, but there's just too much here to ignore: a sober man falling on the rocks behind a house that he literally grew up in after being threatened, and two women believed to be infected with the same type of poison."

"I agree, this is a bit much to expect from natural causes. Alright, Mr. Davies, what do you suggest we do?"

"Well, for starters, please call me Dan."

"Okay, that's easy. I'm Bill…Bill Jenkins. Sorry, I didn't introduce myself before, but you seemed so motivated to get this story out that I wanted to let you talk."

"No problem. I guess you're right. I'm probably energized beyond what I want to be. Now, as to what to do…let's see…I'm going to the Hunter house for dinner tonight. That's Jerry's house. Jerry is the one who made the threat to Tony Kent and acted completely shocked when we told him what had happened. I'm going to see if the fireplace shovel is in the house. If it is, I'll see if there are any visible marks—blood, etc.—on it. If so, then you should get a search warrant for the house and its contents. You probably should do that anyway, since you'll want to do DNA testing if there's nothing visible. If the shovel isn't there, then you probably should get a search warrant for the entire property and his car, assuming that Jerry may have stashed or hidden it somewhere on the property or maybe drove it off the property and disposed of it. Would forensics pick up anything in his car?"

"Maybe. Depends on how careful, or careless, he is. I just can't give you an answer at this time."

"I understand. Excuse me. I may be losing my edge now that I'm retired."

"Oh, I wouldn't worry too much about that. You seem pretty sharp to me."

"Thanks, but let's keep going. We should take all the food and liquid out of the main house—that's where Mrs. Kent and Anita live—and send it to a lab for testing. I've got to believe there's something that has poisoning. I'm getting an impression from the doctor at the hospital that there may be a steady dose of methanol over a prolonged period of time, and that could not come from eating out at a restaurant one or two times or even more. Katherine Kent came close to a complete shutdown of her system and within a whisker of dying, which means that a lot of this toxin had to be in her bloodstream. We may know something more by Monday, assuming she can make it until then."

"Let me make sure I've got this straight," the trooper replied. "You're going to the Hunter home tonight for dinner, and will let me know about getting a search warrant for their place and maybe the entire property. Then, you want us to load up and take away all the food and drink in the other house, the one Mrs. Kent and her daughter live in. We should do that immediately, unless there's a reason for waiting."

"I can't think of any reason for waiting," Dan said. "Can you have someone there tomorrow?"

"Well, I'm supposed to be off tomorrow—that's Sunday—but I don't have anything going on except a morning golf game. How about if I come over there in the afternoon? I'll bring a van to transport everything."

"Sounds like a plan. By the way, I'll provide you with proof of my former life with the NYPD before we touch anything."

"Thanks," the state trooper replied. "I appreciate you offering it before I asked. I'll do some checking after you leave, but I have a sense that you're being straight up."

Dan nodded. "Okay then. I'll see you at two o'clock?"

"You got it."

Dan and Trooper Jenkins got up and shook hands. The trooper then escorted Dan to the parking lot.

The mood was tense at dinner. Susan was making small talk with Anita, but the situation was very difficult due to the affair between Tony and Susan and Tony's serious medical condition. Dan tried to cut through the thick, tense atmosphere by giving a very long and involved answer to a question Susan asked about his retirement and search for a home. He recounted in detail how his life had been impacted by the loss of his wife of many years and his son staying in New York and spending much of his spare time in the Hampton's on Long Island, a more desirable place for a young, single professional than the Connecticut shoreline.

Jon was having a tough time talking about anything, but did comment about the girls that he and Michael had reunited with and how much he enjoyed being with his only cousin—especially their double-dating. Jon mentioned that he had spoken by cell phone to Michael that afternoon about what had happened. Michael was in Newport. When Michael had asked Jon if he should return, Jon suggested staying the night in Rhode Island, driving back the next day and meeting at the hospital. Jerry nodded and stated that he had basically the same conversation with his son and conveyed a similar message, since Michael's car was in Charlestown and he had been driven to Newport in a friend's car.

After Jerry had offered him an after-dinner drink, Dan asked if he could stretch his legs and take a walk outside. He motioned for Jon to join him. Jerry said he would join them in a few minutes after a trip to the bathroom. Anita and Susan were occupied with cleaning the dishes.

"Look, the fireplace shovel is here," Dan whispered to Jon as they walked through the living room and approached the fireplace. "Try to see if there's any visible blood."

Jon looked over his shoulder to make sure no one was looking, then gazed at all sides of the shovel. "I think I see a small red speck, but it's hard to tell," he said softly.

"Good eyes," Dan shot back. "Mine can't pick up very small objects any more, so it's good to have a younger pair. We're going to get a search warrant for the house on Monday and we'll take the shovel in for testing. By the way, did I tell you? A state trooper is coming to the main house tomorrow to take all the food and drink items to a lab for testing."

"No, you didn't tell me. Do you want me to be there? I'm supposed to work the morning—I'm filling in for someone—but I could come home after I finish."

"No, I think the state trooper and I can handle it. Why don't you go to the hospital after work, meet Michael there as you've planned, and check in on your dad and grandmother, assuming nothing bad happens before then. Come on, we're supposed to be going outside. We don't want Jerry to find us wandering around his living room. That would make him more suspicious than he may already be. And remember, don't say anything adversarial to Jerry tonight. Let's give him the benefit of the doubt until we have something concrete."

"Okay…are we going back to the hospital tonight?"

"You bet we are. There are no formal visiting hours for immediate family in the ICU, and Anita signed a document listing me in a special visitor category with no restrictions. I'll finish this drink and then we'll get your aunt and go back."

Chapter 10

Dan was waiting outside the main house at two o'clock Sunday afternoon when Bill Jenkins drove up in a state police van.

Jerry was sitting on his verandah. Seeing a strange vehicle driving on the property, he bolted out of the chair and ran toward Katherine's house. Out of breath as he got there, he recognized Dan and looked at him inquisitively. "What's going on?"

"Jerry, meet State Trooper Bill Jenkins," Dan replied. "You remember we told you yesterday that Anita and Katherine may have similar or exactly the same toxin in their systems? Well, I guess I forgot to tell you that I went to the state police barracks yesterday and suggested that we should test all the food and liquid items in the main house to see if we can find anything suspect."

"I see. What else have you forgotten to tell me?" Jerry retorted.

"Well, let's see…I don't think there's anything else. Look, Jerry, we decided to do this after you left the hospital yesterday. Since this doesn't really involve you, I just didn't think of telling you. I'm sorry." Dan was reverting to his detective tactics, which involved a bit of deception.

"Is there anything that I can do to help?"

Dan felt he had to be careful and not do or say anything that would put Jerry on the defensive. "Sure. If you want to help us load the items from the kitchen into the van, that will get Trooper Jenkins out of here faster, which he'll probably appreciate, since he's here on his day off."

Bill Jenkins nodded in approval.

"Alright, then let's go. Tell me what to do," Jerry said.

"Pack the items in the kitchen in whatever bags and boxes are around," Dan replied. "I brought over several. There are a couple of large coolers that I got out of the garage for refrigerated and frozen items. We're taking everything, but only one of each for packaged food."

After speaking, Dan looked at Jenkins, who nodded again.

Thirty minutes later, the police van was loaded and on its way out of Hunter's Point.

Dan was starting to walk toward his car when Jerry put his arm on his shoulder and said, "So, Mr. Detective, what do you think could have happened?"

"I honestly don't know. All I can go by is what the doctors are suggesting—an apparent continual dose of methanol for some period of time. It's weird!"

"I should say so," Jerry replied, shaking his head and looking very intently at Dan. "I hope I'm not a suspect in either of these incidents."

Dan, having been subjected to this type of question many times, responded with a stoic expression and in, a monotone, said, "Jerry, I don't know what to think or suspect at this time. My main concern and my only thoughts right now are for the well-being of two ladies and a man that I care for along with a boy who is going through a hellish situation that neither you nor I can realistically imagine."

Jerry shook his head. Dan had made his point and there would be no more interrogation of the detective. He shook Dan's hand and slowly walked back to his house. Dan watched him and then walked toward his car.

As Michael strolled into the entrance of the hospital, he pulled out his cell phone and dialed Jon's number, per their arrangement. He then took a seat on the couch in the waiting area. Five minutes later, Jon walked over to him.

"Holy shit, Jon, this is unbelievable! What the friggin' hell is going on?"

"I wish I knew," Jon said, his head shaking from side to side. "I really thought that at least one of them was going to die, but they seem to have stabilized. Who the hell knows, though? They could suffer a relapse and either die or maybe suffer a stroke or heart attack. I don't know what to expect. This whole thing sucks!"

"Amen to that, man. I feel helpless. Wish I could do something."

"Yeah, I know. We're in the hands of these doctors who, by the way, are pretty cool guys. A couple of interns have kept them alive and are in charge until the specialists arrive tomorrow. Do you want to see them?"

"Yeah...is it okay?"

"It should be. I'll say that you're a family member. Hell, Mr. Davies—you know, that retired detective guy from Condor's Nest that my grandmother's friendly with—is here as much as I am. Aunt Anita's up there, also, and I'm sure she'd like to see you."

Michael embraced Anita, who rose from a chair as he entered Katherine's room. The elderly lady's eyes were closed as she remained in her coma. The monitor was indicating a stable condition, even though she was still critical. Anita asked Michael if Miriam knew about the incidents of the past week and that Katherine and Tony were here in the hospital. Michael stated that he had called his mother after she (Anita) had been hospitalized, but didn't know if his mother had been informed about the latest occurrences. He had not yet called her, but said he had planned on doing so after visiting the hospital and knowing more. Anita told Michael that wouldn't be necessary. She would call Miriam, since they hadn't talked in a while and she wanted to relay the latest information herself. After about five minutes, they all went down the hall to Tony's room, where he was still comatose yet breathing normally with a steady, albeit weak, pulse and heartbeat. The three of them were silent as they observed Tony for another five minutes.

Anita then whispered in Jon's ear that she wanted to be alone with her brother for a few minutes, and that Michael should leave now. She stayed with her brother as the two boys went back into the hall.

"Man, this is weird," Michael blurted out as they stood in the hallway. "I've never seen anyone in a coma and now there are two close relatives here."

"Yeah...weird...and scary," Jon countered. "Hey, man, I appreciate you coming here. How was Rhode Island...and Newport?"

"Awesome! The waves were up at Charlestown and Newport was a blast. My friends have some cool places, but not any nicer than Hunter's Point. The weather was dynamite. I'm sorry you had to spend your weekend in this place while I was away having a good time."

"Yeah, me too. This was the just about the worst weekend of my life."

"I can imagine," Michael said softly. "Like I said, I wish I could do something."

"I'll be home tonight. Maybe you can stop over and we'll have a brew and sit out on the deck or take a walk to Rocky Bar. I could use someone my age to talk to." Jon was about to say good-bye to Michael and go back his father's hospital room, when he remembered one thing that he had not done. "There is something you can do."

"What's that?"

"I forgot to call Nicole and tell her about what happened. Can you call her?"

"Of course...let me see, I think I have her cell number. Yeah, I got it. I'll call her when I get back to Hunter's Point. She was going to get a ride back late this afternoon."

"Okay. Tell her I'll call tonight. And thanks for driving her there Friday night."

Michael nodded and then walked away.

A cell phone rang at a town beach about 75 miles away in Fairfield County. "Hello," Miriam said into the small phone.

"Miriam, it's Anita."

"Anita, what a nice surprise to hear from you. How are you feeling? Michael called last week to say you had taken ill. Your voice sounds normal, which I hope is a good indication."

"I'm much better, thank you. In fact, I was just with Michael and he said he had called to tell you about my little episode."

"I hope it wasn't too serious. Michael said you were hospitalized for three days, but never told me exactly what was wrong with you. I called the main house yesterday and today to see how you were doing, but didn't get an answer and didn't leave a message. I guess I feel funny about having my voice recorded at Hunter's Point. I figured I would catch up with Michael later today after he returned from Rhode Island to get an update. It was strange not having Katherine answer the phone. She's usually there when I call."

"Well, Miriam, I hate to tell you this, but Mother is in the hospital, which is where I am now and where Michael was until just a few minutes ago."

"What? Why is Katherine in the hospital?"

"For the same reason, we think, that I was brought here and kept for three days."

"What on earth are you talking about?" Miriam asked.

"The doctors think that Mother and I have somehow been poisoned with methanol."

"Good lord! How is that possible?"

"That's a question we're all trying to figure out—those of us, that is, who are conscious enough to be able to think."

"Now you've got me completely confused," Miriam replied.

Anita told Miriam of Katherine's becoming seriously ill Friday night and finding Tony on the rocks of the embankment off the main house. Anita could detect Miriam gasping on the other end of the phone line as she relayed the events of this past Friday night and the weekend and indicated that both Katherine and Tony had come close to dying and were still in critical condition.

Michael and Jon sat on the deck of Tony's cottage looking out into the Sound. It was ten o'clock at night and each had cracked open a beer. Jon was emotionally exhausted by the events of the past 48 hours. While he wanted to get a respite from them, he was finding it difficult to do so.

"Any change in their condition since I left?" Michael asked, breaking the silence.

"No...they're about the same, which the doctor said is alright. The key is for them not to slip and get any worse."

"Do the doctors know how long they'll be in these comas?"

Jon shook his head. "No one really knows, but if the poison starts to pass through Grandma and she gains some strength, then she may get out of it. Dad suffered severe trauma, and head injuries like his are unpredictable. Some people come out of them quickly, while others stay in comas for a long time."

"Do you know how this all happened?" Michael asked.

Jon shook his head again, a tear appearing in the corner of one of his eyes.

"No clues?"

"Nothing yet...just speculation," Jon replied.

"What kind of speculation?"

"For who?" Jon answered, his face now taking on a look of frustration.

"Oh, yeah…sorry. I still can't believe both your grandma and dad are in there. What are they saying about what caused Aunt Anita and Katherine to get poisoned?"

Jon grimaced and then said, "The only thing the doctors said was that it seems to be an ingestion of methanol, probably over a period of time rather than a 'quick hit'. All the food and liquid in grandma's house was taken away this afternoon and the cops are going to test everything in their lab."

"Yeah, I heard. My dad told me he was there and loaded some of the stuff. This guy, Dan Davies—who my dad said was there with a state trooper—does he think there's any foul play?"

"He's saying we need to investigate, just in case. The other part of this thing is hard for me to talk about—especially with you." Jon grimaced again as the words came out.

"What do you mean?"

"Well…I'm pretty sure Mr. Davies was going to ask the police to get a search warrant for your house…for the fireplace shovel…and I guess anything else that might look suspicious or seem to be connected to what's happened to Dad."

"Oh, Christ!" Michael muttered. "My dad waved that shovel at your dad that night when we were behind the bushes, and then lunged at him another time. Don't tell me. Don't even say it…he couldn't have hit your dad with that damn thing! Before I came over here he asked me if you had told me anything at the hospital about how all this happened. Could this be a big front he's putting on?"

"I hope not, because if he did this to my dad, I may go after him and hurt him bad. I don't know if I can control myself, Michael. Maybe I'll wind up in some prison. Maybe you'll come after me after I go after him."

"Maybe I'll be your accomplice, instead!" Michael blurted out.

Jon looked at Michael in disbelief. "You what? Do you know what you're saying? You'd go after you own father? Are you freakin' crazy?"

"Maybe…but if he did attack your dad with that shovel and almost killed him, then maybe he deserves it. Oh, shit, I don't know. I guess I wouldn't go after him, but I'd get the hell out of here and probably never see him again. Damn it, Jon, things started to go bad when Dad left Mom and married that bimbo, Susan."

"What do you mean by that?" Jon asked. "What does your mom and dad's splitting up and Susan coming on the scene have to do with what happened this weekend?"

"Maybe a lot," Michael replied. "Look, this affair would never have happened if my mother was still here. You know, Jon, it takes two to have an affair, and I'd be willing to bet that Susan came on to your dad and enticed him. I've seen her look at him once or twice, and it's the way you and I like our girls to look at us. And, wait, don't you remember that first night we saw our dads arguing? Your dad said Susan was a 'tease.'"

"Yeah, you're right," Jon shot back, his mind starting to focus on a scenario he had not yet given any thought to. "I had forgotten about that. I've been mad at Dad for screwing around with Susan and wondering what the hell is the matter with him—even after he told me what I already knew and took the blame."

"Yeah, well don't put it past Susan to have 'come on' to Uncle Tony. She may have instigated this whole thing. One thing I know is that she's been a God-damn home wrecker for me and I wish she were out of my life and that Mom was back."

They took a couple of big swigs from their beer bottles and sat in silence, looking up at the stars and out at the water. Jon's tired mind was at work again, now in a different mode

On Monday morning at nine-thirty, state police trooper Bill Jenkins drove his cruiser up to the front of Jerry and Susan's house at Hunter's Point. Susan was walking out the front door, on her way to work at the medical clinic. She stopped in her tracks as the state trooper got out of his car and approached the house.

"Can I help you, Officer?" she asked, staring up at him with a puzzled look on her face.

"Yes, ma'am, I think so. I have a search warrant for your house and I'd like to enter and look around, please."

"A search warrant…for what? Why?"

"Well, there's one thing in particular we're interested in and we want to see if there may be anything else that could relate to the incidents of Friday night."

"Well, can you tell me what this 'one thing in particular' is?"

"When I have it in my possession, you'll know. May I please enter your house?" Jenkins flashed the warrant in front of Susan as he spoke.

"I was just leaving for work. How long will this take?"

"Not too long, ma'am. I can close and lock the front door behind me if you need to leave. You can trust the state police. We document anything we take out of the house."

"I'm not worried about that. Alright, go in. I'll call the clinic and tell them I may be a few minutes late." Her voice was starting to quiver a bit as she spoke.

Susan opened the front door for Jenkins, followed him into the house and watched as the state trooper looked around, and then went into the living room and toward the fireplace. The state trooper was carrying a large sack and had a pair of thin rubber gloves in a rear pocket of his trousers. After putting on the rubber gloves, he took a plastic sheet out of the sack, placed it on the floor, then lifted the fireplace shovel off the holder for the fireplace tools, placed the shovel on the plastic sheet, wrapped the sheet around the shovel, and then slowly put the wrapped shovel in the sack. Susan observed, not certain of the rationale for the state police trooper's actions.

"I assume the fireplace shovel is the 'one thing in particular.'"

Jenkins nodded.

"Can you tell me why you want it? Is it related to Tony's injury? Do you need anything else?"

"I don't comment on police work, ma'am, and at the moment, I don't have anything else in mind, but I would like to look around, if you don't mind." Jenkins knew he had to be polite, even though he wished he could just tell her to sit down somewhere and let him do his job. He was hoping that she would not want to appear too nosy and would not follow him around in the house.

"Does it matter if I do mind?" she retorted.

"No ma'am, it doesn't."

Now out of sight of Susan, who had not followed him past the living room, Bill Jenkins peered into a small powder room off the kitchen. Next, he went into the downstairs guest room and the adjoining bathroom. After gazing around the bathroom, he was about to leave, but leaned down and opened the door to the vanity. There was a stack of towels, rolls of bathroom tissue and cleaning supplies. He reached in and moved the towels away from the back of the vanity. He noticed something in the corner. He grabbed his pocket flashlight and turned it on. There was a plastic bag containing a small syringe, the type used to take blood from a person's finger. *Why would a syringe be here, in a plastic bag?* he asked himself. *It's almost like someone is hiding it. I should take this.*

The trooper put his gloves on and gently grabbed the top of the plastic bag. He walked back into the living room and placed what he had just found in the sack, next to some bubble pack that was also in the sack and would protect it from any contact with the fireplace shovel.

Susan, who had gone upstairs to trim a toe nail and check her lipstick while Jenkins was searching the downstairs, saw the trooper placing something in the sack, but could not see what it was. "Did you find something else of interest?"

"Possibly. We'll just have to see."

"Can you tell me what it is?" Susan asked.

"Not now, but in due course we will."

"I really have to get going. Are you finished?"

"I'd like to look upstairs before I leave." The trooper, based on his recent discovery, didn't want to take any chance of missing any other potential evidence.

"Well, I'm going to leave you alone, then, and trust you to document anything you take."

"Will do."

"We don't lock the doors during the day, so just close the front door when you leave." Susan was shuddering as she walked out of the house.

Jenkins searched the upstairs for ten minutes, but found nothing of further interest. After he placed the sack in the trunk of the cruiser, he walked back toward the house and noticed a tool shed next to the garage. He went into the garage first and gazed around. The cars were gone. There wasn't anything else there, except for a large cooler and some cushions and rope for a boat. He closed the garage door as he left and walked to the tool shed. Opening the door, which let daylight into the windowless shed, he looked around. Garden tools were leaning against the walls and a lawn mower stood in the middle. On a shelf were three cans of paint and a small can of paint thinner. He thought for a moment and then called Dan Davies on his cell phone.

"Dan, it's Bill Jenkins. I've searched the Hunter house and found a syringe along with the fireplace shovel. Both are in the trunk of the cruiser. I went to the garage, but there's nothing there that could be connected to this case. Now I'm in the tool shed. There are a bunch of garden tools, a lawn mower, cans of paint that have been used and a small can of paint thinner that's also been opened."

"Get the paint thinner," said the voice at the other end of the phone line.

"Why the paint thinner?"

"Because it contains methanol, which is what may have been used to poison Anita and Katherine," Dan responded.

"Gotcha. I'll be leaving here now and should be back at the barracks in about fifteen minutes."

"I'll be there within a couple of hours. I'm going to stop at the hospital after running a couple of errands, and then I'll swing over to see you."

Satisfied that he had gathered all that could be potentially important to the investigation, Jenkins returned to his car for the drive back to the state police barracks.

Susan drove her car into the parking lot behind the clinic where she worked. She pulled her cell phone out of her purse and dialed. The phone at the other end answered with a voice mail greeting. "*This is Jerry Hunter and you've reached my cell phone. Please leave a message and I'll get back to you.*"

"Jerry, I need to talk to you," Susan said into her phone. "Call the clinic and ask them to get me wherever I am, since I can't carry my cell phone around in there. A state police trooper was at the house this morning with a search warrant. He took the fireplace shovel and something else, but I'm not sure what. I think he got it from the guest room or the bathroom on the first floor. He said the search was connected to the incidents of Friday night. Do you know what's going on? Is this connected to the trooper and Dan Davies taking all those items from Katherine's house yesterday, which you told me you helped with?" Susan's statements and questions for Jerry were the result of her thinking about the unexpected visit to her home as she drove to work.

After she had closed the top of the cell phone, she looked at her watch. It was ten-fifteen. *He must be in a meeting. His life is one meeting after another*, she thought as she got out of her car and walked quickly toward the entrance to the clinic, upset over being delayed and now troubled by the search warrant.

Chapter 11

It was late Tuesday afternoon and Anita was alone in Tony's room, sitting next to him. She had decided to see him before going to her mother's room. The nurse had just left after checking on his vital signs. Anita saw his right arm move slightly and almost jumped out of her chair. She went over to him. The arm moved again…then again. She saw what seemed to be a slight movement in his right eye, then the left eye, and then a very slight movement of his head. She ran out of the room and down the hall to the nurse's station.

She was choked up and couldn't speak. She opened her mouth, but no words came out.

"Can we help you, Anita?" the nurse inquired. They had come to address each other on a first name basis after Anita had been a patient last week.

Anita gasped and then spoke. "I think he moved, Doris…I think Tony moved!"

The nurse leaped from her chair and said into a microphone, "Paging Dr. Callahan. Please come to Tony Kent's room." The nurses were using first names for the Kents so as not to confuse *Mr.* with *Mrs.* Anita and the nurse walked quickly to Tony's room. They went to his bed, one on each side, and hovered over him. He was moving the fingers on his right hand very slowly. Now, he moved the fingers on his left hand slightly. Anita saw his nose twitch, but his eyes were still closed.

Anita was standing as Dr. Callahan entered the room and also noticed Tony's nose twitching. He leaned over the bed and said, "Tony, can you hear me?"

There was a slight move forward of Tony's head.

"Move your head forward again, Tony, if you can hear me," the young doctor said.

Tony responded with a slight movement of his head.

"I think he's starting to come out of the coma."

Anita, who was on the same side of the bed as the doctor, gently squeezed Tony's right arm with her left hand. She was beaming. "Oh, my Lord, can it be? Is he coming back to us?"

"He may be, but I don't want to say for certain just yet," the doctor said. "We need more responses and it would be nice if his eyes would open. Tony, I want you to move your arm if you can, and then try to open your eyes."

Anita observed that his right arm moved slightly, but the eyes remained shut.

"Okay, that's good. Now, can you move your toes?" Dr. Kevin Callahan pulled back the sheets and observed a very slight movement of the large right toe. "Alright, Tony, that's excellent. How about moving some fingers again?" The right fore and middle fingers moved slightly. "Okay, that's good. Now, why don't you rest a bit and we'll come back in a little while."

The doctor motioned to Anita and the nurse to step away from the bed. "That's enough for now. Anita, why don't you go check on your mother. We don't want to forget about her. Nurse Wily and I will talk about what we think we should do for Tony."

Anita nodded and walked down the hall to Katherine's room. There had been no change since Sunday in her condition, although she had been stable. As she had for the past few days, Katherine lay flat on her back, motionless. "Come on Mother," Anita whispered in her ear. "Come back to us...please. I need both of you back with me."

As she was talking, Dan entered the room. They embraced. "Dan, Tony showed some slight movement. The doctor thinks there's a chance he may be coming out of his coma."

"Fantastic! That makes my day, for sure."

"Have you heard anything about any of the tests?" she asked energetically.

"Not yet, but I did get an update. I was just at the state police barracks. They said the items taken from Jerry's house—the fireplace shovel and syringe—will be analyzed by noon tomorrow, and the analysis of the food and drink items from your house should be done by Thursday."

"Alright," she sighed. "So we'll know something in a day or two."

Dan nodded. "Can I go to Tony's room?"

"I don't see why not. The doctor was talking to Tony and getting some response—not much, but at least a little. I don't know what he's going to do next. He wanted to leave Tony alone and quiet for a while. So when we go in his room, let's observe him, but not say anything."

They spent about ten minutes in Tony's room, hoping to see some movement or other sign of life from him, but he lay perfectly still, as he had since Friday night. Dan motioned to Anita. "Let's visit your mother and then go get something to eat. We can come back afterwards and talk to the doctor. I assume he's on the evening shift. Let's call Jon on our way out of here. He'll want to know about this."

"I spoke to Jon on the way here from the library," Anita said. "He had to work a couple of extra hours and I told him I'd meet him here around six-thirty or seven. That poor boy, he needs some good news!"

At noon on Wednesday, Bill Jenkins called Dan at his home.

"Dan, it's Bill Jenkins."

"Hey, Trooper, what's up?"

"We have the test results on the fireplace shovel from the Hunter residence."

"Yeah…so what have you found?"

"Tony Kent's blood is on it. DNA testing proves it."

"Son of a gun. Anything else?"

"Jerry Hunter's fingerprints are all over it."

"I would expect that, since it *is* his fireplace shovel and I'm sure he's made plenty of fires with it. He also had it in his hands that night he threatened Tony."

"That's true, and this bit of evidence by itself means nothing in terms of incriminating him. There is one other thing, though."

"What's that?"

"There are no other fingerprints on the shovel, based on the test that was done."

"Really! Now that's interesting. You would think that his wife and son would have touched it at some point, since it is in their house."

"Well, maybe Jerry made all the fires. But, with Tony's blood on it and no one else's fingerprint, it does implicate him."

"So, what are you going to do?"

"I'm going to bring him in for questioning. Do you know where he is?"

"I think he's in New York and is returning to Hunter's Point tonight, probably between seven and eight based on the travel time."

"Okay, I'll be at his home at seven. Will you be there?"

"I'll try. If he did this, he's put on one hell of a front and is a great liar."

"He wouldn't be the first," Jenkins said grimly.

"Or the last," Dan replied with a sigh.

Dan, Anita and Jon met at five-thirty in Tony's hospital room. Tony was opening his eyes and responding to the doctor's verbal communication by moving his extremities, but he had not yet spoken and didn't appear to recognize anyone. He seemed to gaze through his three visitors when he looked at them, which was infrequent. After fifteen minutes in Tony's room, they went to visit Katherine, whose vital signs were improving, but who had not yet come out of her deep sleep. They thought they were starting to see some very slight movement, and the doctor now felt that she was out of severe danger and would emerge from the coma. Dan paced the floor and Anita looked at him inquisitively. He motioned for her and Jon to follow him out into the hallway.

"You look like you want to tell us something," Anita said softly.

"Well, I do have something to tell you, but I wish I didn't have to."

"It's about the testing of the shovel, isn't it?" Anita asked.

Dan nodded. "The DNA test has shown traces of Tony's blood on the shovel."

"God damn it!" Jon cried out.

Anita hung her head, but said nothing. She looked at Jon and then at Dan, who said, "The only fingerprints on it are Jerry's."

"That bastard...that lousy bastard. I just felt it," Jon shot back. "What an uncle, and what a liar! Acting so surprised when he found about what had happened to Dad."

"Are they sure?" Anita asked, not wanting to believe what Dan was telling her. "This is so terrible!"

"They're sure. These tests are accurate and you can usually rely on the results."

"So, what's going to happen?" Anita asked Dan.

"A state police officer, Bill Jenkins, is going to Jerry's house tonight and take him in for questioning when he arrives back from New York."

"That damn Uncle Jerry," Jon muttered.

"Just remember, Jon, that Jerry hasn't been charged with anything...at least not yet," Dan shot back.

"Bullshit...he's guilty...he did this...how else could Dad have wound up here?"

"I must say, Dan, that the evidence does look very incriminating," Anita interjected.

"Damn right it does," Jon added.

"Come on, let's go get something to eat. I told Jenkins that I would be at Hunter's Point when he arrived to interrogate Jerry," Dan said, changing the subject.

"Let's go to our house," Anita suggested. "I'm not in the mood for going out, and I can fix something for all of us."

"I want to be there, too, when Uncle Jerry gets back," Jon grumbled. "That son-of-a-bitch! I'll drive home and meet you there for dinner. I'm hungry."

Observing Jon's body language, Dan said, "You seem awfully angry. Don't take that anger out on someone on the road."

At seven-thirty, Jerry Hunter drove his car into Hunter's Point. As he approached his house, he noticed a state police cruiser. His heart started pounding and his mind was racing. Could it be the one that Susan had told him was there Monday morning? If so, why was the cruiser at his home...again? As he got closer, he saw a police officer get out of the car on the driver's side and Dan Davies emerge from the passenger's side. Jerry parked in his customary spot in front of the left garage door and got out. He noticed Susan emerge from the house, walking toward him.

A large, dark-skinned, uniformed man approached Jerry. Dan remained near the cruiser.

"What can I do for you, Officer?" As he spoke, Jerry gazed at Susan, who was now close to him, trying to get some clue as to what was going on. Susan shrugged her shoulders and shook her head. She had gone over to the cruiser a half-hour ago, but did not get a clear indication as to why the state trooper was there.

"I'd like for you to come with me to the barracks for some questioning," the trooper responded.

"Do I have time to get something to eat? It's been a long day, and it appears as though it may get a bit longer."

"We can arrange for some food when we get to the barracks," Jenkins replied, a sullen look on his face.

"Jesus, what did I do?"

"We'll talk about that at the barracks."

Just as Jerry and Bill Jenkins were walking toward the cruiser, Dan saw Jon fly out of the bushes on one side of the house and gallop toward them. The lad jumped on Jerry and started pummeling him with his fists. "You bastard…you rotten bastard," Jon screamed at his uncle. His right fist caught Jerry flush above his left eye and some blood gushed out. Dan sped toward the two of them. He dove on top of the boy and his uncle and put a choke hold on the youngster, pulling him away. Blood had trickled down onto Jerry's white shirt, which was now soiled and torn. Dan and Jon were now writhing on the ground. The retired detective's size and weight, along with having been able to get on top of the lad, served as an advantage. Jerry lay on the ground, stunned more than injured, but his head throbbed from the blow.

As Jon lay pinned on the ground, Jerry slowly got up. Susan came to his side, holding onto him and wiping the blood from above his eye.

"What the hell was that for?" he yelled, glaring at Jon.

"You know damn well what it's for. That's for what you did to my dad!"

"What's he talking about?" Jerry gasped, trying to catch his breath from what had just happened.

"Come on, let's get out of here," Jenkins said, grabbing Jerry by the arm and leading him to the cruiser. "Mrs. Hunter, you can come with us in the cruiser or follow in your car if you like. Dan, you've got to stay here with the boy. I'll call the local police to come here. They're going to have to take him in and book him for assault. You can come to the barracks if you wish after the local police arrive. The kid may have to spend the night in jail."

Dan nodded and he continued to pin Jon to the ground. Jenkins, Jerry and Susan walked toward the state police cruiser.

Anita, who had heard the commotion, came walking as fast as she could toward the Hunter house. "What in the world is going on here? What are you two doing on the ground?"

Dan, his grip still strong on Jon, slowly rose up and pulled Jon up with him. Jon tried to get away and go after Jerry, but the state trooper came over and grabbed the lad, clenching Jon's biceps with his very large hands. "Look, young man, you've already got an assault charge to deal with. Don't make it worse by messing with me. Assaulting a police officer can be a serious offense, which neither you nor your family needs right now."

Jon looked at the officer angrily. "I don't give a damn about your assault charge. That bastard almost killed my father."

"We don't know that yet. Let us take him in for questioning and find out a few things. You're in trouble already for this incident. All you're going to do is get yourself in more hot water by taking the law into your own hands. Let us do what we've been trained to do. Mr. Davies can explain if you don't understand what I'm saying."

Jon glared at Dan and the state trooper. Dan glared back at him and said, "Look, Jon, either you back off or I'll have to do something very unpleasant to calm you down. Get my drift? Let the police do their job. We…they…know how to handle this."

"Okay…okay, let me go."

"Only if you promise me you'll calm down and stay away from Jerry."

Jon nodded.

Dan and Jenkins released their grips and Jon went over to his aunt to embrace her. "I'm sorry, Aunt Anita, but I just couldn't keep my hands off him."

"Fighting violence with more violence won't solve anything. It will only make things worse, if that's possible." Anita sobbed as the stress of the situation caught up with her. Looking empathetically at Jon, she said, "Promise me you won't do anything like this again. We've had enough trauma in our family and I can't take any more. I mean it, Jon… no more."

Jon nodded again.

Michael, just finishing a shower and getting ready to pick up his girlfriend Amy, had heard the yelling, looked out the window and saw Dan and the state trooper restraining Jon. He threw on a tee shirt and pair of shorts and ran out of the house barefooted. "What's going on?" he yelled as he got near the group and saw his father being escorted into the police cruiser.

"I tried to get at your dad and hurt him, like I said I would the other night."

"Why? Is there some evidence that he hit Uncle Tony?"

"Yeah, there may be, and the cops are taking him in."

"Holy shit!"

"Susan is going with him," Dan interjected. "Do you want to go, too?"

"I don't know. If I do, it won't be in that police cruiser. I'll drive myself. Those cars give me the shivers. Where's he going?"

"To the state police barracks, for questioning," Dan answered.

"Has he been charged with anything?"

"Not yet."

"What do you mean, not yet?"

"The trooper is taking him in to question him. If he thinks there's reason to arrest him, he'll do so. If not, he'll probably release him."

Michael looked at Jon. "So, what did you do to him?"

"I caught him with my fist just above his eye. He's bleeding and I think it hurt."

"Well, you said you were going to do it. I just hope you didn't hurt him badly."

"He should be alright. I only landed one good shot."

"Wait a minute, Jon," Dan jumped in. "You mean this was planned?"

"Damn right it was. I told Michael I'd go after him if he did this to Dad."

"Jesus, Lord of the universe…this whole family is going crazy," Dan exclaimed.

"Jon's protecting his dad," Michael shot back. "I'd probably do the same thing if I were in his shoes. Shit, Mr. Davies, Jon's mother is dead and his father came within a whisker of dying. And my dad may be responsible. No, on second thought, I'm not going with him. As long as

I know that he's not hurt badly, I don't really want to see him tonight. Besides, he's got his lovely bride for company."

Michael grabbed Jon, pulled him aside and whispered in his ear, "Remember what I said the other night? Don't discount some involvement of the *Beauty Queen Bitch* in this!" He then started to walk away. After a few steps, he back turned back toward Jon and asked, "Are you in trouble?"

"Yeah, I guess so. Some local pig is coming here to take me in."

"Where?"

"To the local jail, I guess."

"I'll come there later, after I drop off Amy. We're going to a movie and it won't be too late." Michael then jogged toward the house to get a pair of sandals and go out.

Dan watched Michael trot away. Standing silently, he looked at Jon and Anita, trying to imagine the suffering they were experiencing and attempting to justify the actions of an eighteen year-old, who had almost lost his father—his only living parent—due to injuries a close relative may have inflicted.

Chapter 12

It was shortly after noon on Thursday. Just before going out for lunch, Anita had received a phone call from the hospital indicating that her mother had come out of her coma, had opened her eyes and asked for her daughter. Anita immediately called Dan who said he would postpone a visit to the state police barracks to talk to Bill Jenkins about his questioning of Jerry last night and drive to the hospital.

Katherine was lying on her back as Anita and Dan hovered above her. Her eyes opened slowly as she sensed something. The patient saw a fuzzy outline of two faces. She closed her eyes, then opened them again. She was able to focus a little and the fuzziness started to go away. The outline of a familiar face became a bit clearer. "Anita?" she whispered.

"Yes, Mother, it's me, and there's someone with me whom you know."

"Yes? Who's that? Tony? Jon?"

"Actually, Dan is here, and Jon will be here in a little while."

"Dan? Is it you? I can't quite see you. You're fuzzy looking to me."

"That's all right, Katherine. The fuzziness will go away in a while. We're happy you've come back to us. You gave us quite a scare."

"What happened to me? I remember feeling sick in bed, but then everything went blank. Where am I? What time is it? I'm a little hungry."

Dan chuckled and glanced at Anita. It was good to hear that soft voice he liked so much. "Anita's been through quite a bit lately, so why don't I try to answer your questions one at a time. You did get quite sick. We're not sure what the exact cause is, but the doctors will run some tests when you're strong enough. As to what time it is, it's just after twelve noon, so maybe you need some lunch. More importantly, it's Thursday. You've been in the hospital, near the room where Anita was, for almost a week now. If you remember, you got sick last Friday night."

"A week! I've been here for a week?"

"Almost."

"How could that be? How could I be here almost a week? I don't remember anything."

"That's because you've been asleep all this time."

"Asleep? What are you talking about?"

"You've been in a coma, Katherine. We thought you were going to die a couple of times, but I guess it's not your time yet."

"I've been in a coma for almost a week? How could that be?"

"Like I said, we don't know exactly why, but the doctors have some idea and will do more testing to find out."

"You said that Jon will be here later. When is Tony coming?"

Dan looked at Anita, who shrugged her shoulders, signaling that she did not know what to say. Dan winked at her and spoke. "Katherine, do you remember that day we recently met on the beach and talked about how you were feeling? Maybe you should have listened to me when I told you to see a doctor."

A faint smile came across Katherine's face. "Perhaps you're right. I'll listen to you the next time. I assume there's a doctor in this place who's looking after me now."

Dan smiled at Anita, who returned the look.

Katherine then spoke again. "I'm feeling very tired. I'm going to close my eyes. I hope you'll be here when I open them again."

"We will be," Anita replied—crying and smiling at the same time. As they left the room, she looked at him. "Good ploy, Dan. I didn't know what to say about Tony."

"Neither did I, which is why I had to distract her and make her think of something else. Thank goodness she ran out of steam. We're going to have to think of something to tell her about Tony, though, which obviously can't be the truth, at least not yet until she's recovered to the point where she can stand a shock. Let's talk to the doctor. Maybe he'll have some idea as to what we should tell her."

As they were walking down the hall toward the nurse's station, Dan's cell phone rang. "Hello, this is Dan Davies."

"Dan, it's Bill Jenkins. I have some news for you about the testing of the items we took from the Kent house on Sunday. Our most important finding is that all the bags of green tea have methanol in them, and it matches the toxin in the paint thinner we took from the tool shed on the Hunter property. Nothing else we've tested has come up with anything suspicious and we're almost done. And, one more thing…the syringe I took has Susan Hunter's fingerprints on it, only hers, and has traces of the same methanol in it. As soon as I get off the phone with you, we're going to the Hunter house to arrest her. I think we have enough in the way of evidence. Since he has no prior criminal record, Jerry Hunter was released on his own recognizance after we questioned him yesterday. He's still our primary suspect, as he has no verifiable alibi for the time when Tony Kent was almost killed—perhaps by something other than an accidental fall."

"That's quite a mouthful," Dan shot back. "So, now we have Jerry, who may have attacked Tony and has been questioned and released, but is still a suspect; plus Susan, who may have poisoned Katherine and Anita, and is about to be arrested. What a family scenario! By the way, Bill, I've consumed some of Katherine's green tea over the past few months, so I may also have this poison in my system. I wonder who else may have drunk the green tea. I'll come to the barracks as soon as I can. At least we have some good news from this end, which is that Katherine Kent has come out of her coma."

Anita, listening to what Dan was saying, cried out in surprise. "Is this possible? Can it be? Are Jerry and Susan trying to kill Tony and Mother?"

"Don't forget about yourself," Dan said.

"And you, too," Anita moaned as she shook, stumbled and fell into Dan's arms. She was crying and tears were streaming down her cheeks. "How could they do this? Why would they want to do this?"

"Could it have anything to do with a piece of property that's probably worth millions?"

"Oh, God, I hope not. They already own half of it."

"Maybe that's not enough," Dan snickered.

"Could they have been conspiring together? Susan looked so surprised when Jerry was taken in for questioning and she told me she didn't know why the police showed up Monday with a search warrant. And you said Jerry acted surprised when the police showed up last Sunday to take away the food and drink items from our house. Could this be a big ruse? Could my cousin and his new wife really want to destroy our part of the family and take over Hunter's Point…by trying to kill us?"

"I don't know, but it wouldn't be the first time…or the last."

"So, what's going to happen now? I think I'm headed for a nervous breakdown. And, now Jon's in jail. Oh, my God, we get a bit of good news with Mother and then get hit with this! What about Jon? Is he all right? Is he still in jail? There's so much going on that I can't keep track any more. I forgot about him when I woke up this morning and went off to work. I am very upset at myself for that, especially since I was not totally in agreement with your idea of letting my nephew spend a night behind bars."

"Jon was released this morning. I was there early and posted a bond. He agreed to stay with me for the weekend, which I made a condition for posting his bail. He really didn't have much choice, since he didn't have the money and no one in the family was there for him. Jon apologized to me for his actions, and I believe spending the night in jail was a good experience for him in one respect: I don't think he wants to spend any more time there. I drove him home to shower, stayed there, and then drove him to work. He should be calling me sometime soon. I told him to check in before he leaves the lifeguard station today. He's going to spend the next few nights at my place. We're going to talk."

"That's wonderful that he'll be with you," Anita replied. "I'm sapped and would have trouble caring for anyone else now. But won't he spend time in jail if the assault charge sticks?"

"Maybe, maybe not. Let's not worry about that now. We've got bigger issues to deal with, one of which is to visit Tony and see how he's doing."

They left a message with the nurse to have the doctor call Anita when Katherine woke up again, and then went to Tony's room. As they entered, Tony was moving slightly, but his eyes were still shut. Anita went over to him and gently touched his left arm. His eyes opened slightly, and it appeared that Tony was trying to see who they were. His tongue then touched the upper portion of his lip, then the lower portion—the first time they had seen that. Anita said, "Tony, can you hear me?" He nodded slightly. "Do you know who this is?" He nodded again. His left fingers then moved as if he were trying to touch her. She gently placed her hand on top of his. Then, Tony smiled slightly and opened his eyes a bit more. His lips moved. "Anita," came a soft sound from his mouth. "Anita." He then closed his eyes, the smile remaining as he drifted off.

Anita looked at Dan and managed a slight smile of her own. "That's the first word he's spoken…the first, unless he's said something to a doctor or nurse when they've been alone."

"I doubt that," Dan replied. "They would have told us. Let's stop at the nurse's station and give them another message. Maybe they're both going to come out of this. God, I hope so."

After they had left the nurse's station for the second time, Dan's cell phone rang. "Hello…hey, Jon, how are you doing? I'm with your aunt and we've got some good news for you."

"What is it?" Jon asked.

"Well, first, your grandmother has come out of her coma and we spoke to her a bit and second, your father just said Anita's name a few minutes ago when we were in his room, and he seemed to recognize her."

"Really? I was wondering if I was ever going to hear him speak again. Can you pick me up after my shift is over?"

"Of course. We'll come here together to the hospital. There's something else I need to tell you, but I want to do that when we're together. See you soon."

Anita looked at Dan inquisitively as he closed his cell phone. "What are you going to tell him?"

"Have you forgotten already what Jenkins just told me about the methanol tests? I want to be there, just in case Jon freaks out again when I tell him that Susan is going to be arrested. I don't want him going after her!"

Anita's face now had a sheepish look, revealing her embarrassment at suddenly forgetting so many things.

At five o'clock, Jerry was in the living room on the telephone. He had told his people in New York that he wasn't feeling well, and wanted to spend the rest of the week working from Hunter's Point. Fortunately, there were not any important face-to-face customer meetings scheduled for the latter part of the week, and his important communications and customer contacts could be made by telephone. Susan was in the kitchen starting to prepare dinner and was in the midst of cleansing three large chicken breasts with water and kosher salt. She was gazing out the kitchen window, which looked out onto the driveway of the house, when she saw the state police cruiser that she had come to dread driving toward the house. She turned off the water and walked quickly into the living room. "Jerry, the state police are here again," she gushed out.

Jerry sat up in the living room sofa and cradled the phone in his hand, pressing it into his stomach. "Give me a minute," he whispered to Susan. Returning to his business call, he said, "I think we have a consensus here on what your immediate needs are. Can I call you tomorrow, say by noon, and verify what we've agreed to do? Alright, consider it done. Thank you and I'll speak to you tomorrow." He hung up the phone and rose from the sofa. "What the hell is going on now?" he shouted at Susan.

"I don't know, but the police cruiser that's been here twice already is in our driveway again." She was shuddering as she spoke.

There was a knock at the front door. Jerry went to open it. Bill Jenkins was standing there, accompanied by another state trooper. "Good evening, Mr. Hunter. Is *Mrs.* Hunter here?"

"Yes, she is. Why do you ask?"

"May we see her, please?"

"Alright, she's right here. Susan, the officer wants to see you."

Susan, who had gone back into the kitchen, walked slowly into the living room, and stood in front of the state troopers. She was an incredibly attractive sight to behold, dressed in a pair of tight blue denim shorts and a form fitting pale yellow tee shirt. At this moment, however, any thoughts she might have of how men looked at her were very distant. Apprehension gripped her and she felt tense.

Jenkins gulped, gathered himself and walked over to Susan. He looked at her, handed her a sheet of paper, and spoke…"Susan Hunter, I'm here to arrest you for the attempted murder of Katherine Kent via poisoning. A second count of the same charge may be rendered with regard to Anita Kent, but for now you are charged with poisoning herbal tea that Mrs. Kent ingested. Before I ask you to put your hands behind your back so the other officer can hand-cuff you, I want to read you your rights. You have the right to remain silent. You have the right to an attorney. Anything you say can be used against you in a court of law. Do you understand your rights, Mrs. Hunter?"

Susan looked at the uniformed African-American in bewilderment. Jerry did the same. Jerry then looked at Susan and blurted out, "What in the hell is going on? Why are you being arrested for poisoning? What's this that he's saying about herbal tea?"

"I have no idea. Why are you arresting me, Officer? What have I done?"

"We have reason to believe, Mrs. Hunter, that you've poisoned herbal tea that you have been purchasing and delivering to Anita and Katherine Kent for some time now."

Susan's emotions got the best of her and she started yelling at the state trooper. "What? Are you insane? I haven't poisoned anything or anybody. This is completely crazy! Who are you to come into my house and accuse me of this? Are you on a personal mission to make our lives miserable? Why don't you just get out of here!"

Now closer to her, Jenkins stood erect to accentuate his height—he was over a foot taller than Susan—and looked at her eyes and over her left shoulder to avoid staring at the front of her body as he spoke. "I would suggest, Mrs. Hunter, that you be careful about what you say. As I stated, anything that you say can be used against you in a court of law. I ask you again to put your hands behind your back and come quietly with us. Mr. Hunter, you can follow us to the state police barracks in your car, if you wish. Your wife will be treated with the utmost care, assuming she's cooperative. I need to tell you, though, that she will spend the night in detention and we will get an arraignment for tomorrow morning. Be prepared for a significant bond that will have to be posted for her to be released after the arraignment—at least two hundred fifty and maybe five hundred thousand dollars."

"A quarter to a half million dollars! Are you kidding? That's a lot of money."

"The charge is a very serious one," Jenkins responded sternly.

Before Susan could say anything in response, Jerry jumped in with, "Okay, okay. Susan, do as he says and keep quiet. Don't say or do anything. I'll call our attorney…again. I'll try to get him to visit with you. I'll drive my car and be there shortly. A half million dollars—jeez!"

"Bring a pair of slacks and a sweater for me, in case it gets chilly at the barracks," Susan called over to Jerry. The reality of spending a night in a criminal detention facility had started to sink in. "Pigs," she then whispered, just loud enough for the other trooper to hear, but soft enough so that Jenkins, who had started walking toward the kitchen, could not detect.

"Where are you going, Officer?" Jerry called out at Jenkins, who was now in the kitchen. Getting no response from the state trooper, Jerry followed him. "I said, where are you going and what are you doing?"

"I'm sorry," Jenkins replied. He pulled out the search warrant and flashed it at Jerry. "I forgot to mention that we're still authorized to search the premises and, based on the test results, are looking for one more item." Opening the cupboard and pulling out a package of green herbal tea, he looked at Jerry and said, "Here's what I was looking for."

They were gone a minute later. As they drove away, Susan turned her head and gazed back toward the house and her husband, bewildered by the incident.

Chapter 13

It was Friday morning and the nurse on duty at the hospital was giving Dan an update. "Good morning, Mr. Davies. I have good news for you. Tony Kent is finally able to recognize people and is starting to speak normally. And, Katherine is getting better, also."

"Fantastic. Is it alright if I speak to him?"

"Dr. O'Brien, who's on duty today, saw Tony on rounds earlier and told me that it would be okay for you to speak with him and ask a few questions, but not to interrogate him too much." The nurse paused and then said, "The doctor wants me to be with you…not that he doesn't trust you, but he wants me to observe him, particularly as he starts to talk and how long he can be engaged with someone before getting tired or drifting off. We can start with either room."

"Let's see Tony first," Dan said. "I still haven't figured out exactly what to say to Katherine about Tony, and I know that today I'll have to face that question from her. I got away with a diversion yesterday, as she was getting tired after a brief talk with Anita and drifted off to sleep, but today is going to be different."

"I think you're right," the nurse responded. "Katherine has improved and should gain a bit more strength every day. So, we'll see Tony first, and then think about what we want to tell Katherine."

Tony opened his eyes as Dan and the nurse stood over him. A faint smile crept across his lips as he recognized Dan. "Hey, there, Mr. Detective…it's nice to see you."

"It's *very nice* to see you awake," Dan replied with a broad smile. "You've been asleep for a while."

"How long?"

"Well, today's Friday, so it's been almost a week, although you seemed to be coming out of it for the past day or so. Do you remember seeing Anita or Jon…or me?"

Tony slowly shook his head. "How's Jon? Where is he?"

"He's fine and is at work. Can I ask you a couple of questions, Tony?"

Tony nodded and very softly said, "Okay."

"Do you know how you wound up on the rocky embankment near the main house?"

"I was walking toward the house and was hit in the head with something that came fast and furious…like the shovel that Jerry was waving at me and threatening me with one night. I did see an object coming at me—from my left—but it was too quick to react, and I guess I just wasn't prepared. Kind of like a car that comes into your lane, but comes at you so fast you don't have enough time to swerve out of the way. After the hit, I really don't remember much of anything. You say I fell onto the rocks on the cliff?"

"Oh, yeah, you took quite a fall. And I had quite a time getting you off the cliff and to this place."

"You did that?"

"Yes."

Tony closed his eyes, then opened them. "Thank you. The doctor said I have a busted shoulder in addition to my head injury, so the fall would explain that. What else?"

"Did you recognize who hit you?"

Tony started to choke up. He closed his eyes and turned away from Dan, then turned back and opened them. Looking straight into Dan's eyes, he said, "I think it was Jerry. It all happened very fast, and he was dressed in dark clothes, but I'm sure it was someone about Jerry's size—definitely not a really big person and not someone small, either. I could see a forehead and eyes like Jerry's and also his brown hair. And, the clincher for me are the words that were shouted just before I was hit, which I'll never forget…'I told you to keep your hands off her!' Who else could have said that?"

"That's compelling, and traces of your blood were found on the fireplace shovel in Jerry's house," Dan said.

"He must have been a lot angrier than I thought. I knew he was mad, but I didn't think he would actually try to hurt me so badly."

"Yeah, it's hard to believe that someone in your family would do this to you."

The nurse nudged Dan, indicating that he should stop questioning Tony and let him rest.

"Tony," Dan then said, "we're going to talk to the doctor about a couple of things, so why don't you rest for a while."

"Will Anita, Mom and Jon be coming to see me?"

"Definitely…you just rest a while. We don't want to take things too quickly. Okay?"

"Alright, I'll doze off for a while. Tell Jon to come here later."

"Will do."

As they walked down the hall toward Katherine's room, Dan stopped and gently put his hand on the nurse's shoulder. "It's Doris, right?"

"Yes, it is. Doris Wily."

"Well, Doris Wily, I don't want to put you on the spot, but you may be a witness in a criminal case, based on what you just heard in there."

"Great, just what I need," she said with a sigh. "As though there's not enough stress with this job already."

They parted and Dan reached for his cell phone to call Anita. "Anita, it's Dan. Good news: Tony is out of his coma and is conversant. I just talked to him for a short while. He's resting again now. Why don't you come here at lunch and see him? I'll try to be here if I can. Now, I'm off to see your mother." He didn't tell her that he was also going to call Bill Jenkins about what Tony had just told him.

Dan pushed the End Call button and then dialed again. He was calling the state police barracks. "Bill, it's Dan Davies. I have some information that you need to know. I just spoke to Tony Kent, who started to come out of his coma yesterday and is now conscious and conversant. He stated that he was attacked with some kind of an object like the Hunter's fireplace shovel not far from the Kent house, and thinks that Jerry may have been the one who hit him with it. He repeated what the attacker said to him—actually, shouted at him—just before he was hit. Tony seems to think that Jerry could be the only one who would say something like that."

"What did the attacker say?" Jenkins asked.

"Tony said the words were…'I told you to keep your hands off her!'"

"You're *sure* those were the words?"

"That's what he stated. He said he'll never forget those words."

"Hmmm...I guess that narrows the list of suspects and Jerry doesn't really have an alibi for the time the attack occurred. While denying any guilt, he can't account for his time until thirty minutes or so after the incident. That would give plenty of time to commit the crime and get away. This is bizarre—arresting a husband and wife within 24 hours for crimes that are unrelated, yet related."

Dan shook his head and said, "I can't say that I've come across a situation like this before, and I was a detective for a long time."

"Alright," Jenkins groaned into the phone. "I'll get an arrest warrant for Jerry Hunter and go back to Hunter's Point. I'm certainly getting to know that place. Wait a minute, Dan...I've got to get to court first. Mrs. Hunter—Susan—is going to be brought there for arraignment shortly. Maybe I'll be able to arrest Jerry outside the courthouse, instead of at Hunter's Point, assuming he's going to the arraignment. Man, this is really getting crazy!"

"Yeah, it is. I'm just glad it's you rather than me doing the police work. And, I thought all the nuts were in New York. Based on what Tony said a few minutes ago and what you just stated, I think I'll go to the arraignment, also."

Dan walked into the courtroom just as the arraignment was getting started. The presiding judge, a middle-aged man by the name of Julian Frisk, sat behind a large bench at the front of the courtroom. Susan and her attorney, Thad Wilcox, nervously stood before him. Thaddeus Wilcox III was the third generation of attorneys in a firm that bore the family name. His late grandfather had known Jonathan Hunter, the original owner of Hunter's Point, and his father knew Jerry's deceased father—also an attorney.

Dan had just sat down when the judge droned from the bench, "Susan Hunter, do you understand the charge of attempted murder via poisoning that has been brought against you?"

"Yes, I do, Your Honor," Susan replied softly. When asked how she plead, she said, "Not guilty."

"Has the issue of bail been discussed?" the judge then asked.

Dan looked over at Thad Wilcox, who was about to utter his first words in the proceeding. "Based on the fact that the defendant has no prior criminal record, the defense requests that Mrs. Hunter be released on her own recognizance."

"I have a serious problem with that, Mr. Wilcox," the judge stated in his monotone voice. "Mr. District Attorney, how do you feel about this?"

Joel Stein, the district attorney, scratched his chin and approached the bench. "Your Honor, we would normally recommend that bail be set at five hundred thousand dollars, due to the seriousness of the crime. However, I have just been given some information that sheds new light and adds a dynamic to this case that we were not aware of when this arraignment was scheduled."

"Would you like to share this information with me, Mr. Stein?" the judge asked, a puzzled look on his face—an expression that Dan could detect from where he sat.

"Certainly, Your Honor. The state police have informed me that Mrs. Hunter's husband, Jerry Hunter, was questioned about a possible crime against another member of the Kent family two nights ago on Wednesday and is going to be arrested immediately after this arraignment by State Trooper Bill Jenkins, who is in the rear of the courtroom."

"What?" Susan gasped, turning her back to the bench and looking into the spectator rows to see where Jerry was seated. Dan also looked around as he tried to spot Jerry.

Jerry shot up out of the bench he was seated in. "What are you talking about?" he shouted at the D.A.

The judge grabbed his gavel and pounded it loudly so everyone could hear. "Order...order in the courtroom. Sit down, Sir, and be quiet, but first answer one question. Are you Jerry Hunter?"

"Yes," Jerry replied as he sat down again.

"Turn and face the bench, Mrs. Hunter, and stay quiet," Judge Frisk then stated. "Continue, Mr. Stein."

Dan leaned forward as the district attorney began to speak again. "Based on this new information, that both Mr. and Mrs. Hunter may be implicated in crimes against their own family members, we feel there's a risk of flight and therefore recommend that Mrs. Hunter be held without bail."

"That's preposterous," Thad Wilcox blurted out. "She shouldn't be jailed any more. Mrs. Hunter spent last night as a guest of the state and that should be enough. Certainly, there is a reasonable bail that can be set. I should add, Your Honor, that the Hunters have a 20-year-old son who is on summer recess and living with them."

"Well, I can't make a judgment based on the situation with Mr. Hunter, because I don't know anything about the charge and the cases have to be treated separately," the judge interjected. "You say, Mr. Wilcox, that there is a 20-year-old son at their home?"

"Yes, Your Honor," the young defense attorney answered.

Dan, who had sat through many such proceedings in New York, looked intently at the judge to see if he exhibited any mannerisms that might signal how he would rule, but could not detect anything. He was startled out of his reflective thinking as Jerry stood up again and shouted, "I'll get a five hundred thousand dollar bond and spend the weekend in jail. Just let my wife go."

The judge, now visibly angered, stood up and looked at Jerry. "I will say to you again, Sir, sit down and be quiet or leave my courtroom. The state police will decide your place of domicile for the weekend. In fact, maybe it would be appropriate if you leave now and meet with the state trooper at the rear of this courtroom, who I assume wants to see you and has something to present to you."

Dan's gaze shifted to Susan, who had turned and tearfully watched as Jerry got up and walked to the back of the courtroom, where Bill Jenkins was waiting with an arrest warrant. The two walked out of the courtroom together. Another trooper was waiting in the hallway. Susan then turned back to face the judge again.

After a brief moment of silence, the judge spoke. "I'm going to allow bail for Mrs. Hunter in the amount of five hundred thousand dollars, after her passport is turned in and with the stipulation that she wear an electronic bracelet and not leave New London County until her next court appearance. I will reconsider the issue of Mrs. Hunter's status until the time of her trial next Thursday morning at ten o'clock, when I am ordering her to reappear in this courtroom. Mrs. Hunter, I trust that someone will be able to turn in your passport by the end of the day, which will enable you to spend the weekend at your home instead of behind bars."

Glancing at her attorney, who nodded back, Susan said, "We'll get it done, along with posting the bond, and I promise you, Judge, that I'm not going anywhere. I wouldn't know where to go."

"Well, let me give you another perspective. If someone can come up with a bond for the amount I've stipulated, then there are plenty of places that person could go, some of which may be far away from here. I would encourage you to abide by my ruling about staying in the local area. At least with us having your passport in our custody, I don't have to worry about you leaving the country."

Dan, reflecting on the proceedings so far, looked over at Thad Wilcox and noticed a heaving of his shoulders. He wondered if the young attorney was contemplating *two* criminal defenses for his firm and the prospect of Jerry Hunter spending the weekend in police custody. *Well, at least one of his clients is out of jail,* Dan thought.

After looking at both attorneys to see if either of then had anything more to say and not getting any reaction, the judge picked up his gavel and, pounding it more gently this time, said, "Trial date for Susan Hunter is set for 60 days from today."

Dan, who was seated on the opposite side of the courtroom from where Jerry had been sitting, rose and walked out as the judge closed the arraignment. Outside the courthouse, Dan saw Jerry being escorted into Bill Jenkins' police cruiser, his arms handcuffed behind his back. Dan picked up Jerry's scornful look as the newly accused glared at him.

Dan turned around and noticed Michael standing behind a pillar, observing his father being taken away by the police. Dan walked over to Michael and said, "I didn't know you were here today. Were you in the courtroom?" Michael nodded, but said nothing. "I feel for you," Dan stated empathetically. "I feel for you *and* Jon, although for different reasons. Both of you are going through situations that guys your age shouldn't have to deal with."

Michael shrugged his shoulders. Then he began to speak. "I took the morning off to be here, after I heard about Susan's arrest. I didn't know Dad was going to be arrested, though, until the attorney in the courtroom made his statement when the bail for Susan was brought up. I thought that when they let him go the other night after the questioning, they didn't think he had anything to do with Uncle Tony being so badly injured."

"Tony came out of his coma and said something this morning that implicates your father," Dan said.

"What was that?"

"I'm not at liberty to say anything specific, but Tony made a comment about his fall onto the rocks and words shouted at him that he thinks could only have come from Jerry."

"Those words wouldn't be about Susan, would they? I mean, what else could it be—something that only my dad could say that would put the finger on him."

"I really don't want to get into it," Dan said, not wanting to reveal exactly what was said by Tony, but also knowing that almost the entire family knew about the affair and the nature of what Tony had said would be fairly obvious.

Michael shook his head in disgust. "I think I can figure it out for myself. In a way, Susan may be involved in both the poisoning and what my dad did, or may have done. This is nuts! It's about as crazy a family fiasco as I could ever imagine. And, it's my family! You know, it used to be pretty good around here before Susan arrived. I'm going back to work, finish out the day, and go out with Amy tonight. I think tomorrow I'll go see Mom and spend the weekend with her. I need to get away from here and be with someone who's normal. She won't believe this!"

"I can appreciate that. It's been pretty bizarre and nutty around here lately."

"Does Jon know what's happened?" Michael asked. "Maybe I should call him."

"He doesn't know everything yet, but will shortly. I'm going to see him for lunch and fill him in. Maybe it's better if I tell him. You two seem to incite each other, which I guess, is understandable, but we don't need any more incitement. So, I'll take care of informing Jon."

"Okay by me, if that's what you think is best. Tell Jon I'll see him tonight with the girls."

Dan picked up a couple of roast beef sandwiches, chips and sodas, and went to the beach where Jon was life guarding to have lunch with him. As they began to eat, he told Jon about the charges filed against Susan and Jerry.

Jon tensed up as he listened, his mind racing. "Wow!" he exclaimed after Dan was done. "This is some family. Maybe Michael was right."

"What do you mean by that?"

"Well, last Sunday night Michael said that maybe Susan has some involvement in this. You know, the affair with Dad that started the bad blood between him and Uncle Jerry, and the home wrecking that he feels in his own house with his mother being tossed out. And this was before we knew anything about the tea poisoning."

"Alright, now I understand what you mean," Dan said. "I saw Michael at the courthouse as Jerry was being taken away, and he said something about Susan having either direct or indirect involvement in both incidents."

"Do you think Uncle Jerry and Susan could have devised a plot against our side of the family? Maybe to get rid of us so they can take over and control Hunter's Point?"

"It's funny you should ask that question." Frowning, he said, "Anita was thinking the same thing yesterday, after I told her about the results of the tea poisoning."

"Yeah, well maybe we think alike. She is my aunt, you know... really my second mother. So, Mr. Davies, *could there be* some type of plot here?" Jon's mind was now totally focused on the possibility of Jerry and Susan being co-conspirators.

"I don't know, Jon. I just don't know. This situation is puzzling...real puzzling." Looking at his watch, Dan said, "Let's finish eating. You've probably got to get back to ensuring the safety of all these people on the beach and I've got a couple of things to do. Maybe I'll see you at the hospital at the end of the day. If not, you know you're at my place for the weekend, with a one o'clock curfew tonight and tomorrow, and midnight on Sunday. And don't even think of doing anything stupid. Got it?"

"Yeah...I got it. And, thanks, Mr. Davies. Thanks for everything. I mean it. My dad would probably be dead if it weren't for you and the doctors."

"Glad to do anything I can to help. I like this family, and don't like what's happened. Remember that you can talk to me about anything that's on your mind. And, one last thing."

"What's that?"

"Call me Dan. Mr. Davies makes me feel old."

Jon nodded as he took a bite of his sandwich and reached for a chip.

Jon and Nicole embraced and kissed tenderly on the deck of Nicole's cottage at Crystal Sands, another of the area's beach communities.

"Hmmm, this is nice," he whispered in her ear. "At least one aspect of my life is good."

She pressed her body closer to his. "I'm glad that I can make you feel good. You've been through so much suffering. You and Michael don't deserve this. He looked a little spaced out tonight. Having both parents arrested in the same week is too much!"

"Yeah, it sucks…big time!" Jon then looked at his watch and saw it was getting close to his curfew time. "I've got to go, Nicole. Dan will be waiting for me."

"Will I see you tomorrow night?"

"You bet. Maybe we'll do a movie. I'll pick you up at seven-thirty." As he walked back to his car, he felt something in the front left pocket of his denim shorts. *Oh shit, I forgot to give Michael his cell phone after I borrowed it to call Dan,* he muttered silently. *I'll bring it to him tomorrow morning before he leaves to go see his mom.*

Chapter 14

"Good morning," Dan said to Anita as she opened the front passenger door to his car and got in. He was picking her up at the home of her co-worker and friend. She had spent the night there, because her car needed work and had been taken to a local garage late Friday afternoon.

"Good morning, Dan. What a nice one it is. I can't believe we're spending so much of the summer we crave for during the cold season at the hospital."

"Yeah, neither can I. This wasn't exactly what I planned for in my retirement. But, that's how life goes. We roll with the punches and play the cards we're dealt. Let me tell you about the latest developments with Jerry and Susan," he continued. "Jerry got bail posted for Susan. Can you believe it was half a million dollars? He's in police custody for the weekend, but she's out—wearing an electronic bracelet and having had her passport confiscated to minimize any risk of flight. Susan's trial is scheduled for 60 days from now, and I guess Jerry's trial date will be set on Monday when he's arraigned. We may have two trials going on at the same time. Can you imagine that?"

"Dan, I can't believe any of it!"

"It is tough. I try to put myself in your shoes, but I have trouble doing that, so I can only try to empathize with you."

"You've been a dear friend through all of this. I don't know what I would have done without you." Wiping a tear from her eye, she then said softly, "So, Susan is at Hunter's Point and Jerry's in jail for the weekend. How are we going to live together on the same property with this going on—preparing for a criminal trial? How could I possibly even see Susan after she's apparently poisoned mother and me…and maybe you? What would I say to her?"

"You know, these are powerful questions. I hadn't thought much about them," Dan said, scratching his chin.

"Neither had I, until now. And what about Jerry? Is he going to have to stay in jail for the whole time between now and the trial?"

"Another good question, Anita, that I don't know the answer to and haven't thought about…until now. I'll go to the arraignment on Monday morning and find out what the judge orders."

"And what about you, Dan? Do you think you've been poisoned?"

Dan scratched his chin again. "I felt a little queasy for a day or so this past week, but didn't think much of it. I guess I should get some tests done," he said softly.

They were quiet for the remaining time it took to drive to the hospital, each of them contemplating the bizarre events of the recent past and what might transpire in the near future.

Michael was taking an orange juice container out of the refrigerator as Susan sauntered into the kitchen.

"Well, well, look who they let out of the cage," he turned and said with a snicker.

"I don't need any of your wisecracks, Michael. I've got enough trouble to deal with and would appreciate at least a little support from you."

"Yeah, well don't count on it, lady. You're right about being in a shitload of trouble, but don't look to me for any help. A lot of this wouldn't have happened if you hadn't invaded our family and our lives."

"Can't you stop persecuting me for the attraction between your father and me? I'm sorry that it didn't work out between your father and mother, but it's not my fault. It may have been another woman if it weren't me."

"I'm not so sure about that. You have a way of going after men. Look at your affair with Uncle Tony!"

"What's that about my dad?" Jon had come in through the front door, unheard by Michael and Susan, and he had only heard the words "Uncle Tony." When he saw Susan, he stopped dead in his tracks, holding Michael's cell phone in his left hand. He placed the phone on the kitchen table, lunged at Susan and grabbed her by the throat, forcing her to the kitchen floor. She gasped as she fell on to her back.

Michael raced over and grabbed Jon, pulling him back and allowing Susan, still lying on her back, to breathe. She started to cry. Michael stood over her. "We probably should beat the crap out of her, Jon. God knows, she deserves it."

Susan rose up and glared at Jon and Michael. "You two little bastards!" she yelled. "Is this what you want? Well, go ahead. Two young men against a woman. That's probably what you guys would call a fair fight." She glanced at a carving knife lying on a cutting board on the counter and reached for it.

Reacting quickly, Jon clamped his hand on top of her wrist, pulling it back before she could reach the knife. Remembering the admonitions from Dan and Anita, he said, "We've had enough violence around here, so let's not have another episode." With his other hand, Jon motioned to Michael to get the knife.

"Let me go," Susan cried out, as Michael grabbed the knife.

"As long as you keep away from the knife," Jon shot back. Releasing his grip, he then said sarcastically, "You know, I'd almost like to see you beaten up a little, so you wouldn't look so pretty any more. Maybe then my dad wouldn't want to look at you again. But I've already got one assault charge to deal with, and you're not worth another."

"Well, maybe you *will* get another charge if I tell the police about this."

"Yeah, and who's going to be your witness?" Michael retorted. "Let's see, a woman about to go to trial for attempted murder filing an assault charge, with no visible marks of injury and no witnesses. That ought to get the police excited."

"Why don't you just get the hell out of here, Susan," Jon growled. "No one except Uncle Jerry really wants you here and you're trouble... big trouble."

"I'm staying until someone orders me out. This is my home and I plan to stay here."

Jon was getting agitated and clenched his fist. While he really wanted to go after her, he thought again about Aunt Anita and Dan Davies. He backed away. "Michael, I came over here to return your cell phone, which I forgot to give back after I borrowed it last night. She isn't worth any more of my time. I'm going to the hospital and you're better off getting out of here and going to see your mother."

"Yeah, you're probably right, although I did enjoy scaring the crap out of her. Okay, I'm outta here, too. Enjoy your castle, Bitch Queen. We'll see how long you're here. If I had anything to say about it, it wouldn't be for long."

"Who's going to care and cook for you?" Susan scowled.

"Hopefully anyone but you," Michael said. "Maybe I'll get lucky and my real mom can come back, especially if you and Dad get sent away for what you've done."

Jon walked quickly out of the kitchen and toward the front door. Michael grabbed his cell phone and sprinted up the stairs to his room. He had packed an overnight bag, which he grabbed, then ran out of the house, catching up with Jon and leaving Susan alone—shuddering as she gazed out of a window and saw the two boys pumping their fists at each other.

"Good morning, Dr. O'Brien," Anita said as she and Dan walked past the nurses station on their way to Katherine's room. Dr. Jack O'Brien, on duty today, had just finished his morning rounds visiting patients and was giving instructions to the nurses on the floor.

"Oh, Anita, I'm glad you're here," the young doctor called over to her. "I wanted to give you an update on your mother and brother. And good morning to you, also, Dan. Here's the latest. Katherine is coming along well, but with the poisoning and her age, we have to be extra careful, so we expect her to be here for a maximum of ten more days. In about a week, Tony should be strong enough to have the shoulder surgery he needs, and with the recuperation from that and continued treatment for his head injuries, he should be released in two weeks. Now, there is something about Tony that you need to be aware of. Based on some tests done yesterday by a specialist, he may suffer some short-term memory loss. He's lucky he doesn't have serious brain injury. However, he may exhibit some behavior that would normally occur ten or twenty years later."

"Kind of like what I experience," Dan interjected, a wry smile appearing on his face. "Are you talking about the onset of dementia?"

"No, I wouldn't say that," the doctor replied, "although a sooner than normal onset is a possibility. We really have to wait, since it's just not possible to make that kind of prediction based on what we know now. The short-term memory loss might be a frustration for Tony, but it should not affect the other workings of his brain. One of the reasons we've waited on his shoulder surgery is to make sure he's able to go through it without any complications from his head injuries."

"Alright," Anita sighed, her head slumping down and her fingers stroking her forehead. "I guess we should be thankful that Mother will come out of it soon and Tony will be able to function normally at some point." A wrinkle had developed on her forehead from all the stress and she had a look of consternation on her face.

"That's a good attitude," the doctor said, forcing a smile. "Why don't you go see them now?"

Katherine smiled at Anita and Dan as they entered her room. "Now, my darling daughter, are you going to tell me when my son is going to visit me?"

Anita looked over at Dan, who nodded back at her, the signal to tell Katherine what they had agreed on. "Well, Mother, we have to tell you something about Tony."

Katherine gasped. "Please don't tell me it's something bad. Is he all right?"

"He is, but he did suffer an injury that, believe it or not, has put him in the hospital— just down the hall for that matter."

"Down the hall? Tony is down the hall from me? How long has he been here?"

"Since the day after you arrived. He had a fall on Rocky Bar—out near the end."

"A fall on Rocky Bar? How?"

"Just an accident," Anita answered. "He slipped on a wet rock and his legs went out from under him and he landed on his shoulder, which shattered as it broke his fall, and then on his head, which caused him to be unconscious for a while."

Dan, sensing that Katherine was going to ask questions until she found out all the facts surrounding Tony's condition, touched Anita on the right elbow and winked, the signal for him to do the talking now. Dan told Katherine that Tony had been unconscious for a couple of days, but was not in any real danger even though he could not move around, explaining how cautious doctors are with head injuries. Thus, they had confined him to a bed. When the elderly lady asked if her son knew that she was a patient, Dan said that the doctors had not yet told him about her condition, but would do so soon, saying they didn't want to run any risk of upsetting him. He then said that Tony had asked about her during their last visit with him.

"My, my, this is strange," Katherine responded. "Do they know what's the matter with me? The doctors, who I like and seem very nice, either can not or do not want to give me a straight answer."

Anita looked lovingly down at her mother and said, "They want to run a few more tests, which they couldn't start until you regained consciousness. It's definitely not a heart attack or stroke. They think it has to do maybe with a lack of oxygen flow, which caused you to lose consciousness."

"I didn't just lose consciousness. I was out for almost a week."

"That's why they can't just give you a quick answer, Mother. They have to run some tests."

"Test...tests...now you know why I don't like these places. I want to go home to Hunter's Point. How long do I have to stay here?"

Anita looked at Dan, who nodded, indicating she should say what the doctor had just told them. "It's going to be about another ten days," Anita said.

"Ten days? That's preposterous! I want to get out of here tomorrow. Call the doctor and get him in here. He didn't say anything about that when he was here earlier...but, I guess I didn't ask him."

"Mother, you're just going to have to grin and bear it. These medical people know what's best for you, and want you to leave well enough so you don't have to come back."

"Ten more days...I can't believe it. I miss the sound of the waves at night. This place is totally silent at night...it's too quiet."

"Well, Katherine, I definitely think you're getting better," Dan said. "You sound like the feisty lady that I know and have affection for." He smiled at her as he spoke. "Listen up now. Let Anita and me go to Tony's room and visit with him for a while, and then we'll come back and see you again before we leave. Okay?"

"Alright. I'm getting a bit tired and maybe should doze off for a while, so you go to see Tony and give him a kiss for me. Tell him that his mother loves him, hopes that he's feeling better and wants to see him soon."

As Dan and Anita entered Tony's room, he was awake and propped up in his bed. He smiled at Anita, who said, "Hey there, Little Brother, how are you feeling today?"

"Much better, Sis. Hi, Dan. Thanks for coming here. Anita, there's something I can't figure out. Why isn't Mom with you when you come to visit me?"

"We thought you would ask us that question," Anita stammered, looking again at Dan for support and direction. A subtle nod indicated another fabricated tale. "Mother, surprisingly, took ill just before you were attacked and had to be rushed to the hospital. She's been here, with some kidney and breathing problems, since last Friday. She's doing all right, though, and is responding to the treatments the doctors and nurses have been giving her. Please don't ask me exactly what the illness is, since it's very technical and I don't understand everything the doctors tell me. She's just down the hall. Now, Tony, we had to tell Mother a little lie, since we didn't want to upset her with what exactly happened to you. So, you must go along with what we said."

"Yeah, so what's that?"

"We told Mother you had an accidental fall out at the end of Rocky Bar; that you slipped on a rock and fell on your shoulder and then your head, causing your injuries. So, Mother knows that you're here and are injured, but doesn't know the actual cause."

Dan then said, "Another thing you should know is that Jerry has been arrested, charged with criminal assault, and will be arraigned in court on Monday. He'll probably go to trial."

Tony lay there silently, nodding his head. "I assume that Mom knows nothing about this."

"That's right," Dan said. "She knows nothing and won't know anything until she's back home. By then, we figure she'll be able to deal with it."

Tony nodded again. "That's the right thing to do. I'll keep your story to her intact. On another matter, how's Jon? Is he coming today?"

"He's as good as he can be under the circumstances," Dan replied. "He's staying with me for now, and should be here momentarily."

Just then, Jon bolted into the room. "Hi, everyone! Hey, Dad!"

"Hi, Son...nice to see you. How are you?"

"I'm okay. Dan is taking care of me and giving me some good advice."

"Well, thank goodness for something positive in this crazy scenario," Tony sighed.

"How's Grandma doing? Have you heard what happened to her?"

"Well, your aunt just told me. It's strange...kind of mysterious."

"Mysterious?" Jon blurted out, looking at Dan and Anita in bewilderment.

Dan grabbed Jon by the arm and said, "Oh, Jon, your girlfriend called the house and asked to give you a message. Tony, let me tell him before I forget. Jon, come with me out in the hallway. Tony, we'll be right back." Motioning with his head and tightening his grip on Jon's arm, Dan nudged the youngster out of the room. As they got outside the room, Dan turned to Jon and, putting his forefinger to his lips, whispered, "We didn't tell your father the whole truth about what happened to Katherine."

"What do you mean? What did you tell him?"

"We told him that she's sick and in the hospital. In fact, he knows that she's down the hall. But we did *not* tell him that she was poisoned. We said she got sick and is undergoing tests to find out the cause. You've got to go along with our story. The doctors agree with what we've said and don't want your father having any kind of bad mental reaction to what is an attempted murder charge. Also, we told your grandmother that your dad had a fall out at the end of Rocky Bar. She doesn't know about the attack and the charge against Jerry, or the charge against Susan, for that matter. Trust us, Jon, this is the right thing to say at this time. When they're stronger and get home, we'll tell them the truth."

Jon nodded. "I guess you're right. Can we go back in Dad's room now?"

Chapter 15

"All rise. The Superior Court of Connecticut, New London County, is now in session, the Honorable Willard Thomas presiding." The bailiff's voice was sharp and clear as he opened court proceedings Monday morning. The judge entered the courtroom and took his seat.

Judge Thomas pounded his gavel lightly and spoke. "Case number NL35063832—the People of Connecticut versus Jerald Hunter. Defendant and counselors, please approach the bench."

Now seated, Dan gazed toward the front of the courtroom as Jerry Hunter and Jason Wilcox, Thad's younger brother and a junior partner in the law firm, rose and walked slowly to the railing separating the front of the courtroom from the center and rear. On the other side of the aisle, assistant district attorney Allan Bentley rose and strode briskly to the rail.

"How does the defendant plead to the charge of criminal assault?" the judge asked, looking down at Jerry.

"My client pleads not guilty, Your Honor," Wilcox replied. Jerry nodded as his attorney spoke.

"Does the assistant district attorney know the condition of the victim, Mr. Anthony Kent?" the judge inquired.

Allan Bentley cleared his throat and, looking at the judge stated, "As of early this morning, your honor, Mr. Kent was in stable, yet guarded, condition at the hospital. He was taken off the critical list over the weekend."

Dan noticed Jerry's shoulders droop slightly, which he took as a sigh of relief.

"I see," Judge Thomas said. "So, the district attorney's office is sticking to a Criminal Assault charge against the defendant?"

"Yes, Your Honor," the youthful Assistant D.A. said solemnly. "We have no way of knowing what the intent of the defendant was beyond the charge that has been filed."

"Very well, then," the judge continued, leaning forward. "Let's talk about the issue of bail and a trial date."

Jason Wilcox, wanting to be heard before Bentley said anything further, looked first at Jerry, then at Judge Thomas and blurted out, "The defense proposes a one hundred thousand dollar bond and Mr. Hunter's release, with no travel privileges outside a four state region—Connecticut, Massachusetts, New York and New Jersey—until the trial begins and no airline travel privileges within this four-state region or outside of it. This condition will enable Mr. Hunter to conduct his business affairs and keep him close by."

Bentley had been prepared for a bail and release request by his boss, district attorney Joel Stein. The young prosecutor responded, "Your Honor, there is an extenuating circumstance that you may not be aware of, which makes the issue of releasing Mr. Hunter one that we have to argue against. You may have notice of this in your file for this case. We, therefore, request that bail—which would normally be in the two hundred fifty thousand dollar range for a charge of this nature—be denied."

Judge Thomas leafed through the papers in front of him as Bentley was speaking. "Hmmm…I read here that on Friday Judge Frisk imposed a five hundred thousand dollar bond on Mrs. Susan Hunter, regarding a charge of attempted murder. Is this your wife, Mr. Hunter?" The judge had a puzzled look on his face as he queried Jerry.

"Yes, Your Honor," Jerry replied, his voice barely above a whisper.

"And, Your Honor," the Assistant D.A. interjected, "Mrs. Hunter's alleged crime is against another member of the Kent family, Mrs. Katherine Hunter-Kent, mother of this crime's victim and the defendant's aunt."

"I see," the judge murmured, scratching his chin. "Well, I've been on this bench for almost twenty years now, and I can't remember anything like this. While the two cases have to be treated separately, I'm going to support Mr. Bentley's request and order a temporary denial of bail, pending my further review of *this* case."

Jerry's face turned beet red as anger started to burn inside him. He was about to say something, when a strong grasp on his lower right arm from Jason Wilcox's left hand told him to remain quiet. "Could you define what you mean by 'temporary', Your Honor?" the young attorney asked.

The judge looked at everyone in front of him and then stated, "We will reconvene here on Wednesday morning at this hour to review the issue of bail for Mr. Hunter. As to a trial date, is everyone comfortable with sixty days from now?" All the heads nodded. "So be it, then. Is there anything else before I close this arraignment?"

Allan Bentley stepped forward slightly and, looking straight ahead at the judge said, "Actually, there is one more item, Your Honor. Based on the fact that Mr. Hunter's charge and his wife's attempted murder charge are for alleged crimes against family members, along with the fact that the defendants and victims all live in a family enclave on a piece of property known as Hunter's Point, we feel that Susan Hunter—who has been released on a bond—should be removed from the property within forty-eight hours." Looking at his watch, Bentley said, "District Attorney Stein will petition Judge Frisk on this matter within the next hour. Regarding this case, we request that Mr. Hunter be given forty-eight hours to remove his personal belongings plus an additional week to remove any furnishings from his home, and be ordered to leave the premises if and when the court decides to release him from police custody."

"Are you freakin' crazy?" Jerry shouted. He lunged toward Bentley, but was held back by Jason Wilcox, who stepped between them and gripped Jerry in a bear hug.

Dan instinctively felt his knees starting to rise, but restrained himself.

"Bailiff, please have Mr. Hunter handcuffed and taken out of this courtroom," Judge Thomas thundered.

"You son of a bitch!" Jerry yelled at Bentley, glaring at him as two police officers, stationed at the side of the courtroom, ran to where they were standing, cuffed Jerry's hands behind him, and quickly escorted him out by the side entrance.

"Request is granted," the judge stated, pounding his gavel to signal the closing of the arraignment.

Dan leaned back and sighed, shocked by the recent outburst and starting to think about the implications of Jerry and Susan leaving Hunter's point followed by two criminal trials going on at the same time. As Dan turned to leave, he noticed Michael, seated in the last row, rise and walk out of the courtroom.

Later that afternoon, Jason Wilcox met with Jerry at the state detention facility.

"What am I going to tell my company? How do I deal with being in jail for most or all of the week?" Jerry was despondent and venting to his attorney, as they sat across a plain wooden table from each other.

"Let me think about that," Jason answered. After pondering for a moment the predicament his client faced, he said, "I think the two most viable options right now would be to feign illness or concoct some personal emergency. We certainly do have a personal type of emergency on our hands," he muttered, his voice shaking a bit. "Let's think about making up something that's in line with what's happened and can be disguised. Maybe an incident with your son, which is always happening with college kids. Maybe that can buy us the rest of this week."

Jerry nodded. "Damn it!" he cried out. "I'm at the peak of my career and could lose everything because of this."

You stand to lose a lot more than your career if we can't win this case, the defense attorney thought to himself.

"What about Susan and her situation?" Jerry asked.

"I talked to my brother about Susan having to leave Hunter's Point and he gave her the other judge's order about an hour ago."

"Oh yeah? How did she react?"

"She was very upset, but said she'd go to her parents' home in the New Haven area."

"I figured that. If I ever get out of here and they let me leave the state, I have an apartment in New York City that I use almost every week, where maybe we can stay." Jerry then stared blankly at the ceiling, as the impending incarceration and uncertainty of his future started to sink in.

Tuesday evening, an hour after Susan left Hunter's Point and headed for her parents' home, Michael entered the verandah of the main house where Anita was sitting alone, looking out at the ocean. He walked over and gave her a gentle kiss on the cheek. "Thank you for inviting me to dinner, Aunt Anita. I don't have anyone to cook for me anymore, now that Susan has left and Dad's in the pokey."

"You poor boy, you've been through a lot. The least I can do is feed you. Besides, I'm almost always alone, with Mother and Tony in the hospital. Thank goodness Jon is here to provide company for me, and thank the lord also for Dan Davies, who has been such a great friend and always available."

"Yeah, this has been an incredible ten days, capped off by the arraignment this morning," Michael said.

"I didn't have the strength or inclination to attend the arraignment. Tell me what happened."

"Well, I sat in the back of the courtroom out of sight. I didn't want Dad to see me. He went 'nuts' when the prosecutor asked that he be removed from this place and the judge granted the request. He had to be taken away by the cops in restraints. It was unbelievable, like in a movie. As I told Jon one night, you can't make this shit—excuse me, stuff—up. By the way, is Jon coming for dinner tonight?"

"Actually, he is. I thought it would be nice to surround myself with two handsome young men." Anita smiled fondly at him. "Now, Michael, we still have most of the summer ahead of us. I assume you're going to spend it here at Hunter's Point."

"I guess so. I've got my summer job and I need the money for college. And there's Amy, who I'm really starting to like. Jeez, I don't know where else I'd go. The only other place would be Mom's home, but that's so far away and I'd have to give up everything here—my job, my girlfriend, this place and all the beaches and parties around here. I haven't really given it too much thought. There's just been too much going on."

"Hmmm," Anita muttered softly, thinking about Michael's predicament. "Along with Jon, you've suffered from all of this turmoil. This bothers me and I believe the two of you deserve a normal summer life. Maybe we should think about asking Miriam to come back here for a while."

"Mom…coming back to Hunter's Point? I remember Dad saying to her she'd never again set foot on this property. I don't think he knew I overheard that conversation. Mom's leaving and not being allowed back was a major part of the divorce settlement."

"I know that, but under the circumstances, I'm wondering if she'd be willing to come. I'll ask Dan if he thinks we need to get a court order and how hard it is to get one."

"Well, you know how much Mom loves this place, and with Dad

and Susan gone, she just might come back. Do you want me to ask her?"

Anita nodded. "Yes, I do, but we need to think about where you should stay."

"I don't think we could live in the house, but how about the vacant cottage?"

"That makes sense. Tell her I suggested it."

Anita and Michael turned to see Jon approaching and waving to them. Anita served marinated chicken, a large salad, boiled potatoes and fresh bread, all of which she and the boys devoured. She felt good to be with them and away from the hospital. She opened a bottle of white wine to make the meal more enjoyable. After dinner, Jon and Michael, sensing that Anita wished not to be alone, called Nicole and Amy, who joined them for the rest of the evening.

"I can't believe I'm back here," Miriam exclaimed as, three days later, she and Michael embraced in the living room of the vacant cottage. They held each other tightly, then let go and smiled at each other.

"What a turn of events, Mom. Dad kicks you out and now he's out and you're back. What we've both wanted since Susan came into the picture has happened. We can thank Aunt Anita for suggesting that you come back here."

"Yes, life can certainly have its twists and turns," Miriam whispered in her son's ear. "Let's hope that you and I can stay together and Susan gets sent off for a long time for what everyone seems to think she's done." She gently grabbed Michael's arm and embraced him again. She then looked up at him and said, "I love it when you hold and hug me like this. I've missed this so much since I've been away from here."

"I'll always be here for you, Mom. I'll never abandon you the way Dad did."

Miriam smiled. Her head was resting on her taller son's shoulder and her thick brown hair nestled under his chin. "I know that and I love you, Son, more than anything on this earth. I always want to be close to you...very close."

Chapter 16

On Tuesday morning of the following week, Katherine was released from the hospital and returned to Hunter's Point. As Dan was driving Katherine home, Tony was being taken by ambulance to Hartford Hospital for shoulder surgery and a brain scan.

Arriving at the main house, Dan helped the elderly woman out of his car. As she held onto his hand, she said, "Dan, you've become more than a friend. I consider you to be one of my family. You saved Tony's life and you were there for me, and I'll always remember that." Starting to sob quietly, she whispered, "I hope you will continue to accommodate an old lady and come back here this afternoon for a cup of tea with me, one without any poison in it. By the way, I appreciate you and Anita telling me yesterday what really happened to Tony and me, along with the surrounding circumstances. I also think it's a good idea to keep the truth from Tony until he gets back home." As they approached the house, she exclaimed, "Goodness, how I've missed this place and our afternoon chats. Let's call Miriam. Anita told me about her returning and that you helped get a court order allowing her to come here to help take care of Michael. I've been looking forward to seeing her again, and this will give you a chance to get to know her."

"Alright, I'll do as you wish. I've missed our occasional afternoons together and this will be a lot more pleasant than standing over you in a hospital room," Dan said, smiling.

On Friday, Tony was released from the hospital and returned to Hunter's Point. Jon had taken the day off, driven to Hartford, chauffeured his father home and spent the afternoon with him, after which Tony ordered his son to go out for the evening with his girlfriend.

Katherine had asked Dan to join her, Anita and Tony for dinner at the main house. There was much to tell Tony.

After they had finished eating, Anita suggested they all go to the verandah. As they were getting seated, Anita glanced at Dan, who turned toward Tony and started speaking. "Tony, there are a few things you need to know about what happened three weeks ago and what's transpired since then. We just couldn't tell you everything at the hospital."

"Has it really been three weeks?" Tony said inquisitively. "Yes, I guess it has, although I can only recall the last two. I lost the first week. I still don't know exactly what happened to you, Mom, so maybe you can tell me."

Katherine replied that the hospital tests confirmed she was poisoned, apparently by Susan. When her son cast a puzzled look at her, Katherine continued by saying that the evidence gathered so far pointed to Susan injecting paint thinner into the herbal tea she'd been buying and bringing to the main house over the past few months.

"Poisoned...by Susan?" Tony was dumfounded. A look of utter disbelief now distorted his face. "You've got to be joking! Why would she poison you? She's had it so good here."

"Well, maybe it's not been good enough," Katherine countered. "Perhaps she and Jerry wanted me...and you...and Anita...out of the way to get *all* of Hunter's Point. Oh, Lord, I don't know, but that's one theory—a conspiracy plot that seems far fetched, but perhaps everything, including Susan's affection for you, was contrived."

Tony leaned back and sighed. His shoulder was still hurting from the surgery and he grimaced as he looked out at the water. "This is incredible. Jerry hits me with the fireplace shovel and Susan puts paint thinner into your herbal tea bags? Wow! Is this how you also got sick, Anita? Are you sure this isn't some bad dream we're all having and we just need to wake up?"

"It's been a nightmare for sure," Anita said, "but it's also our reality. Both you and Mother came within a whisker of dying and, as you noted, I also got pretty sick. And, since Dan drank the contaminated green tea on occasion, he's going to be tested."

Tony looked incredulously at the three other people with him on the verandah and asked, "So, where are Jerry and Susan?"

Dan leaned forward in his chair and spoke directly to Tony, telling him about Susan's release on a bond, leaving Hunter's Point to stay with her parents in New Haven, her weekly check-ins at the probation office there, and the requirement to wear an electronic device to track her whereabouts. He then explained Jerry's situation, whereby the judge was allowing him to stay in his New York apartment and travel on a restricted basis in the northeast until a week before the trial date, as long as he wore his electronic device and was monitored. He then mentioned that Jerry has to be at the local jail by seven o'clock every Friday night to spend the weekend there. Dan concluded by stating that both of them had their passports revoked, Susan was not allowed to leave the state, and they were not permitted to see each other."

Tony sighed again and looked out at the Sound. "I suppose, Mom, based on what you just said, that you know about the affair, which could have something to do with all of this, or at least my getting attacked."

"Yes, unfortunately I do," Katherine scowled as she stared at her son. "Anita told me yesterday. How could you be so selfish and thoughtless?"

"I don't know, Mom…weakness, I guess. It was purely a physical attraction, nothing else."

"Without any regard to the consequences for this family!" the elderly lady said forcefully. "You put yourself and your desire for having a sexual affair ahead of everything and everyone else."

Dan gazed out at the water, which was starting to darken as nighttime approached. He was sensing the pain that was gripping this family. *I feel a part of them,* he thought.

Tony rose from his chair. "You're right, Mom, about this situation. Well, now that everything is out in the open, maybe something Susan said to me after one of our encounters—the night of Jon's graduation party—has some bearing on your situation…and Anita's."

"What was that?" Anita asked with a sneer.

"I'd like to hear about that," Dan chimed in.

"Susan was wondering how it would feel to have Hunter's Point all to herself. She put it in the form of a thought of how Grandpa Jonathan must have felt as he walked along the beach in his early years here, knowing that this place was all his…his alone. Then she said something that took me by complete surprise."

"What was that?" Dan asked.

"She said she sometimes imagines what it must be like to say to yourself...'this is mine...all mine'."

Dan looked over at Katherine who gazed at her son and then out at the ocean. He noticed a stone cold look on her face.

Silence pervaded the group on the verandah as Tony's last comment and the events of the past three weeks started to sink in.

Dan peered at each of these people who had been enduring so much physical and emotional pain. "Folks, I think that while you can't sweep away the devastating events that have occurred, it's time to now band together as a family and recognize that anyone can make a mistake. For one thing, you need to show Jon that the grown-ups have their priorities in order and give him some idea as to how you're going to approach these trials, which are probably going to be two of the most difficult and bizarre situations you'll ever face."

"Oh, goodness, I hadn't given much thought to that," Katherine exclaimed. "Is it true that we'll have *two* criminal trials going on at the same time, starting shortly after Labor Day?"

"That's my understanding," Dan replied. "It's going to be something. I've been in law enforcement all my adult life and have never encountered circumstances like these."

"Great...just great," Tony sighed. "Just what we all need, on top of everything else. You said, Dan, that we should give Jon an idea about how we're going to approach the trials. Can you elaborate?"

"I think you need to remember that Jon is convinced that Jerry attacked you, Tony, and you may also be certain that it was Jerry. I really don't know if he believes as strongly about Susan being guilty of poisoning his aunt and grandmother, but let's assume he believes this, since the evidence gathered so far along with the comment you just made is compelling. You need to keep him from getting emotional. Make sure he appreciates the spirit of our judicial system, which is that people are presumed innocent until proven guilty. In order to do that, you need to stay away from prosecuting Jerry and Susan while we await the trials. The attorneys will take care of this in the courtrooms."

Katherine, who had been listening attentively, said, "Well, Dan, once again your logic is probably what we need to think seriously about. My grandson needs his life simplified and made less stressful." She then got up, went over to Dan, and gave him a tender peck on the cheek. "You've been wonderful through this ordeal and all of us Kents owe you so much." Tony and Anita raised their hands in a "thumbs up" sign.

Dan blushed a bit and smiled.

"How about an after dinner drink?" Tony blurted out. "We all probably need to relax a bit."

"Sounds good," Anita countered. "I'll get it."

As they were all sipping a liqueur, Anita turned to her brother and said, "Tony, there's one other development you should know about."

"What's that?"

"Miriam is back."

Tony gasped and almost spat the liqueur he was sipping on the floor. "Miriam…back here at Hunter's Point? Is this for real? I thought she was banned for life!"

"Well, that's true according to the divorce settlement, but with all that's happened, especially Jerry and Susan being removed from the property by the court, I felt that Michael needed his mother at this time. We've still got several weeks before he goes back to college. You and mother will need some care, which I hope to provide, and I felt we could use another adult around here. Besides, Michael is very close to his mother and is very happy to have her back and living with him. After all he's been through with Jerry and Susan, I thought that asking Miriam to return was the right thing to do."

"Well, I certainly have no objections," Tony said. "What's the old saying? What goes around comes around? How does Miriam feel about being back here?"

"She seems to have mixed feelings," Anita responded. "She said she's shocked by what has happened, but happy to be back at the place she loves and with the boy she adores. It's really wonderful to see the love she has for Michael."

"Anything else?" Tony asked, raising his liqueur glass and sipping from it.

"I think that's about it," Dan answered, looking first at Anita and then at Katherine—who nodded and stated that it was her bedtime, excused herself and went upstairs.

With Dan guiding them, Tony and Anita spent the next half-hour going over everything that had transpired during the past three weeks, along with what could have motivated Jerry and Susan to commit the acts they were accused of. Neither Tony nor Anita could reach any definitive conclusions. As they talked to each other and to Dan, the two siblings often shook their heads in disbelief at what had happened.

Chapter 17

Katherine invited Miriam for breakfast Saturday morning to start the weekend. Miriam offered to cook. As she surveyed the French toast and sausages lying on a platter and ready for the skillet, Katherine said, "Miriam, about the only good thing that's happened during the past month is that you and I have had a chance to get reacquainted. I've missed you and never did approve of Jerry ending your marriage, and taking up with Susan."

"I've missed you, too, Katherine, especially our afternoon teas."

"We'll be resuming them on a regular basis starting this coming week. I'm so glad you were able to come here when I returned from the hospital and that you had a chance to spend some time with me and get to know Dan a bit."

"Yes, it was nice to see him again. We had only met briefly before I had to leave last year. You seem to be fond of him."

"I am. Dan Davies has become a *very* good friend and also enjoys afternoon tea with me, as you do. At least that's what he tells me," Katherine said, chuckling softly. "I sometimes wonder if he's just trying to humor an elderly lady, or if he's lonely and enjoys the company."

"You think he may be lonely? What else can you tell me about him?"

Katherine told Miriam of Dan moving to Condor's Nest after retiring from the NYPD over a year ago, how they met by accident at Rocky Bar, and then got to like each other. She choked up a bit as she explained Dan's carrying Tony off the cliffs and driving him to the hospital, and then helping to care for Jon. Then, she spoke about how he's always there when needed and does a host of little things that mean a lot.

"Yes, I heard some of this from Anita," Miriam said. "You said he's retired. Do you know how old he is?"

"I'd guess around sixty. I think he took an early retirement package."

"He looks good for sixty," Miriam replied.

"Well, I haven't given that much thought, but now that you mention it, I guess he does. With the sides of his hair turning gray, he looks rather distinguished."

"You've never mentioned a *Mrs.* Davies. Is he divorced? Or, just never married?"

"Actually, neither. He was married, but his wife—her name was Sarah—died. I don't know exactly when, but it was before he moved here last year from New York."

"Oh, that's sad. Does he talk about her much?"

"No, not very often, but when he does it's with affection."

Katherine then heard a familiar sound—the shuffling of feet and soft footsteps. Tony, who was staying in the first floor guestroom for a week or so, sauntered into the kitchen. "Good morning ladies."

"Good morning, Tony," Miriam and Katherine said in unison.

Tony walked over to Miriam and gave her an affectionate hug. A tear ran down the right side of his face as they silently embraced. "It's good to have you back here, even if the circumstances aren't exactly the best," he whispered in her ear.

The sound of a car approaching caused all of them to turn toward the kitchen windows.

"That should be Anita and Dan," Katherine stated. "We needed some groceries and, last night when he was here for dinner, Dan offered to drive Anita to the store and help carry the bags."

"That was nice of him," Miriam said softly.

"Good morning everyone," Anita said, smiling at them as she carried a bag of groceries into the house. "Dan is behind me with the rest of what we bought." Anita placed the bag of groceries on the kitchen counter, and then went to the back door to open it for Dan, who had six grocery store bags—three in each hand. Then she turned to her brother and said, "It's so good to see you up and about rather than lying in a hospital bed."

"You can't imagine, Sis, how good it feels for *me* to be getting around by myself and not having nurses and doctors all over me, although I do appreciate everything they did."

Miriam prepared the French toast and sausages that everyone enjoyed. After eating, Katherine and Tony, dressed in robes that covered their night clothes, excused themselves to get dressed. Katherine, on her way out of the kitchen, stated very emphatically that this would be the last day she would appear without being properly dressed. Anita picked up the morning newspaper she had purchased at the store and made her way to the verandah.

Alone together in the kitchen, Miriam and Dan looked at each other, neither saying anything. "Well, here we are…just the two of us," Miriam blurted out. "Katherine told me that you and she met last year at Rocky Bar."

"That's right. We both like walking to that spot. Katherine doesn't venture out onto the Bar any more, so we usually sit at the edge and talk. We're usually there in the early morning. In fact, if she hadn't become ill and hospitalized, we probably would have met there this morning."

"How sweet. You know, I like Rocky Bar very much and walked there all the time when I lived here with Jerry. In fact, I think I liked those walks more than he did."

"Well, I could use some exercise after that calorie-loaded meal we just consumed…which, by the way, was superb. Would you like to take a stroll there?"

"Sure, why not? That would be nice."

Miriam and Dan had gone about half-way to Rocky Bar and had been chatting as they walked along the beach. Then Miriam asked, "So, Dan, how do you like the serenity of the eastern Connecticut shoreline after spending most of your life in the Big Apple?"

"If I could sum it up in a couple of words, I'd say peaceful and pleasant, until the past few weeks, that is. It's such a change from the fast pace and daily stress that was basically all I knew in New York for many years. I hope I can return to the life I was enjoying here before all this madness began. That was the good life I was seeking for my senior years. I want it back."

"Yes, I can appreciate that. What made you pick this area so far from New York?"

"Well, I've always liked Long Island Sound. I prefer it to the open ocean because I like to swim and I'm getting too old for body or board surfing. Besides, it's tough to buy a place at the Hamptons or the better places on the North Shore of Long Island on a city cop's retirement pay."

"Did you look anywhere else?"

"Oh, yeah...I spent my last working year investigating and visiting places along the North Shore and this area. I guess what it came down to was wanting to break away from New York, which brought me here instead of over there." Dan pointed toward Orient Point, the last land mass connected to Long Island's north shore, as he spoke. "This place is like a postcard—very picturesque. The clincher was the home I found, nestled at the dead-end of a road near the beach, which I liked the moment I set foot in it."

"This is *such* a special place," Miriam said. "I've missed it so much this past year. I actually thought about selling my house—the one I got in the divorce—and moving back somewhere in the vicinity, maybe even Rhode Island, which is close, yet far away. There's something about the beaches and shoreline in this area that I truly love, and I miss that when I'm not here. And, with Michael going to college in the Boston area...." Miriam's voice drifted off as they reached Rocky Bar and sat on a large rock at the edge of the beach.

Dan looked at her and said, "I can imagine that the past year has been hard on you. Divorce is a messy situation. No one wins, except the lawyers."

Miriam started sobbing and nodded her head. "It's not easy, losing the things that mean so much to you—your marriage, your home, your extended family. Thank goodness I didn't lose Michael, who has been so close to me all his life and who is the most precious person I know."

Dan looked at her again. Miriam's thick brown hair was radiant in the morning sun, streaming in over the eastern horizon. *She's quite attractive and seems to have a mature manner,* he thought to himself. *Not exactly the type of woman a normal guy would cast aside. Jerry must be turbocharged sexually for someone his age. His priorities must have been going in that direction to swap Miriam for Susan.*

She looked at him and said softly, "I understand you've suffered a loss in your life."

Dan wiped a tear from his eye. "Yes...yes...my sweet Sarah—my one and only love. Hard to believe it's been almost three years now since she passed away. That was another reason for retiring here. I wanted to get away from the anxiety I felt in New York. We had lived together there for so long. Here, I can think about her in my own space and in my own way. It's better in this setting."

"That's very touching. I envy you, having had such a long, enduring relationship. I thought I was going to have that with Jerry. What a shock when he came home one night and told me I was being traded in for a younger model. His timing was incredible—just after my fiftieth birthday. I had no idea he was seeing someone else, and still have a hard time coming to grips with being tossed. I had this long-term view of marriage, just as you obviously did, and felt so worthless when the man I had given my life to told me that the 'feelings' were no longer there."

They sat silently, staring out at the water. After a few minutes, Dan stood up, picked up a stone and tossed it into the water. "How's your energy level, Miriam? Can you handle a walk out to the end of the Bar?"

She thought for a moment and then said, "I think so, but I haven't done this for a while, so let's go slowly."

When they reached the far end of Rocky Bar they sat on one of the rocks that formed a natural ledge, their legs dangling over the side of the large rock.

"Do you ever swim off these rocks?" she asked him.

"Sure, quite a bit. The water is beautiful out here."

"I used to swim out here, also."

"Well, then, we'll just have to come here again with our bathing suits."

"I'd like that," she said, smiling at him. "This brings back fond memories."

They sat and gazed out at the water and the tip of Long Island's north shore to their right and Plum Island to their left. The water glistened in the morning sunlight. Miriam leaned toward Dan and gently let her head fall onto his shoulder. He flinched ever so slightly, but didn't move. *She seems to be at ease out here,* he thought. She then lifted her head, looked at him and said, "Thank you for walking with me to this place that I love. This has been fun!"

"You're very welcome. Let's do it again."

After walking back along the Bar and reaching the edge of the beach, Miriam had to sit and catch her breath for a moment.

"What have you been doing since leaving Hunter's Point?" Dan asked her.

"Mostly developing a new group of friends in Fairfield County to try and get my life back together and, I guess, start a new one. I'm not a career person and there's enough money so I don't have to work. If nothing else, Jerry has provided for me financially, so my main challenge has been the emotional aspect of this divorce and separation from Jerry's family. I'm an only child and my parents are both gone, so my family life was here. I've been volunteering three days a week for a non-profit agency in Stamford that has a satellite office in New London. I offered them two days a week while I'm here, which they gladly accepted. I cut back a day each week, since I have a son to look after now, at least until the end of the summer. What about you? Any post-retirement activities?"

Dan talked about starting to play tennis again, which he had enjoyed in his younger days, and taking up bowling in the winter months. When Miriam said that she had played tennis competitively as a teen-ager, Dan suggested they play together sometime on the courts at his beach. As he thought about his new lifestyle as a retired person, he then said, "The last thing of any significance, I suppose, is that I joined a church—which was not part of my former existence in New York."

"Really? What caused you to want to do that?"

"Oh, probably a delayed reaction to losing Sarah, when I had time to sit back and reflect on things. She attended a church occasionally in New York and tried to get me to join her, but I just never got into it. Too many Sunday morning sleep-ins after Saturday night incidents, I suppose."

"That's interesting. I went in the opposite direction. When I lived here, I went to the big white church in Old Lyme, but after leaving I guess I got so bitter that I lost my faith, or at least the part of it that kept me going to church. Maybe that was a mistake."

"You said you used to attend the big white church in Old Lyme?"

"Yes, at least once every three weeks. Usually twice a month."

"Well, that's the church I joined."

"Really? Maybe I should go back there. I could probably use a spiritual revival."

"I'm going tomorrow morning if you'd like to join me. The service is at nine o'clock."

"Yes, I remember. Oh, goodness, what will I say to all the people I know there who felt so badly for me when I left last year?"

"There's one way to find out. Come on, let's walk back to Katherine's house. I'm going to our beach and work on my tan today...should be a good day for it. You can call me later and let me know about church."

"I can tell you now, Dan. I'd like to go."

"Good. I'll pick you up at eight-thirty."

As Dan drove away from the main house, he thought, *this is quite a lady. I can't figure out why Jerry would just up and leave her, regardless of how beautiful Susan is.*

Dan dropped Miriam off in front of her cottage after they had attended Sunday church service together. "Thank you, Dan," she said. "Thank you for the walk and conversation yesterday and for taking me to church this morning."

"You're very welcome. I enjoyed the company and I think quite a few people were happy to see you again today."

"Hope to see you soon," she said, smiling at him as she got out of the car.

"I think you will. Katherine invited me to the barbecue this afternoon, so I'll see you later."

"Fantastic! I enjoy being with you. You make me feel comfortable about being back here." She closed the car door and walked quickly toward the cottage.

Dan sighed as he put the car in gear and started the drive out of Hunter's Point. *I know I'm repeating myself, but she seems nice...very nice,* he said to himself.

Both main houses at Hunter's Point had large fieldstone patios looking over the waters of Long Island Sound. The Hunters and Kents, minus Jerry and Susan, along with Dan, Nicole and Amy, were gathered on the patio of Katherine's home for a late Sunday afternoon barbecue.

Tony felt so much better that he offered to grill the main course—

steak and striper filets—for the group. Katherine smiled, for one of the few times in what seemed to her a long while, as she surveyed the people. Jon and Michael were near her, with their girlfriends close by. Family-style hugs and kisses were being shared generously. Dan was chatting with Anita and Miriam. In the midst of this chatter, Dan cast a glance over at Katherine, noticing the peaceful look on her face. He sensed tranquility in the air, which he had not felt for the past few weeks.

Michael left Jon and the girls and sauntered over to his mother, who had moved away from Dan and Anita toward a table where liquid refreshments had been set up. "Hey, Mom," he said tenderly. "You and Dan seem to have hit it off nicely. Anything you want to tell me about?"

"Oh, don't be silly, Son. We've just gotten to know each other, took a walk out on Rocky Bar yesterday, and went to church together this morning."

"Well, that's a good start. He's well liked and respected around here, which I guess you know by now."

"Indeed I do. Katherine and Anita—and Tony, for that matter—can't seem to say enough about him."

Just then, Jon and Nicole came over. "Aunt Miriam, this is Nicole, the prettiest girl at the beach."

Nicole blushed and extended her right hand to Miriam. "Oh, he's so embarrassing—but in a sweet way. It's nice to meet you, and welcome back."

"Thank you. It's nice to be here again."

"I know Michael is happy, having his 'real' mother here," Jon said, smiling at her.

"We both are," Miriam replied…sighing and smiling.

Katherine then cleared her voice and, tapping a bottle of wine with a spoon to get everyone's attention and raising a glass of wine, said, "Here's a toast to the Hunters and the Kents…and to Hunter's Point. May we all enjoy this place and each other for a long time to come."

After dusk, Dan and Miriam took a walk along the beach. The boys and their girlfriends had left for a night out. Katherine, Anita and Tony were cleaning up after an enjoyable dinner. As they walked silently near the water's edge, Miriam felt her left hand touching Dan's right hand. Then, upon instinct, their hands became clasped together as they approached the beach edge of Rocky Bar. They stopped and looked at each other. Miriam, arched her feet and was now standing on her tiptoes. She arched her neck and moved her lips toward those of the man who was close to her. She put her arms around his waist as his arms found their way to her shoulders and down her back. They embraced as they gently kissed each other, holding each other tightly for about a minute.

"Oh, my goodness," Miriam blurted out. "I just couldn't stop myself, Dan."

"It's alright," he whispered in her ear. "I guess I felt it coming."

The next kiss was more passionate and the embrace stronger…and longer.

Chapter 18

The following evening, Jon and Michael were sitting on the deck of Tony's cottage, sipping sodas and watching the sun descend in the western sky. Jon had calmed down after his father and grandmother returned home and appeared to be recovering fully from what had happened to them. He had also spent some more time with Dan and had come to respect him. "Can you believe it, Michael? It's August! We'll be off to college in less than a month...well, I'll be off and you'll be returning. My dad tells me that the older you get, the faster the summer goes by. Maybe he's right, because this one has gone by really fast."

"Yeah, it does go by quickly," Michael shot back. "Seems like we just got here for the summer. While it's gone fast and it certainly has been crazy, I'm glad we've had a chance to get close. This is a small family and you're the only cousin I've got."

"Likewise," Jon replied. "I look at you as more of a brother—the one neither of us had—than a cousin. There's a bond here that I feel. I thought that the 'incident' might drive us apart, but instead it's made us closer. I really appreciate your concern for Dad and me, and for not siding with your father and blaming mine for what happened."

"As I've told you, what Uncle Tony did may not have been right, but I feel that Susan had something to do with it—like luring him to her. And, my dad...Jesus, nothing can justify what he did. I've basically disowned him. Screw him! I don't need him. With Mom here, I'm happier than I've been in quite a while."

They stared out at the water, which was starting to be illuminated by a rising full moon. Jon went into the cottage and returned with some munchies, feeling really relaxed and content for the first time since that fateful Friday night.

The following afternoon, Tony was sitting on the verandah at the main house with his mother and Miriam, sipping iced tea as the sun shone over the water. "Tomorrow I go back to work," he exclaimed gleefully.

"You look so much better," Miriam said, smiling first at him and then at Katherine.

"And, I feel so much better…almost back to normal. I should be able to handle a short work week."

"All of which makes me very happy," Katherine chimed in.

Miriam stared intently at Tony and Katherine and then spoke. "You two have suffered terribly. Did either of you have any indication, or any feelings, that something like this was going to happen to you?"

Katherine and Tony looked inquisitively at each other and then at Miriam. Katherine cleared her throat. "Well, Miriam, I had not been feeling well at all for a few months—I'd say starting in the late winter or early spring. I was tired a lot, didn't have all my strength—not that there's much left in this old body—and I would get these bouts of nausea from time to time."

"Did you ever go to see a doctor?"

Tony chuckled, as he cast a wry smile at Miriam, and then snipped, "Mom doesn't have much use for doctors."

"I guess that's going to change," Katherine responded. "I'm on quite a schedule now with visitations and monitoring of my condition."

"Isn't that a good thing?" Miriam asked.

"I suppose so," the elderly lady responded, "but I preferred my former existence when I consumed food and beverages that had not been poisoned, didn't need any medical care, and enjoyed myself right here—my favorite spot in the whole world. I was feeling fine until Susan arrived with that herbal tea. Oh, my, I still can't believe she could have done this to me…and Anita…and, possibly, Dan. In spite of what she did to upset your life, Miriam, she was very nice to me. Even though I missed you and the times we had together, I must admit that I enjoyed being with her. Maybe I just reconciled myself to accept what was inevitable."

"Maybe it was all an act—or a plot on her part."

"Perhaps so. I just don't know. That's one theory being proposed." Katherine had a blank expression on her face, perplexed by the circumstances and still not having any sensible answers as to why the incidents occurred.

"That's crossed my mind a few times," Tony added, "especially with this affair we had and something she said during one of our encounters. Susan knows how to 'come on' to you and get you interested in her. With me, she used her physical beauty, and it was obviously effective." He looked away from the two women, still very embarrassed by the affair. Then, looking back at them, he said, "Jerry made some threats, which Jon and Dan witnessed, but I never thought he would attack me the way he apparently did."

"Are you sure it was Jerry?" Miriam queried. "He still is the only man I've been married to and, in spite of what happened, I do have some feelings for him."

"Well, it was dark, I'll admit. But the man was Jerry's size and had brown hair like Jerry and the same eyes and forehead. That much I was able to notice and remember. And, then those words he shouted at me…'I told you to keep your hands off her'. Who else could have said that? The only others who knew about the affair were Jon and Dan… and, oh yes, my sister, but she certainly didn't do it, and I can't imagine Dan or my son doing this."

"Hmmm," Miriam murmured. "As much as I detest Jerry for what he did to me, I have a hard time believing he would attack you like that. But who knows? Maybe for Susan he would resort to just about anything to keep her affection. Perhaps they *were* conspiring against you."

"Oh, goodness, this is so distressing!" Katherine said with a sigh. "All I've wanted is to live out my remaining years peacefully at this place I love so much. Now, our lives have become a nightmare. Those trials starting in early September will be another ordeal."

Miriam came over to Katherine, kneeled down and put her hands on the matriarch's knees. "Well, we can't undo what's been done, but whatever I can do around here to help out, please let me know." Then standing up and turning to Tony, she said, "And that goes for you too, Tony." Looking back at Katherine, Miriam said, "I'm a pretty good cook, so why don't we have a few family dinners before the boys go back to school? I've got some dishes that you should like."

"I know what a good cook you are and that's a wonderful idea," Katherine said, forcing a smile.

Early Friday evening, after Tony had returned from working the past three days, he and Jon were eating pizza and salad at Teddy's, a popular place on the shore road. "Hey, Dad, do you realize this is the first time we've been together to eat outside of Hunter's Point since we were in Newport at the beginning of the summer?"

"You're right, Jon. I hadn't really thought about it, with all that's been going on. It's good to be back at work and to be able to get out with you again. I've missed this. I can't apologize enough to you or say how sorry I am about having the affair with Susan. I mean it, Son. I'm the one who's supposed to be an example for you, and I failed miserably."

"Dad, I know you made a mistake, but I've gotten over it. And I think you may have been seduced. Michael and I have talked about it, and he thinks that Susan probably coaxed you into this affair. In fact, he's really pissed about what Uncle Jerry did and doesn't want to have much to do with him right now. He feels for you and me. That we're the real victims…especially you."

"That's kind of surprising, but it feels good to know that maybe I wasn't totally at fault and the cause of all the trouble this family's been through."

"Dad, have you forgotten? You were almost killed by a vicious attack. Michael said, and I agree, that nothing justifies that sort of reaction, which is why he doesn't want to have anything to do with his dad for a while."

"That's an interesting way for him to view this situation which, frankly, I hadn't given much thought to. So, Michael has turned against Jerry on this?"

"Yeah, for sure, assuming Uncle Jerry was your attacker. That makes two of us, since I'd like to rip him apart for what he did."

"I see how you feel. It's just intriguing to hear that Michael feels this way about his own father."

"Yeah, I guess it is."

"Did he know anything about what was going on between Susan and me before it all came out?"

Jon answered by saying that Michael was there with him when he hid behind the bushes near their cottage and observed the first encounter with Uncle Jerry.

Tony sighed and sank down into the chair he was sitting in across the table from Jon. "Hey, not to change the subject, but I've got some news that I hope you'll like."

"What's that?" Jon asked.

"We're going to be having some family dinners, with Miriam cooking, before you and Michael go back to school."

"Now, that's something I do look forward to. Michael and I have gotten close this summer and enjoy being with each other, with and without the girls. And Aunt Miriam can really cook. No offense, Dad, you're good on the barbecue, but she can really prepare some dishes—especially seafood and pasta. I've always liked Aunt Miriam, much more than Susan. She's easy to talk to. This summer has been a real bitch, Dad, but maybe we can salvage the rest of it."

"I think we can, Son."

After seeing each other twice during the ensuing week and following through on their "talk" about taking a swim off the far end of Rocky Bar, Dan and Miriam were having dinner at Cristo's, a seafood restaurant on the water in nearby Niantic, on Saturday evening. Dan had been on the beach at Condor's Nest for a good part of the warm and sunny day. Miriam had spent the late afternoon chatting with Katherine and Anita on the verandah of the main house and was rehashing some of what the women had talked about. Dan noticed her blush slightly as she told him how Anita, after complementing her for cooking a delicious family meal last night, teased her about how she and the man sitting across the dinner table seemed to have taken to each other. She seemed to blush a bit more when she said that Katherine called herself cupid for getting the two of them together.

Dan smiled at Miriam and said, "Seems like they've got it in for us."

"Maybe they do," Miriam said with a sigh. "Oh, well, I think that's enough of what we ladies spoke about today." Looking onto his eyes, she then said, "Dan, I can't believe it's been three weeks—three *enjoyable* weeks I must say—since I dropped my bags at the cottage at Hunter's Point. Katherine's right when she says that the summers go by too fast here."

"I suppose that's true," he replied. "This one's only my second, but it has gone by fast so far. Maybe that's because I spent so much time at the hospital just as this summer was getting started."

The dinner at Cristo's was superb. After an appetizer of steamers that they shared, Miriam ordered striper and Dan salmon. Both dishes were broiled. Miriam raised her wine glass and, taking a sip, said, "Dan, you've brought back something to me that I was wondering if I'd ever experience again: the touch and feel of a nice man."

Nodding, he said in return, "You've done the same for me. I never dreamed of getting close to another woman after losing Sarah. And, I don't feel as though it's wrong. Rather, everything that's happened has been natural. She's still out there in my mind and in my heart, but I know she's gone and I can't have her physically with me anymore."

"I know…and I'm comfortable with you wanting to never let go of her emotionally. I just hope that I'm the one you want to be with physically."

"You are…and I want to have you…that is, I'd like for us to have each other in a special sort of way," Dan said.

"I want that, too."

"I'm glad. How about spending the night at my place?"

Dan lay naked beside Miriam in his bed. He was feeling a bit strange, experiencing emotions that had never before existed for him. Miriam had started to slumber after their lovemaking, feeling the effect of the wine she had consumed, at the restaurant and again at his place. He was still awake, however, and thinking. *I hope you can understand, Sarah,* he said silently, turning on his side and away from his companion for the night. *Until the other day, I never gave any thought to making love with another woman. But this one is different. I hope you can accept my having a relationship. Maybe the tough old cop is human after all and needs someone. She won't ever replace you. No one could ever do that. Let's just say that perhaps we can each fill in a void in each other's life…at least for a while.*

Chapter 19

Labor Day weekend has always been a special time at the shore for many of the seasonal inhabitants, signaling the end of summer and a last blast before returning to the real world. It was Sunday, the middle day of this holiday weekend, and Dan was reflecting on Katherine's comment of a few days ago about this last of the big summer weekends as he sipped a cup of morning coffee in his kitchen.

Nearly a week ago, on Monday of the previous week, the boys had left for their respective colleges—Michael just outside of Boston and Jon in southern New Hampshire. Tony had driven Jon to his new school. Michael, entering his third year and with a car on campus for the first time, had driven himself.

The Hunters and Kents had a tradition of a Sunday afternoon family barbecue that Tony had been in charge of for years. While the group was altered and the circumstances were still a bit bizarre—with Miriam living in one of the cottages and Jerry and Susan in police custody awaiting trials that would begin this coming week—Katherine wanted to have the Labor Day weekend event. Her logic was that she could not do anything about the boys getting older and going off to college. The only missing long-time family member was Jerry. Miriam had been there at last year's gathering, just before the break-up of the marriage. With Miriam and Dan now apparently starting a relationship, there was almost a new person in the family—one that Katherine was very fond of.

Katherine turned her head toward the driveway as she heard the sound of an approaching car. She was just getting ready to walk over to Tony's cottage for the barbecue. She smiled as Dan walked in carrying a small package.

"I picked this up yesterday at the natural food store. You said you were running low on the herbal tea you like so much and I was in the area, so I picked up a package. I actually bought two, so I have another that I can bring over here when this one is gone. I made a cup at home at lunchtime and can assure you that these packages are not tainted."

"Thank you, Dan. You're so considerate to remember the things that mean a lot to me. I'm relieved that your tests turned up only a small trace of poison and you're not in any danger. After all that's happened, I was thinking of switching to another brand, but I really do like the flavor of this one." Taking the package, she said, "My, isn't this interesting? They seem to have added a logo on the front of the packaging. It's quite attractive."

"What do you mean?" Dan asked.

"The yellow sunflower with the green border in the upper corner. That's the logo for the brand name, *Sunflower Green Tea*. It's on the tea bags and now I guess they've put it on the outside wrapper."

"So, that's a new wrapper on the package?"

"I guess so...never noticed it before. Maybe it was there and I just didn't see it, although I usually notice things like that. Oh well, let me put it in the cupboard. Are you going to walk me over to Tony's?"

"That was my thought. I figured you might like an escort."

"Tony, that was delicious," Dan exclaimed as he walked over to Tony who was sitting on a lounge chair on the deck of his cottage.

"Well, thank you, Dan. And, I must say it's a pleasure to have you here with us. It's a smaller group with the boys not here, and we love having you."

Dan, happy to be with his friends at Hunter's Point instead of spending the day alone, said, "Thanks. I appreciate your saying that. So, how are you feeling and how's the injury?"

"I'm feeling good for the most part. The periodic headaches that I had have mostly gone away. I only get them one or two times a week. Look how I can move my shoulder...not bad, huh!" Tony said emphatically as he rotated his right shoulder blade. "And, here, take a look at my head."

"It is healing nicely. From a blow that seems to have hit you square on the left temple and caused such a nasty contusion, I'd say it's almost unnoticeable."

"Yeah, the doctors did a great job fixing me up. I'm very grateful."

Dan scratched his chin and nodded, reflecting on a few other experiences he had witnessed where attacks such as the one Tony endured resulted in more tragic outcomes. He began to think about the coming trials, something he had not done much of since Jerry's arraignment, and how Jerry's trial would, at some point, focus on the actual attack—where and how it took place. He figured that the prosecutor would go through some type of re-enactment. "Let me ask you a question, if I may," he said. "When you were returning to the main house that night you were attacked, do you remember if you were walking slow or fast?"

"Hmmm, let me think. I'd say I was probably walking slowly. I was feeling down in the dumps with a lot on my mind, and you don't walk very fast in that condition."

"That was my thought," Dan said.

"Why do you ask?"

"Oh, no special reason. It would give the attacker plenty of time to observe your movements and carefully plan when to come out of hiding to hit you...more so than if you were moving faster. It also helps to deliver a more accurate blow. I'm just rambling here—the old detective coming out, I guess. Would you mind if we walked over to Katherine's house and re-enacted the incident as you remember it? The ladies are cleaning up the remnants of that great dinner you cooked and I could use some exercise before biting into one of Katherine's scrumptious pies."

They walked to the edge of the property—about two hundred feet from the main house. Tony motioned to a large rock at the edge of the property and said, "I sat here for a few moments, pondering all that had been going on between Susan and me, the impact on Jon, Jerry's reaction and how it would probably affect Mom if she found out. Then, I got up and started walking...slowly...yes, definitely slowly...back to the house where I was going to spend the night, since I was helping to take care of Anita after she had come home from the hospital. I guess I was looking at the ground, which is normal when you're depressed or concerned about something. About three-quarters of the way back, there was a rustling sound in the bushes next to the house where Jerry must have been hiding. The bushes were now almost directly to my left and I had just looked up when I saw what I think was his face and an object—I guess the fireplace shovel—coming at me from this direction." Tony, now standing at the spot where he was struck, pointed toward the edge of the bushes on their left.

Dan walked over to the bushes and then back toward Tony. He raised his right hand high above his head and made a downward motion toward him, as Tony nodded. He then looked over the embankment to verify the location of the spot from where he had lifted Tony. "Okay, now I have a good image in my mind of what happened," Dan said. "Let's get back to your place for dessert."

After returning, Dan sat next to Miriam on a love seat on Tony's deck as they both consumed an apple-raspberry pie, one of Katherine's finest.

"Well, this has been a nice day," Katherine exclaimed, taking a final sip from her tea cup. "Anita, are you ready to go home? The sun is starting to set and it will be getting chilly in a little while."

"I'm ready, Mother. Let's go. Good night, all."

"I left one of my best pipes at your place, Mom," Tony said, getting up to return his plate to the kitchen. "I'll walk you and Anita back and then I'm going to visit a friend at Crystal Sands Beach."

Dan and Miriam got up and walked back to the cottage where Miriam was living. They sat on the deck of the cottage and watched the sun fall below the horizon. As the sky began to darken, a chill started to fill the air. "I think we may need a sweater or sweatshirt if you want to sit out here any longer and then take that walk to Rocky Bar," Dan said to her. "And I forgot to bring one."

"Well, then, let's take a look in Michael's room to see if he left one here. I can't imagine he would have taken all his warm clothing, since he always comes here once or twice in the fall. His room is the one upstairs facing the water. Take a look in the dresser and the closet. There should be something there." Smiling at him, she then said softly, "I'll keep you warm after we get back."

Dan went up to Michael's room. Except for a couple of tee shirts with the logo of the marina where Michael had worked during the summer, the dresser had been cleaned out. He opened the closet door. It was empty. Returning to the deck, he shook his head. "Nothing there."

"Alright, then, let's go to the big house. It's locked, but Michael gave me the key before he took off last week. Maybe he left some clothes there."

Miriam went to her bedroom and came back with the key to the house that she had called home for many years and a cotton sweater, which she put on. They walked hand-in-hand from the cottage to the house. She put the key in the latch on the front door and opened it. Turning to Dan, Miriam said, "You go in by yourself. I feel uncomfortable going in there. Michael's bedroom is to the right at the top of the stairs."

Dan ascended the stairs and went into Michael's bedroom. He looked in the dresser. There was a pair of shorts and a couple of old tee shirts, but no sweater or sweatshirt. Then he opened the closet door. He was in luck, as there were two fleece sweatshirts on the shelf above the hanging racks—one dark blue and the other gray. He chose the dark blue one, which was larger. As he pulled it over his shoulders and was straightening up, his eyes caught something in the far left corner of the closet. Without a light in the closet, it was hard to see exactly what was there, but it was some type of metal device, roughly a foot and a half long and a foot wide, with what looked like a black handle or lever connected to it. A roll of something lay next to it that appeared to be clear in color and about the length and width of a roll of aluminum foil or Saran wrap. It definitely wasn't aluminum foil based on its clear color, and it looked a bit shinier than Saran wrap. He shook his head as he closed the closet door.

Dan pulled the sweatshirt down, fixed the collar on his pullover shirt and walked back to the front porch where Miriam was waiting for him. "Voila," he said. "Now we can face the great outdoors. You know, I think this is the first night since about the middle of June when I've had a sweater or jacket on. Maybe that's why I hadn't thought of it when I came over here this afternoon. Out of sight…out of mind."

As they walked silently along the beach, Dan's thoughts reverted to their first night together at his home and the words he had spoken silently to "Sarah" before falling asleep. When they reached the end of Rocky Bar, darkness had descended and they were alone. They held and kissed each other tenderly. After sitting and watching the stars for another fifteen minutes or so, they returned to Miriam's place, where they watched a TV movie and spent the night together.

Chapter 20

The bailiff gave the traditional command at the opening of a court proceeding. "All rise!"

Susan Hunter trembled as she rose from her seat in the front of the courtroom. Her attorney, Thad Wilcox, who was sitting next to her and shuffling his papers, rose slowly as Judge Julian Frisk entered the courtroom. It was Monday morning, exactly one week after Labor Day. Wednesday and Thursday of the previous week had been consumed with jury selection. Dressed conservatively and with hardly any make-up, trying to appear as humble as she could, Susan looked at the twelve people who now held her fate in their hands. She could not stop shaking and grabbed Wilcox's left arm to maintain her stability as she stood up. For a moment, she thought she was going to faint, but regained her composure as the judge made his opening remarks. Then Judge Frisk looked at Joel Stein, the district attorney, and directed him to begin his case.

The balding, slightly built, middle-aged man who had spent most of his career as a state prosecutor, walked to the edge of the jury box, gently touched the railing and then backed off a bit as he began to speak. "Ladies and gentlemen of the jury, what we have here is an open and shut case of attempted murder against Katherine Hunter-Kent and Anita Kent, mother and daughter. The state alleges that these two women were poisoned by the defendant, who is related to the victims by marriage and was living in a family compound in a home adjacent to one occupied by the victims when the crimes occurred. Susan Hunter contaminated herbal tea bags with methanol by injecting paint thinner into the tea bags using a syringe that we believe she procured at the medical clinic where she worked. She did this with the knowledge that the Kents would drink this tea on a regular basis. Mrs. Kent, who I may refer to as Katherine on occasion, to distinguish her from her daughter

Anita, had asked Susan Hunter to buy the tea for her at a natural food store near where Mrs. Hunter worked, as it was convenient for Mrs. Hunter to do so. We will present testimony related to the discovery of paint thinner in a tool shed near the Hunter home. State police lab tests have matched this paint thinner to the methanol discovered in the Kents' blood streams. Fingerprints on the syringe match Mrs. Hunter's. Further, we will present testimony related to finding a package of contaminated tea in the kitchen cupboard of the Hunter home. We also have as a witness the store owner who can identify Susan Hunter as purchasing the brand of tea that was subsequently poisoned."

The D.A. paused for a moment before continuing. "Now, regarding motive....we believe there has been an attempt on the part of Susan Hunter to eliminate two members of the Kent family—Katherine and Anita, who are the victims in this case. We suspect that Susan Hunter has a desire to gain effective control of the property, known as Hunter's Point, where she has lived since her marriage to Jerald Hunter, who may be mentioned in this trial by his nickname, Jerry. What we do *not* know with certainty is whether Mrs. Hunter acted alone or was collaborating with her husband, but Susan Hunter's guilt is not affected by this distinction. What we *do* know is that with the two aforementioned relatives gone, along with another who came close to death in a separate incident, Jerald Hunter would be the only living legal heir to the Hunter's Point property, triggering a provision in the property's deed that would transfer a fifty percent Kent ownership to him. This would leave Jonathan Kent, the eighteen year-old son of Anthony (the other relative who came close to dying) homeless and indigent, since he is a minor with no property inheritance rights at this time. With all the Kents of legal age gone, we contend that Susan Hunter could gain effective control of the entire property through her marriage to Mr. Hunter. As a note, Jerald Hunter divorced his first wife last year to marry Susan Hunter. The divorce decree stipulated that Miriam Hunter, his first wife, had to give up any and all rights to the property and, further, was banned from even stepping foot on it for the rest of her natural life. This set of circumstances could be worth millions to the Hunters, given the value of the property. People have maimed and killed others for much less money than could potentially be involved here."

Joel Stein made a few more administrative type remarks about the state's case and then returned to his seat.

The judge looked down from his bench at Thad Wilcox. "Does the attorney for the defense wish to make an opening statement?"

"Yes, Your Honor, I do." The young defense attorney strode over to the jury box and, trying to appear confident, began his opening remarks. "You have heard a baseless accusation against my client for crimes that she has not committed. The prosecution's evidence is mostly circumstantial and Mrs. Hunter can not be directly connected to these criminal acts. She has been undergoing a significant amount of criticism since marrying Jerry Hunter and moving onto the family's property, mainly due to a divorce between Mr. Hunter and his first wife, which the district attorney alluded to in his opening remarks. This marriage has caused friction among members of the Hunter and Kent families. We believe this emotional state of affairs has created a prejudicial atmosphere that is influencing the charges and prosecution of my client." Stammering a bit, he then stated, "And, furthermore, Mrs. Hunter had no plausible motive for poisoning the Kents. We categorically reject the state's conspiracy theory. Jerry Hunter is what most people would call well off and not in need of money. Thus, even though the value of the Hunter's Point property is significant, it is not enough to cause Jerry and Susan Hunter to risk their futures, particularly the prospect of spending many years incarcerated. Susan Hunter liked these two ladies and enjoyed spending time with them, along with enjoying her life in general at Hunter's Point, where the extended family resides. To reiterate my earlier point, she had nothing to gain personally by making them sick or attempting to kill them."

Wilcox was struggling for some more concrete commentary to refute the prosecution's opening remarks, but he really did not have any. He concluded by saying, "We will demonstrate that Mrs. Hunter is not the perpetrator here, but is the victim of being falsely accused." He had no clue as to how he was going to be able to prove this, since he had come up with nothing during the preceding weeks to back up this statement. Nevertheless, he felt he had to make the statement and hope that in the next few days he could find something that would exonerate his client.

Dan Davies was seated in the middle of the courtroom, almost filled with spectators due to the local publicity the Hunter trials had received during the past week. Susan noticed him. She stared at him, and Dan saw a look of bewilderment and desperation on her face. *This is one very frightened lady,* he thought.

"The prosecution calls Katherine Hunter-Kent as its first witness." Dan's eyes moved back to the prosecution's side of the courtroom as Joel Stein spoke forcefully to begin his formal trial proceedings. Based on his experience in several trials of this nature, Dan knew that that the district attorney's goal was to get the jury sympathetic toward the state's case by seeing how an elderly lady had been poisoned, suffered, and almost perished by consuming contaminated green tea as part of her daily intake of liquids; and then begin a process of connecting Susan Hunter to the poisoned tea.

Standing in front of her, the bailiff asked Katherine to raise her right hand and then said in a monotone, "Mrs. Kent, do you solemnly swear to tell the truth, the whole truth and nothing but the truth, so help you God?"

"I do," the elderly lady, dressed in a dark blue dress, stated softly.

After going through a standard procedure of getting her to state her full name, age and address, the district attorney smiled at Katherine and said, "Mrs. Kent, while this may be a bit difficult for you, would you please tell the jury how you've been feeling for the past few past few months and then, as best you can, recount the events of that Friday night in the fourth week of June of this year when you became very ill and were taken to Shorehaven Hospital?"

Dan leaned back, crossed his legs, and folded his hands on his lap. He gazed at his friend, who was clearing her throat and preparing to speak from the witness stand. *I hope this is not too stressful for her,* he thought.

Katherine began testifying, with words similar to those she had used with Dan on a Saturday morning in early June at Rocky Bar when she had described her constant fatigue, nausea and occasional cramps in her legs. She talked about getting into bed that fateful Friday night and starting to feel very sick and vomiting before everything went blank. She then spoke about waking up in the hospital several days later and about the treatment she had received there, and concluded with her recuperation activities over the past several weeks, ending this portion of the testimony by saying what an ordeal it had been and that she had just recently started to feel better. The courtroom was silent and attentive as she talked for about ten minutes.

Joel Stein returned to be near the witness stand after sitting down in his chair and gazing back and forth at the jury and then at his witness during Katherine's opening testimony. "Katherine, would you state for the record the brand of herbal tea that Susan Hunter had been purchasing for you and bringing to your house."

"Yes. The brand is called *Sunflower Green Tea*."

"And is this tea bag similar to the ones that Susan Hunter brought to you on a regular basis?" The D.A. was holding a clear, small plastic bag that contained a tea bag taken from the package at Katherine's house and tested by the authorities for methanol. He held the clear plastic bag which contained the green tea bag toward Katherine so that the side of the tea bag with the logo was in front of her.

"Yes, it's a *Sunflower Green Tea* bag. You can tell by the sunflower logo—a yellow flower with a green border."

"Thank you, Mrs. Kent. Your Honor, the prosecution presents this tea bag, taken from Mrs. Kent's home and tested positively for containing methanol, as Exhibit 1. We have several more bags—approximately twenty—from the same package that have also been tested and contain methanol. These are in the custody of the state police."

"So noted, Counselor," the judge replied.

"Now, Mrs. Kent, can you tell us for about how long Susan Hunter had been delivering this brand of tea?"

"Objection...calls for speculation," Thad Wilcox interjected, rising out of his seat.

Stein was quick to react. "Your honor, we're merely trying to establish the fact that Susan Hunter had been delivering this brand of herbal tea for a sustained period of time, which is a basis for the charges brought against her."

"The objection is overruled," the judge intervened. "The witness may answer."

Dan continued to gaze at Katherine, who was now looking at the district attorney for direction. The D.A. nodded at her, indicating that it was all right for her to respond to the question. She spoke slowly and clearly. "Well, it has certainly been since early this year. Yes, I believe that's right. I remember that Susan brought some during the Christmas holidays for me to try when the family was all together, shortly after she had married Jerry and moved into Hunter's Point. Yes, that's right. Even the boys were home from school, since one of the get-togethers was to welcome them home for the holidays. We were all together between Christmas and New Year's Day at least once and more likely a couple of times. I commented on how much I liked the tea and Susan said she'd be happy to buy it for me and bring it to my house." Dan then caught a glance that Katherine cast at Susan as she uttered the last sentence. Susan shuddered and turned her head toward the jury. Dan knew, again from his experience, that Susan wanted to assess the jury's reaction to Katherine's comments and did not want to look her in the eye.

"How often did Susan Hunter bring a package of this *Sunflower Green Tea* to you, Katherine?"

"Oh, let's see. I drink one or two cups of herbal every day and Anita usually has one, so that would be two to three tea bags a day, or fifteen to twenty a week. There are, I believe, eighty tea bags in a package, so that would make…oh, now, I remember, Susan would usually bring a package every four weeks or so. Yes, that's right. Usually she would bring a package about once a month. It became sort of a routine. I remember one time in the spring when we had run out and she had not brought a package. I think she forgot to go to the store where she purchased the tea that month. I made a comment about it, and she said she felt bad. She even offered to drive there and get one, but I told her that would be silly and that I could survive for a few days on regular tea. After that episode, I think she kept an extra package just in case I ran out again. That's why the police found one in her kitchen. I'm sorry, Mr. Stein. I hope I'm not rambling here."

"You're doing just fine, Mrs. Kent, and you can just keep talking as much as you want and however you want," Stein interjected.

"Move to strike…no question pending!" Thad Wilcox thundered, leaping out of his seat.

"Sustained. The jury will disregard the last statement made by the district attorney. Watch yourself, Mr. Stein. I won't allow that type of remark in my courtroom."

"My apology, Your Honor; it won't happen again."

"It better not," the judge admonished the D.A.

Dan uncrossed his legs and leaned forward slightly as the district attorney walked over to the jury box, turned back to Katherine in the witness stand and asked, "Is it safe to say, then, Mrs. Kent, if the tea bags that you and your daughter Anita were brewing into herbal tea were poisoned—similar to those just entered into evidence—then the two of you had been consuming methanol for almost six months before you became so seriously ill, which would be consistent with the medical testing that indicates a sustained intake of small methanol dosages into your system?"

"Objection…calls for speculation," Thad Wilcox interjected again.

"Your honor, we're merely trying to establish the probability, which medical tests have corroborated, that the Kents—Katherine and Anita—appear to have consumed poisoned herbal tea for several months before becoming ill."

"I'll sustain the objection," the judge replied. "Rephrase your question, Counselor."

Stein gathered his thoughts for a moment and then spoke again. "Have you and your daughter, Anita, been consuming this *Sunflower Green Tea* brand since Susan Hunter began bringing it to you?"

"Yes…so if we started in January, then that would be about six months," Katherine said. "It's funny; you'd never know that the tea had been contaminated. I drank this tea almost every day and it tasted just fine."

"Finally, Mrs. Kent, when did you start feeling ill?"

"About three months before I became seriously ill that Friday night in June."

"Thank you. Your Honor, we have no more questions at this time for Mrs. Kent."

"Mr. Wilcox, do you have any questions for this witness?"

"Yes, Your Honor, I do. Mrs. Kent, do you have any reason…let me say this another way…was there any type of dispute between you and Susan Hunter, or any bad blood or festering arguments or feuds, that would make you believe that the defendant would have any motive for injuring or killing you or your daughter?"

Dan leaned forward a bit more as Katherine said, "No, sir, I can't say that I know of any. That's what is so strange about this situation. I can only speak for myself. My daughter can speak for herself if she is called to testify."

"She will be, you can be assured of that. But, if I understood you correctly, you've stated that you know of no reason as to why Susan Hunter might want to harm you."

Dan's eyes quickly moved toward the prosecutor, anticipating a reaction. But then remembering that an attorney is allowed to lead a witness on cross-examination, he leaned back and awaited Katherine's response.

"That's correct."

"Let me ask you this question," Wilcox then said, trying to strengthen his cross-examination. "Did Susan Hunter ever act nervous or strange in any way when she personally delivered the herbal tea or when she was with you?"

"Not that I can recall. She would often join me for afternoon tea on her days off from work, even though she didn't drink tea."

"I see...so no nervousness or strange behavior on the part of Susan Hunter?"

"No, nothing that I can recall. That's what I just stated."

"Do you believe that any member of the Hunter or Kent family resented the fact that Susan Hunter had become a family member through a divorce and remarriage, in which a well-liked member was cast out?"

Dan shook his head and quickly glanced at the district attorney and then at the robed man behind the bench. He had a notion as to what was coming.

"Objection...calls for speculation—wild speculation, I might add," the D.A. shouted.

"Sustained," the judge thundered back. "Now, you had better watch it, Mr. Wilcox!"

"Yes, Your Honor," the young defense attorney replied, embarrassed by the judge's admonishment. Regaining his composure, he said, "Let me ask the question this way: Did you have any personal feelings of animosity toward Susan Hunter, since a divorce occurred in a family that I assume wants stability, as most families do?"

"I don't think I would call it animosity toward Susan. I was upset by the divorce, but more because I had grown to like Miriam—that's Jerry's first wife and the mother of his son, Michael—and enjoyed her company very much. I believe in people working together to resolve marital difficulties, which is why I was upset at the actual divorce. But I never blamed Susan, just as I never blamed Miriam for the break-up between her and Jerry. I must say that I was surprised, though—I think we all were—when it occurred. In terms of my feelings, I like *both* Miriam and Susan, who were always nice and pleasant to me."

"Thank you, Mrs. Kent. Your Honor, I have no further questions for this witness."

"Mr. District Attorney, do you have a redirect?" the judge inquired, looking at Stein.

"Just one or two more questions, Your Honor. Mrs. Kent, if Susan Hunter didn't drink tea, why did she join you for these afternoon get-togethers?"

"Mainly for the conversation and the chance for us to get to know each other, since she was new to our family and was now my nephew's wife. She said that Jerry had told her I enjoyed being with people in the afternoon, since I'm not a night owl and usually go to bed fairly early at night."

"Did she indicate that she wanted to get to know you better?"

"Yes, she said this any number of times, and I said the same thing to her."

"Did she drink anything when you were together?"

"Yes, coffee—hot in the colder weather and iced when it was warm. I always brewed a small pot when she came over, even though I don't drink coffee myself."

"So, Susan Hunter *never* drank the green tea that she delivered to you."

"No, she did not."

"Thank you, Mrs. Kent. No further questions."

Dan leaned back and sighed, feeling relieved that Katherine had held up under the questioning and didn't seem at all stressed out from the testimony. *She's definitely back to her normal self—straightforward and resilient,* he thought. *The last give-and-take about Susan never drinking any of the contaminated green tea is intriguing. I hadn't thought about that.*

"Next witness," Judge Frisk stated in a monotone voice.

"The state calls Anita Kent." Joel Stein put Anita through a series of questions, essentially the same as those presented to Katherine, with Thad Wilcox cross-examining. Anita's responses were a bit shorter, but contained messages consistent with those conveyed by Katherine. She had taken ill at the library with symptoms similar to her mother's (although not as severe or life threatening), she had consumed the tea alleged to have been poisoned by Susan for about six months (albeit in lower daily doses than her mother because she drank at most one cup of the tea per day). She was shocked by the divorce but did not hold a grudge or feel personal animosity toward Susan for what had happened, and she also spent time with Susan to get to know her better. The D.A. concluded his questioning by asking Anita if there was anything that Susan had mentioned about a desire to effectively control Hunter's Point. She responded with the revelation that Tony made after he had returned home from the hospital—the one about Susan wondering how it would feel to have the property all to yourself.

After Anita's testimony, the judge ordered a morning recess.

Dan and Bill Jenkins almost ran into each other as Dan was exiting the courtroom and heading for the men's room. The state trooper was on his way to the courtroom, being the first scheduled witness after the morning break. D.A. Stein had told him he was going to testify, and Jenkins had requested that it be after ten o'clock, as he had an early morning meeting he needed to attend.

"Hey there, Dan. I see you decided to show up for the day's events. You gonna watch me?"

"You bet. Wouldn't miss it. I drove Katherine and Anita here this morning and said I'd stay at least for the morning to get a sense of how this trial is going. This case, along with Jerry Hunter's, has me interested, and I actually want to talk to you about a couple of things. Can we see each other later today? I can come to the barracks if that would be convenient for you."

"Sure. I'll be back there after lunch, so any time after that."

As the court session reconvened, the prosecutor called Bill Jenkins to the witness stand and had him sworn in. Dan, now back his seat, gazed at the jury to see if all of them were focused on the third witness. They appeared to be attentive. After nodding to the judge, Joel Stein began his questioning. "Officer Jenkins, can you describe the events that took place on the last Sunday afternoon in June of this year?"

Dressed in his state police uniform, the trooper began his testimony, providing details of the process of hauling away a stock of food items that had been gathered in the kitchen of the Kent home after Anita's illness and poisoning diagnosis by the hospital. In response to the next question about the type of food items that were taken away for methanol testing, Jenkins reached into his pocket for a slip of paper on which he had written the items. He read the items from the list. Responding to the next series of questions about the state police's lab tests and results, Jenkins stated that all the confiscated items were found to be non-toxic except for the herbal tea, which contained traces of methanol—believed to be from a paint thinner.

Dan nodded as Jenkins spoke, confirming to himself the accuracy of what had been stated for the record. *I wonder how deep the D.A. is going to go with Bill,* he mused. The answer came quickly.

"Officer, will you describe how the paint thinner containing methanol found its way into the herbal tea?" Stein then asked.

"It appears to have been injected with a syringe."

"Objection. Calls for an expert opinion and, while we respect the officer, he is not a scientist or a laboratory specialist," Thad Wilcox interjected, standing up as he spoke.

"Your Honor," Stein responded, "we're asking Officer Jenkins to simply tell the court the results of the testing that has been done by the state police laboratory. If the defense wishes, we can call the scientist who actually performed the tests, but we thought it would save the court time and money if at this time we could have a summary of what are documented test results. Furthermore, Officer Jenkins is very familiar with the testing procedures and has testified in other criminal cases on the subject of laboratory tests."

"Overruled...I'll allow the question and the response," the judge replied. "You may continue, and I will direct the witness to speak strictly to documented facts and not get into any area where there is not a specific laboratory test result."

Bill Jenkins continued his testimony, stating there was evidence of small holes, consistent with those made with a small, sharp object such as a syringe, in the back bottom corner of all the tea bags from the package of herbal tea that was taken from the Kent home and tested by the lab. He then summarized his search of the Hunter home and property, during which he discovered two items related to the case.

"Can you describe what you found in and around the Hunter home relating to this case?" Stein asked.

"We found two things," Jenkins replied. "One was paint thinner with the type of methanol found in Anita Kent's and Katherine Kent's bloodstream by the hospital. Our lab people corroborated this with the hospital staff that performed the tests there. The second was a syringe in the corner of a vanity in a downstairs bathroom of their house."

"And what is the significance of these discoveries?"

"There were traces of the paint thinner found in the tool shed on the syringe needle, and Mrs. Hunter's fingerprints are on the syringe."

"Did you find any other fingerprints on the syringe?"

"No."

"Did you find any other items of interest on a subsequent visit to the Hunter home?" Stein asked.

Jenkins answered by stating that he found a package of *Sunflower Green Tea* in the kitchen. When asked about tests run on this package, he stated that two bags were tested and these bags contained the same paint thinner found in what was taken from the Kent home. He then mentioned that the remaining tea bags from this search were in the secured storage area at the state police barracks.

As Dan reflected on the seemingly conclusive nature of the testimony given so far by the state trooper, Joel Stein held up another clear plastic bag, similar to the one previously presented. This one contained two contaminated bags of *Sunflower Green Tea*. "Your Honor, I would like to enter into evidence Exhibit 2—two tea bags from the package taken from the Hunter home the day that Susan Hunter was arrested."

After confirming that there were not any other significant findings from Jenkins' two searches of the Hunter home and surrounding property, Stein excused his witness.

"Do you want to cross-examine this witness, Mr. Wilcox?" the judge asked, looking directly at the defense attorney.

"Not at this time, your honor; but we would like to reserve the right to question Officer Jenkins at a future time."

"So granted," the judge replied. "We'll adjourn for lunch and return at 1:30," he said, pounding his gavel lightly.

Dan waited for Bill Jenkins outside the courtroom. Motioning him aside, Dan said that he was going to drive Katherine and Anita back to Hunter's Point, have a quick lunch with them if time allowed, and return to the courtroom for the remainder of the day's session. When queried by the state trooper, Dan said that his interest in the case was growing as he listened to and thought about the proceedings. He complemented Bill on the completeness of his testimony and reiterated his desire to meet later that day.

After the lunch break, Joel Stein strode to the front of the courtroom just as Dan was taking his seat. "The state calls Dr. Kevin Callahan to the stand." After the swearing in formality, the D.A. began his questioning. "Doctor, could you please state your position and your relationship to Katherine Kent?"

Kevin Callahan settled into the witness chair. "I am a second year resident intern at Shorehaven Hospital. I treated Katherine Kent, but not Anita Kent when she was a patient, although I learned of Anita's case after the fact. With regard to Katherine Kent, I was very involved in her initial treatment and care when she was admitted to the hospital's emergency room in a very critical and comatose condition."

"Can you describe her condition, doctor?"

"She was almost clinically dead."

"Can you be more specific, doctor?"

Doctor Kevin Callahan explained Katherine's physical state: renal failure, low pulse rate and cyanosis. With some prodding from Stein, the doctor mentioned his fear of losing Katherine on a couple of occasions during the night, due to these serious conditions. Not wanting to miss a word of this testimony, Dan leaned forward, his elbows on his knees and his chin perched in the palms of his hands.

"So, what type of treatment did you administer?" the prosecutor asked.

"Well, Sir, soon after her admission to the emergency room, Katherine Kent's daughter, Anita, mentioned to me that she had been a patient earlier in the week and was diagnosed as having methanol in her blood stream. She thought there was a possibility that her mother was suffering from the same ailment."

"And, doctor, what was your reaction and what did you do?"

"My immediate reaction was that methanol poisoning was consistent with Katherine Kent's symptoms, so I took a calculated risk and ordered a series of procedures and medications based on this hypothesis."

"Did this hypothesis prove to be correct?"

"Yes. Our lab tests confirmed that she suffered blood poisoning as a result of methanol entering her system, most likely from a series of small doses sustained over a prolonged period of time."

"What was the substance that was found to contain the methanol?"

"Our tests concluded that the poisoning came from paint thinner or a similar type of liquid substance."

"Are you convinced that the poisoning came from small doses of paint thinner taken over a period of time—say, five to six months?"

"I am now," the doctor replied. He went on to explain the process of running blood tests and the conclusions that he made in collaboration with his colleagues at the hospital. Responding to another question from Stein, Dr. Callahan stated that the medical team confirmed that Anita had the same symptoms, only not as severe.

Joel Stein looked at the jury, then at the judge and stated, "I have no further questions."

The judge looked at the defense lawyer and asked the obvious question, "Do you wish to cross-examine, Mr. Wilcox?"

"Just one question for this witness, Your Honor," Attorney Wilcox replied. "Dr. Callahan, you said that it was your opinion that Katherine and Anita Kent suffered a prolonged period of ingestion of methanol in small doses. But is it not possible that a sudden, heavy dose could produce similar results?"

"It's possible, but not very probable. In fact, it's not very likely."

"But, is it possible? Please, doctor, just a yes or no answer."

"Yes."

"No further questions," Wilcox groaned. He returned to his chair and slumped into it. Susan looked at the attorney. An expression of despair covered her face.

Dan gazed at Wilcox and read his body language, thinking that the young attorney should work on this aspect of his demeanor in court. The retired detective's mind was in full investigative gear as he reflected on the proceedings so far and where he felt that Susan's attorney stood. *He's struggling and can't find any ammunition to refute the testimony of the prosecution's witnesses so far. He knows that Stein is building the case against his client—brick by brick—and he can't do anything to derail it. That last effort with the doctor was feeble, since I'm sure the jury will be reminded that "probabilities", not "possibilities" are what count in testimony. Every time I look over at Susan, she seems to be looking desperately at him. She must be praying for a smoking gun to move the jury away from believing and acting on the evidence that the D.A. is presenting.*

The prosecutor was back at the witness stand to question the other doctor involved with the Kents. "The state calls Dr. Jack O'Brien as its next witness."

Jack O'Brien gave testimony that corroborated and reinforced the "small methanol dosage over time" theory and then provided a significant amount of detail about Anita during the time that she was in the hospital.

"We have time for one more witness today and we'll take that one after a twenty minute recess," the judge droned.

"Thank you, Your Honor," Stein replied. "We'll call our final witness for the day after the break."

Dan leaned back in his seat and cast a glance, first at Susan, who was now sitting with her head in her hands, and then at the district attorney, who was moving papers in and out of his briefcase. *This is pretty hard evidence,* he thought. *It almost does seem open and shut: the syringe with the paint thinner and Susan's fingerprints on it, the holes in the poisoned tea bags that match to the size of the needle, and the consistency of the police and hospital lab tests for Katherine and Anita. It's a tight case…very tight!*

As the courtroom was brought back into session, the prosecutor called Natalie Ferguson. After she had taken the oath, Stein faced her and asked, "Ms. Ferguson, could you state your occupation for the record?"

"I am the owner of Natalie's Naturals, a specialty food and beverage store."

"And, Ms. Ferguson, is green tea one of the products you sell?"

"Yes, it is."

"And is *Sunflower Green Tea* one of the brands that you carry?"

"Yes, it is."

"Ms. Ferguson, do you recognize any of your regular customers in this courtroom?"

"Yes, I do...you, Mr. Stein...and the woman sitting over there." She pointed toward Susan as she spoke.

Turning to the judge, Stein said, "Let me assure you, Your Honor... and the jury...that this is not meant to be a trite question. There is a reason for asking it."

The judge looked at the D.A. with a frown on his face and motioned for him to get on with his questioning.

"Ms. Ferguson, can you tell the judge and jury what products I typically purchase?"

"Objection...this is irrelevant! I don't believe anyone here cares what products you purchase," Wilcox interjected, staying seated as he spoke.

"Your Honor, I'm trying to establish the fact that Ms. Ferguson has a good knowledge of her customers and what they purchase, and that the jury can rely on the accuracy of her testimony."

"I'll allow the question. Objection overruled."

Thad Wilcox again slumped in his chair, trying to hide a feeling of utter dismay at the way the trial was proceeding. He turned away from Susan to keep her from seeing his facial expression, which he knew would only make her more fearful than she already was. As he turned away from Susan, though, his face and the message it conveyed was visible to Dan, who shook his head slightly as he leaned forward to rivet his attention on this new witness and her testimony.

With a nod from the D.A., Natalie Ferguson began speaking again. "Mr. Stein, you purchase about four or five items on a fairly regular basis. Let's see...whole grain wheat bread, unsalted nuts, dried tangerine skins, natural lemonade and one of the new power drink beverages, although I'm not sure of the specific brand."

"Now, can you tell us what product or products the defendant purchases and how often?"

"She has been buying the *Sunflower* brand of green tea about once every month, and occasionally purchases one of our brands of natural mixed snacks. I believe it's *Dave's Delight*."

"Nothing else?"

"Not on a regular basis. She may buy other items, in fact I hope she has, but those are the ones that I remember she always seemed to leave with."

"How can you be so sure?"

"There are only a handful of customers who buy the *Sunflower Green Tea* brand—it's not a big seller for my store—and she's one of them, although she hasn't been to the store in a while. As for the *Dave's Delight* product, it has a very unique and colorful package that you just seem to notice and remember."

"Finally, Ms. Ferguson, do you know me in any capacity other than as an occasional customer in your store?"

"No."

"And, one last question…do you know Susan Hunter in any capacity other than as an occasional customer in your store?"

"No."

"Thank you, Ms. Ferguson. Judge, I have no further questions for this witness."

"Mr. Wilcox, do you wish to cross-examine?"

Thad Wilcox shook his head, not having a clue as to what he might ask this witness that would be of any value to his case.

The judge looked at his watch, and then closed the proceedings for the day.

Susan Hunter's body shook convulsively as she rose in response to the bailiff's order for adjournment and then gazed nervously at the jury walking out of the courtroom.

Dan looked at Susan as he rose to leave and she caught his glance from across the courtroom. She stared at him with the same look of bewilderment and desperation that she had given him in the morning. Then he noticed her lips moving. He looked around. She was speaking to him and saying something…just two words. What were they? He looked at her again. Her lips moved again as she mouthed the same two words. The second word was "me", but he wasn't certain about the first. As he started to walk out of the courtroom, he saw her sobbing and shaking. She was then cuffed and escorted to a side entrance where those on trial entered and exited the courtroom.

Chapter 21

It was almost five o'clock Monday afternoon and Bill Jenkins was seated in his office with Dan Davies sitting across the desk from him. "So, what is it, Dan, that you wanted to talk about?"

"Well, Bill, I sat through and listened to all the testimony today. After driving Katherine and Anita back to their home shortly after we spoke, I returned to the courthouse to hear the witnesses the D.A. put on the stand during the afternoon."

"Who was that?"

"The two young doctors at the hospital who provided medical treatment for Katherine and Anita, plus the owner of the store where Susan bought the herbal tea."

"So, what's up? I'm sure you didn't drive here for the enjoyment of seeing me."

"I'm not sure. Maybe it's the old detective in me that doesn't want to go away. I've been thinking about a couple of things for the past few days. Can I see the packages of tea that you mentioned in your testimony today? The ones that are in your secured area?"

"Well, I can't let you back there. I'm sure you can understand why, but I can have someone get them and bring them here." Jenkins rose out of his chair and went to the main area of the barracks, where he spoke to one of the younger troopers who was manning the front desk. Returning to his office, he said, "We'll have them here in a few minutes. We have to document the removal and then the return, but you know all about that. Anything else?"

Dan scratched his chin and said, "I think you should go back to Hunter's Point, specifically to Jerry and Susan's home which is now unoccupied. There may be something there of interest to this case. With Jerry and Susan not living there, the house is locked, but Katherine and

Miriam have keys to get in."

"What is it that you want me to get?"

"I don't know."

"Well, I'm not sure what I should be searching for if you can't tell me what it is."

"I don't know *what* it is...I only know *where* it is," Dan said

"Okay, then, *where* is it?"

Just as Dan was about to speak, the young trooper strode into Jenkins's office with the two packages of herbal tea, the first about one-quarter full and the second containing seventy-eight bags. Two bags from the second package had been introduced into evidence a few hours ago in the courtroom. Wearing rubber gloves, he placed the packages on top of Jenkins's desk and then left the office.

"Let me remind you, Dan, that you can't touch these packages."

"I don't need to touch them. I just need to get a good view of them," Dan replied, looking at the packages from every angle as he walked around Jenkins's desk. "Hmmm...maybe there's something here...just maybe."

"Care to explain?"

"In due course. I need to check out one thing first. Now, regarding the visit back to the Hunter's home, here's where you should go...."

Having enjoyed their recent dinner there, Dan and Miriam were back at Cristo's that evening.

"So, what was it like in court today?" Miriam asked.

"Compelling, I'd say, in terms of connecting Susan to the poisoning of Katherine and Anita."

"I assume Katherine and Anita testified," Miriam said.

"Yes, they did. And, the prosecution also had Bill Jenkins—you know, the state trooper who arrested Susan and made the searches, the two young doctors at the hospital and the lady who owns the natural food store where Susan bought the tea that was poisoned."

"So, what were the highlights?"

As they sipped a glass of wine, consumed an appetizer, and began eating dinner, Dan recounted the day's testimony, pausing occasionally to gather his thoughts as to what each of the witnesses had said. Miriam had a few questions, but was quiet for the most part. He concluded with…"Susan's fingerprints on the syringe that has the traces of paint thinner, coupled with the holes on the back of all the tea bags into which the syringe fits perfectly, seem to place her as the person who injected the methanol into the tea bags. This theory is strengthened by finding paint thinner in the Hunters' tool shed, along with the owner of the food store identifying her as buying the tea on a regular basis."

"You're right, it does sound compelling."

"I guess it does, but I'm not totally convinced she did it."

"Why do you say that, with all the evidence that's being presented?"

"I'm not sure why, but I've got this feeling that's hard to explain. When I looked into Susan's eyes this morning, just as the testimony was about to begin, I saw a very distressed woman. It was almost as if I were looking at a frightened little girl, who seemed bewildered by the whole situation and was desperately crying out for help…searching for someone to get her get out of something she didn't do. She had the same look again this afternoon at the end of the court session when I was leaving. And, then she looked straight at me and said something. In fact, she said it twice. I think it was 'Help me'! She was speaking to *me*—I know that. I can't get that look and those words out of my mind."

"Don't you think it could be the act of a desperate person trying to salvage her life?"

"Maybe, but I saw this look of bewilderment, this total disbelief at the charges and proceedings, and desperation—by that I mean not knowing where to turn to for help—on the faces of only a few defendants in all my years in New York. In every instance there was a false accusation or a set-up, and the accused person wound up being innocent. A couple of them, both women, were convicted and then won on appeal. Chasing down the evidence and bringing in a witness who did not testify in the original trial led to the real criminal in each case."

Miriam looked at Dan silently, as if she were wondering what was going through his mind. "Is there anything else you would like to talk about?"

"Of course, but these trials are consuming me now. There are some things that don't add up in my mind. Oh, well, tomorrow's another day to roll some of these thoughts around. I have to testify tomorrow when

Jerry's trial begins. Are you going to be there?"

Miriam shook her head. "I don't think I can take it. And I don't think Jerry would want me there."

"Yeah, I suppose you're right, he probably wouldn't. Okay, we've beaten these trials enough. Let's move on to something else. What do you hear from Michael?"

"He's fine…enjoying being an upperclassman, having a car so he can now drive to see Amy occasionally, and getting into his major. He also went out for the soccer team."

"Really? I didn't know he played at that level."

"Well, he hasn't for a couple of years, but he was quite a star in high school, in soccer and baseball. He played striker and was the highest goal scorer on the soccer team, and he played third base and had the highest batting average on the baseball team. He didn't want to pursue varsity sports in college…until now, that is. I think one of their better players got injured. The coach heard about Michael's high school achievements and asked him to try out for the team. Maybe the baseball coach will do the same in the spring."

"That's great. We should go to a game this fall. Now that I think about it, I remember that he and Jon played in a few pick up softball games during the summer. Maybe he was unconsciously getting prepared. You said he played third base in baseball? What a coincidence. That's what I played…'way back when'!"

"Yep, that was his position. He was good, with a strong arm and batting swing."

Chapter 22

As the bailiff made the opening remarks, Judge Willard Thomas entered the courtroom and took his seat, motioning for those in the courtroom to sit down. The trial for Jerry Hunter's criminal assault charge was about to begin. Dan, dressed in a dark suit and sitting on the same side of the courtroom, albeit a different one, as he did yesterday and a row closer to the front, leaned forward as the judge got settled and cleared his throat. After making a number of administrative remarks and giving the jury their instructions regarding the charge they would be rendering a decision on, he gazed at Allan Bentley and said, "Does the prosecution wish to make an opening statement?"

The thirty-three year-old assistant district attorney, short and stocky, with thick brown hair that was closely cropped, nodded at the judge, rose out of his chair, and walked toward the jury box. "We do wish to make a statement, Your Honor. Ladies and gentlemen of the jury, this case is a crime of passion, involving a jealous man who took revenge on another man—a relative, I might add—who had an affair with his wife, whom we have reason to believe he considered to be his 'trophy,' belonging solely to him. Jerald Hunter, widely known as Jerry, found out about Tony Kent, his cousin, having at least three sexual encounters with his wife, Susan Hunter. He threatened Mr. Kent on two separate occasions, both of which can be documented—and will be through the witnesses we'll present—and then attacked Mr. Kent between nine and ten o'clock at night on the fourth Friday in June of this year. Mr. Kent almost died. We don't know if Mr. Hunter was trying to kill Mr. Kent, but we have strong reason to believe he wanted to harm him. He used a heavy fireplace shovel to strike him down. Thus, we will prove that Mr. Hunter is guilty of Criminal Assault as charged by the state."

After pausing for a moment, Bentley continued. "We will present, as witnesses, the victim of this crime, his sister (who knew of the affairs), a friend of Mr. Kent's who happens to be a former police officer and witnessed one of the threats made by Mr. Hunter, plus the victim's son, who witnessed both episodes when Mr. Hunter threatened Mr. Kent. Regarding Mr. Kent's son, Jonathan Kent, his testimony will be read into the record from a deposition taken this past Friday at the district attorney's office in Manchester, New Hampshire and attended by the defense attorney. Further, we will provide testimony from a state police officer who confiscated the weapon used to commit the crime, the doctor who treated Mr. Kent when he was admitted to the hospital, and a hospital nurse who witnessed Mr. Kent name Mr. Hunter as his attacker after he came out of a coma he was in for almost a week."

Dan gazed at Allan Bentley, thinking that the young prosecutor was probably pleased with his opening statement. Bentley then strode quickly back to his seat, nodding toward Judge Thomas as he walked in front of him.

"Mr. Wilcox, does the defense wish to make an opening statement?" the judge asked, now looking straight at Jerry Hunter's lawyer.

Jason Wilcox, the tall and slender younger brother of his even taller family law firm partner, Thad, rose and nodded toward the judge. "We do, Your Honor. The state has a case built on circumstantial evidence and innuendos. They cannot directly connect my client, Mr. Hunter, to this crime, and will try to lead you with a bunch of hypotheses that simply can't be supported by hard evidence. The only piece of 'hard' evidence is a fireplace shovel with a trace of blood that is of the same type as Mr. Kent's, with Mr. Hunter's fingerprints on it, which is normal since he made many fires using this tool. While Mr. Hunter was upset and may have threatened Mr. Kent, he did not commit this crime. I would also remind the jury that, as the judge stated in his opening remarks, the prosecution must convince you beyond a reasonable doubt that Mr. Hunter committed this crime. We do not believe the state has the evidence to prove the allegation against my client and that you will find the case lacking in concrete evidence, thus requiring an acquittal."

Dan observed the judge leaning back in his large chair as Jason Wilcox returned to his seat. He then noticed Jerry looking suspiciously at Judge Thomas, the defendant's face reflecting consternation and concern.

"The state calls as its first witness, Mr. Anthony Kent, the victim in this crime," Bentley said in a matter of fact tone. After being sworn in, Tony sat down in the witness chair. "Mr. Kent, would you please start by describing your relationship with Susan Hunter, the defendant's wife."

Dan leaned back and folded his arms as Tony went into a lengthy explanation of how he and Susan had become physically attracted to each other, and how his loneliness over the loss of his wife, along with Susan's longing for companionship when Jerry was away and her physical attractiveness, which was overwhelming for him, had led him into sexual encounters with her. He spoke for over ten minutes about how their relationship had started, how they would arrange their encounters, where they would meet to engage in sex and the discussions they had about the need to end the affair. Bentley was silent as Tony spoke, waiting until he had finished before resuming his questioning. From his seat, Dan could observe Jerry glaring at Tony with a look of disdain on his face. At the conclusion of this initial testimony, Tony leaned back, stretched his legs out and breathed heavily. *That must have been hard for him to say,* Dan thought, studying Tony's body language.

Taking the cue, Bentley resumed his interrogation. "Mr. Kent, would you tell the court, to the best of your ability, the settings and the words that Mr. Hunter said to you on the two occasions when he threatened you?"

Tony sat up, thought for a moment and spoke again. "The first time he threatened me was after we had a Friday night barbecue at my place."

"I assume you mean your home at Hunter's Point?"

"Yes. I was getting ready to watch a movie, when Jerry came running over to my place. He was waving a fireplace shovel and he said he would bash my head with it if I didn't keep my hands off Susan. He was screaming at me. The second time was about a week later. It was a Thursday night—the night before I was attacked. Susan and I had gotten together the night before and Jerry found out. He came after me in my cottage. He ran past my son, Jon, who was on the deck, and into the cottage. Dan Davies, a friend, got between us and prevented what would have probably been a fight. Jerry called me a nasty name and said he ought to kill me for having sex with Susan."

"Let me be sure I've got this straight, Mr. Kent. Mr. Hunter said that during the first encounter between the two of you that he would 'bash your head in with the fireplace shovel if you didn't keep your hands off his wife'...and during the second incident he said that he 'ought to kill you' for what you were doing with her. Is that correct?"

"Objection...leading the witness, Your Honor," Jason Wilcox interjected, rising out of his seat.

"Your Honor," Bentley countered, "I'm simply trying to get Mr. Kent to state, as accurately as he can, the words that the defendant used when he confronted the victim."

"Overruled...the witness may answer the question," the judge stated.

"Yes, those were the words he said to me...actually, shouted at me," Tony replied.

Dan, now leaning forward in his seat, nodded to himself at the recollection of the words spoken during the second incident.

After glancing at the jury, Bentley looked back at Tony and said, "To continue, Mr. Kent, you said there were witnesses to both of these encounters?"

"Well, definitely the second one...Mr. Davies and my son, Jon. And Jon told me later that he and his cousin, Michael, had witnessed the first encounter and overheard what was said between Jerry and me."

Jason Wilcox rose out of his chair and forcefully said, "Move to strike the last statement about the first encounter. It's hearsay!"

"Sustained," the judge said in a monotone. "The jury will disregard the last statement made by the witness concerning the first incident. Continue, Mr. Bentley."

"So noted, Your Honor. We will present testimony regarding the first encounter later on today. Now, Mr. Kent, please describe—as best you can—the events of the evening on the fourth Friday in June of this year."

"Well, we had a family dinner at my mother's house. I was staying there to take care of my sister, Anita, who had just come home from the hospital. I think everyone here knows the circumstances, since there is another trial going on regarding that situation."

"Yes, I think we do," Bentley stated, nodding at the judge. "Please continue."

Tony responded by recounting the conversation with his sister after his mother had gone to bed, and how Anita queried him on who knew about the affairs with Susan and confrontations with Jerry. Tony gave a recap of his walk outside the main house and his commitment to end the affair with Susan. He concluded by saying, "As I was returning to the house, a man came quickly out of the bushes. I assume it was Jerry."

"Objection…objection!" Jason Wilcox shouted. "We don't want to hear about Mr. Kent's assumptions. We need to stick to the facts."

"Sustained," the judge roared. "The jury will disregard the remark, 'I assume it was Jerry'. Continue, Mr. Kent, but stick to the facts as you know them."

"Yes, Your Honor. As I said, I was returning to the main house where I was staying to help my sister who was recovering from blood poisoning, when a figure—I'm sure it was a man about the size of Jerry—came out of the bushes to my left that border the house and hit me with something on the head. It was an object of some sort—definitely not a fist or an open hand. While it was dark outside, I could see it descending toward me. It came fast. The last thing I remember is that object hitting my head and the sharp pain I felt." Tony pointed toward his left temple as he made the last remark.

"And, Mr. Kent, did your attacker say anything to you…or shout anything at you just before striking you with the object?" Bentley asked.

"Yes. He shouted words I will never forget…'I told you to keep your hands off her!'"

"Thank you, Mr. Kent. No further questions."

"Attorney for the defense, do you wish to cross-examine?" the judge droned.

Jason Wilcox had told Jerry before the trial began that he would have to find a major hole in Tony's testimony to do an effective cross-examination. The affair with Susan had occurred, Jerry had threatened Tony, and Tony had been attacked. Since there was nothing Tony had said that could be disputed and the judge had sustained his objection about assuming it was Jerry who had come out of the bushes and struck the blow, Wilcox did not want to make his first appearance a weak cross-examination. Thus, he replied, "Not at this time, Your Honor, but we would like to reserve the right to question Mr. Kent at another time."

"So granted. Call your next witness, Mr. Bentley."

"The state calls Anita Kent." After Anita was sworn in, the assistant district attorney began his interrogation. "Ms. Kent, can you please relate to us what your brother told you about his affair with Susan Hunter, along with anything you know to be true about the encounters between Jerry Hunter and your brother, Tony?"

"Tony and I had two or three conversations about his affair with Susan, during which we discussed the encounters you stated in your question." Anita continued by stating her shock and dismay over the affair and her admonishment to end it. She then provided specifics about what Tony had told her about his relationship with Susan and the incidents with Jerry.

"Are you certain that all the references you've made are true?"

"Yes, Sir, they are, to the best of my knowledge."

"Thank you. No further questions."

"Cross-examine, Mr. Wilcox?" the judge asked, leaning forward.

Wilcox shook his head. "Not at this time, Your Honor."

"Next witness," Judge Thomas said.

Allan Bentley responded with, "The state calls Mr. Daniel Davies."

Dan strode to the witness stand, took the oath and sat down.

"Mr. Davies, could you state your occupation and where you live?"

"I'm retired now and am a year-long resident at Condor's Nest Beach. Prior to my retirement, I was a detective with the New York City Police Department."

"So, is it safe to assume that you've testified in a number of criminal cases?"

"Yes, Sir, quite a few."

"Were you present at Anthony Kent's cottage on a Thursday night in the fourth week of June of this year?"

"Yes, I was."

"Can you tell us what happened at Tony Kent's cottage that night?"

"Well, I had been at the main house—Katherine Kent's home—for dinner that night. I went to Tony's cottage with him after dinner. We were going to talk about a couple of things related to Anita Kent, his sister, having been diagnosed with methanol poisoning. We were in the cottage when Jerry Hunter came bounding through the door and lunged at Tony. I was able to get between them and stop what I thought was going to be a physical confrontation."

"Did the defendant, Mr. Hunter, say anything to Mr. Kent?"

"He yelled out a couple of things…'I told you to stay away from her' and 'I ought to kill you'."

"Anything else?"

"I think he said something about Tony not being able to control what's in his pants."

"Anything else?"

"Oh, yes, there was another exchange of words between Tony and Jerry. Tony ordered Jerry out of the cottage and said they would deal with this privately, and Jerry replied with something like 'you bet we will,' and 'be prepared for the worst'. That's about it. After that last exchange, I was ready to leave, since Tony had to deal with his son—who was on the deck and presumably overheard everything."

"Thank you, Mr. Davies. I have no more questions for this witness."

"Does the defense wish to cross-examine?" Judge Thomas, anticipating the same response from Jason Wilcox that he had heard regarding the first two witnesses, was preparing to announce a morning recess.

"Yes, Your Honor, I have a few questions I'd like to ask this witness."

"Proceed, Mr. Wilcox. We'll take a recess after your questioning."

Dan looked directly into the eyes of the defense lawyer, who said, "Mr. Davies, is it your experience, as a career police officer, that some people suffer what I would call random attacks? That is, the reason behind the attack is not clear?"

"Yes, that's certainly been part of my experience."

"Now, Mr. Davies, is it safe to say that in the years you served as a police officer and detective, you've either heard personally or been made aware of many expletives and threatening statements similar to the ones that my client made to Mr. Kent?"

"Yes, that's true. People often threaten others, particularly where I come from. And, the language is not always what you would hear in church."

"Do you have any idea of how many you've heard, directly or indirectly, over the years?"

"More that I could possibly count easily. Hundreds, maybe thousands."

"And do all or most of these threats result in violent actions and attacks, such as those suffered by Mr. Kent?"

"Certainly not. Typically only a very small percentage of threats actually result in some type of physical attack."

"So, even though my client made accusations and threats against Mr. Kent, your last statement would suggest that, based on your experience with many years in police work, there's actually a very low probability that the person making the threatening remarks would actually follow through on the threats. Would you agree with this?"

Dan thought for a moment and then replied, "Yes, I would have to say that I agree."

"Thank you, Mr. Davies. I have no further questions at this time for this witness, Your Honor."

"Assuming the prosecution does not wish to redirect, we'll take a thirty minute recess," the judge ordered, pounding his gavel. Bentley looked at the judge and shook his head, indicating he had no further questions for Mr. Daniel Davies.

Dan visited the restroom during the recess and started to ponder the last line of questioning from the defense attorney.

Allan Bentley stood up once the trial reconvened. "Judge, our next testimony will be from a deposition of Mr. Jonathan Kent, son of the victim of this crime. Jonathan Kent is an eighteen-year-old college freshman. We took the deposition this past Friday at the district attorney's office in Manchester, New Hampshire. The defense was present and participated in the proceeding."

"Is this correct, Mr. Wilcox and do you have any objection to the admission of this testimony?" the judge queried.

"I was present at the deposition and we do not object to its admission, Your Honor."

Dan, who had returned to the courtroom, and Bill Jenkins, who was to be the next witness and wanted to hear what Jonathan Kent had to say, sat next to each other and listened attentively as the assistant district attorney and the defense attorney made their remarks. Dan had thought some more about the questions the two lawyers had asked him and his responses as he walked back to take his seat in the courtroom, wanting to ensure that his testimony was accurate and complete. However, after sitting down, Dan turned his attention to Allan Bentley and what he was about to read into the record. Bentley had told the courtroom that, except where indicated, he was the one asking the questions.

Bentley then read the deposition…stating first the questions that were asked and then Jon's responses. He indicated to the judge and jury that he and the defense attorney had agreed to address him as 'Jonathan' instead of 'Mr. Kent' due to his age and all the stress that he had been through. The deposition began with the two encounters between Tony and Jerry, which rehashed much of the testimony of Dan Davies regarding the second one, and added the shouting and brandishing of the fireplace shovel from the first confrontation between the two men. The initial phase of this deposition was intensive and consumed nearly thirty minutes, as the prosecution and defense had interacted with Jonathan Kent during the interrogative session.

Bentley was now in the final phase of reading Jonathan Kent's deposition.

Question: "Jonathan, are there any additional comments you would like to make?"

Response from Jonathan Kent: "Michael, my cousin—well, sort of my cousin—and I have talked about this situation a couple of times. We've talked about the possibility that Susan seduced my dad—realizing he was vulnerable and taking advantage of what she perceived as a weakness on his part."

Question: "What makes you and your cousin, or your 'sort of' cousin, think that there was a seduction?"

Response: "Susan just has that way about her. It's hard to explain, but she's very attractive and seductive. You have to be around her to feel it, but it's there."

Question: "So, Jonathan, how does this relate to this case of Criminal Assault?"

Response: "I'm not sure, but maybe Uncle Jerry was so jealous or felt so jilted by Susan seducing my dad, that he went nuts and reacted violently. I kind of did the same thing when I went after Uncle Jerry when I learned that his fingerprints were all over the fireplace shovel and my dad's blood was on it. I also beat up some kids when I was in grade school who made fun of my grandmother and my aunt raising me, because my mother had died when I was a little boy. People can do strange things when they're enraged."

Question: "But, Jonathan, I'm still not connecting your statements to this case."

Response: "My dad told me that one of the times he and Susan had sex was the night after my high school graduation party in early June, when Uncle Jerry got drunk and passed out in his home. My dad said that Susan came looking for him after finding Uncle Jerry passed out and asleep. She had also been drinking, was apparently feeling good and wanted to make love to her husband. Since he was totally out of it, she came looking for my dad, who happened to be around after the party, seduced him, and they rendezvoused in a thicket at the end of the beach. Another incident occurred in Uncle Jerry's house—in his own bed, no less—when he was on a business trip and Susan must have felt horny and again seduced Dad. Maybe Uncle Jerry couldn't take the embarrassment of having his beautiful wife—some of us call her his 'trophy'—not being totally satisfied by him alone and wanting to be with another man, because he went crazy when he found out about these encounters, based on what I witnessed when he threatened my dad. That's all I have to say."

"This concludes our deposition of Jonathan Kent," Allan Bentley stated.

"Does the prosecution have any more witnesses?" the Judge Thomas asked.

"Yes, we do, Your Honor…we have three more."

"Then, we will call them after lunch. Court is adjourned until 1:30."

After the break for lunch, during which Dan and Bill Jenkins went to a local diner to eat together, Allan Bentley stood at the front of the courtroom. After the swearing in procedure, he began his interrogation. "Officer Jenkins, can you please tell the court the result of your search at the Hunter home on the Monday following the Friday night attack against Mr. Kent."

"We found a fireplace shovel that we suspected might be involved in the attack."

Bentley went over to the prosecution's table and picked up a large, clear plastic bag, through which a black fireplace shovel was visible. Striding back toward the witness stand, and holding the top of the bag open so that Jenkins could look inside and view the shovel, he asked, "Officer, is this the fireplace shovel that you took from the house owned and occupied by Jerald Hunter?"

"Yes."

"Your Honor, the state introduces this fireplace shovel, taken from the Hunter home under a valid search warrant and alleged to be the implement that struck the victim in this case, as Exhibit A."

"Alright. Bailiff, please take the plastic bag," the judge responded. "Proceed, Counselor."

"Officer Jenkins, were you looking for this shovel?"

"Yes."

"Can you please tell us why?"

Jenkins gave the pertinent details of Dan's visit to the state police barracks the day after the attack and the rationale for confiscating the fireplace shovel from Jerry's house, including what he had learned concerning the prognosis of the doctors at the hospital who treated Tony Kent for his injuries.

"And, what did you find on the fireplace shovel as a result of your lab tests?"

"We found two things of significance. First, we found traces of Mr. Kent's blood type, which no one else in the family has, so we felt there was a strong possibility that Mr. Kent had been hit with this shovel. Second, we found Mr. Hunter's fingerprints all over the shovel—particularly prints from his left hand."

"Well, wouldn't you expect this, since he probably made a lot of fires using the shovel, since the Hunter's live in their home all year round?"

"Yes, that's correct, but there were no other prints on the shovel."

"Thank you, Officer. We have no further questions."

"Does the defense wish to question this witness?" the judge droned.

"Yes, Your Honor," Attorney Wilcox replied. "We have one question."

"Please proceed."

"Officer, could someone other than the defendant, Jerald Hunter, have been the attacker and used, say, some type of rubber glove, so that Mr. Hunter's prints would remain and that a lab test would uncover no other prints? A simple 'yes' or 'no' answer will suffice."

"Yes."

"Thank you. We have nothing further for this witness, Judge, at this time."

Dan winked at Jenkins as the trooper walked past him and out of the courtroom.

Allan Bentley was back at the witness stand. "The state calls Dr. Kevin Callahan. Dr. Callahan, I have just one question for you. Officer Jenkins, in part of his testimony just given, stated that he was told that the doctor who treated Mr. Kent on the night of the attack indicated that the injury to the victim's head was most likely the result of being struck by a blunt object rather than a fall on the jagged rocks that border the ocean side of Hunter's Point. This led to the search of the Hunter home and confiscation of the fireplace shovel. As the doctor who attended to Mr. Kent, is that your prognosis—that is, without naming a specific object or implement, that the head wound was caused by some type of blunt object?"

"Yes, it is, and this prognosis has been confirmed by further testing."

"Could you elaborate, please?"

"Mr. Kent's head wound resulted from being struck by a blunt object. Since they are jagged, a fall on the rocks alone would have produced lacerations in the head region, similar to what he suffered in his shoulder, which is the part of his body that the evidence indicates hit the rocks. The evidence is almost indisputable in support of this statement."

"Thank you, Doctor. We have no further questions for this witness and are prepared to call our last witness for the day, unless the defense wishes to cross-examine Dr. Callahan at this time."

Wilcox shook his head.

After getting a nod from the judge, Bentley, remaining where he had been while questioning Kevin Callahan, stated emphatically, "We call Doris Wily to the stand."

The gray-haired, middle-aged nurse from Shorehaven Hospital, wearing a white blouse and gray skirt, walked quickly to the witness stand. Dan noticed her hand shaking as she took the oath. *I figured she'd be nervous about testifying,* he thought. *I'll bet she's never been in a court of law before, much less a witness in a criminal trial.*

Bentley motioned for her to be seated. "Good afternoon, Ms. Wily. I'd like to ask you a few questions. First, could you tell us what your position at the hospital is?"

"I'm a senior staff nurse in the Intensive Care Unit."

"Thank you, Ms. Wily. How long have you worked in this unit?"

"Let's see…it's been eighteen years now."

"Ms. Wily, were you present on the day when Mr. Kent came out of his coma and had his first conversation with anyone?"

"Yes, I was."

In response to Bentley's next question, Doris Wily recounted the dialogue between Dan and Tony about what happened the night of the attack.

"What did Mr. Kent say in response to a question that Mr. Davies asked concerning who the attacker might be?"

"He said he thought it was Jerry," the nurse answered.

"Just to clarify, Ms. Wily, by 'Jerry', we're referring to the defendant in this case?"

"Yes."

"Is there anything else?"

"Yes. Mr. Kent said…'The words shouted just before I was hit, which I'll never forget were, *I told you to keep your hands off her*! Who else could have said that?' was the way he put it."

In response to a final question from Allan Bentley, the nurse stated that Dan Davies made a comment that these words were compelling and then told Tony that traces of his blood had been found on Jerry Hunter's fireplace shovel.

"Thank you, Ms. Wily. This concludes our testimony for the day, your honor."

"Mr. Wilcox?" the judge asked, looking at the defense attorney.

Dan turned his gaze from the nurse to Jason Wilcox, anticipating the response. The lawyer shook his head. *That figures,* Dan thought. *Wilcox is not going to attempt to refute anything that Doris Wily has stated, especially since it's been corroborated by other testimony. While damaging, it still doesn't prove conclusively that Jerry committed the crime.* Dan surmised, by the way the young attorney slumped into his chair before being roused by the bailiff's voice to announce the court's adjournment, that Wilcox felt the state's testimony was damaging and it would be difficult to muster a strong challenge.

Dan looked at Jerry, reflecting on how stoic and silent he had been for the entire day's proceeding, unlike Susan who was so emotionally distraught during her first trial day. Suddenly, Jerry's head fell into his hands as the judge and jury filed out of the courtroom. Dan cringed slightly as he saw tears slowly stream down the side of Jerry's face and neck. Dan started to muse about what Jerry might be thinking. *He's kept his emotions and feelings in check, but is now feeling the intense pressure of a criminal trial and thinking about the possibility of spending a long time in jail and never returning to his job, Hunter's Point, his son, and Susan.*

Chapter 23

On Tuesday evening, a few hours after court had adjourned, Dan and Miriam met at another of their favorite restaurants. Dan had told Miriam he would give her a summary of the opening day events for each of the two trials, since she felt she could not attend.

"So, you said there were seven witnesses?"

"Yes," he replied. "It started with Tony, next was Anita, then me, and just before lunch a deposition from Jon was read by the Assistant D.A. Bill Jenkins testified after lunch and the day ended with the doctor (Callahan) and Doris Wily, the nurse who was with me when Tony came out of his coma and began to talk."

"So…any 'smoking guns'?"

"Plenty…where do I start?"

"Why not at the beginning."

"Alright…here goes." As he had done the previous evening, Dan recapped the highlights of the day's proceedings, taking breaks to eat his meal when she would chime in and ask questions about certain aspects of the testimony.

"My goodness," Miriam exclaimed when he had finished. "While I still have a hard time believing that the man I was married to for so long could commit this type of crime, this seems to be a very tight case. Kind of like the one against Susan."

"Yes, it certainly appears to be. This case against Jerry has been *so* tight that maybe I haven't stepped back and given enough thought to anyone else who might have gone after Tony."

"Well, who could that possibly be?"

"I don't know, but maybe I need to think about this some more."

"Hmmm…well, I was shocked to think that Jerry could react like he's alleged to have. But I can tell you, based on being married to him for almost twenty-five years, he can have a volatile personality at times. So, it's possible that he could have just lost it for a brief time and done something like this. If he did, I'll bet he had serious regrets when he got back to thinking more clearly. I've seen him *very* angry a few times and was a little scared—not that I felt in any real danger—just uncomfortable, and everyone says he was definitely enraged when he learned that Susan was 'doing it' with Tony."

"Yeah...maybe so. One thing I started to think about is that when Bill Jenkins gave his testimony, he mentioned that most of the fingerprints taken from the shovel were from Jerry's *left* hand."

"So, what's significant about that? He's naturally left-handed and doesn't use his right hand much. If Jerry's prints are all over the fireplace shovel, they would be from making all those fires where he would stoke the logs with the shovel using his left hand."

"I guess that makes sense. Now that you mention it, I do recall Jerry lunging at Tony like a left-handed fighter would that night he came to the cottage and threatened him. I hadn't given that any thought." Dan sat back in his chair, as they had now just about finished their dinner. "Anything else you'd like to know? If not, I'm almost ready to leave. Can we forego coffee and dessert tonight?"

"Sure. Just one more thing."

"What's that?"

"Are we staying together tonight? I've missed you this past week."

"Don't take this the wrong way, but I'm emotionally and physically drained, and am going to bed real early. I don't think I'd be much of a companion tonight. I also have to get up early tomorrow morning and do a couple of things."

"Okay, but I'll be at home...by myself...if you change your mind."

Dan awoke startled. He squinted and looked at the clock on the night table next to his bed. It was four-thirty in the morning and dark outside. He had been dreaming and suddenly awoke with some startling thoughts...*Left handed...the package with the logo... that thing in the closet...the first confrontation...the Friday night timeline...Susan's look and those words...idle threats...*that he said silently as he rolled over in bed. *Am I missing anything?* He checked the alarm to make sure it was set for six-thirty. *Let me sleep for two more hours. I'll call Wilcox and Jenkins at home after I take a shower and shave, and then maybe the hospital. I'll call Katherine after breakfast. I need to get hold of Jon also, but I probably can't reach him until later today. Ah, screw it, I'll call Jon later this morning, even if I have to wake him up!*

Chapter 24

"Katherine…it's Dan. I just finished breakfast and I'd like to come over to your house. There's something we need to talk about."

"Well, why didn't you call me earlier and tell me you were going to come here? I could have made you a nice breakfast. Anita left early today and I ate by myself."

"Sorry, but I didn't want to impose. Besides, I had to make another call and was eating while I was moving around my place doing a couple of things. By the way, Bill Jenkins is going to join us. I just spoke to him and he'll be on his way there shortly. There's something we want to get from Jerry's house and I told him you had a key."

"Yes, I do, and so does Miriam," Katherine said.

"Yeah…I know. I think we'll use yours this morning."

"Alright. I'll see you shortly, then."

Dan soon arrived and Katherine let him in. As he seated himself in Katherine's kitchen, he placed a package of *Sunflower Green Tea* on the table and said, "This is just like the package I bought and gave to you when I was here for the Labor Day weekend barbecue. I've had this one at my home."

"Oh, yes, I remember," the elderly lady replied.

"Do you remember making a comment about the packaging—with the logo on it? You said something about them adding a logo on the front of the package."

"Yes, I remember saying that."

"Do you have the package I brought to you?"

"I have the package of tea, but the outside wrapper has been ripped off and thrown away, which I always do when I open a new package."

"I thought you probably did that, which is why I brought this one. What I'd like you to do is look at this package, with the logo in the upper corner on the front, then close your eyes and see if you can recall whether or not the packages you've been opening for the past several months had this logo on the outer wrapping."

Katherine looked at the packaging with the sunflower logo and then closed her eyes. After a minute or so, she opened them again. "I don't remember seeing that logo on the outer wrapping, even though it's been on all the tea bags that Susan brought here and the ones you brought to me before."

"Are you sure?"

"Well, I can't say that I'm absolutely certain, but I don't believe I've seen this logo on the packages I had been given before. That's why I made a comment about this wrapping when you brought me the package on Labor Day weekend, since it catches your eye. Is this important?"

"It may be. Before I came over here, I called Natalie Ferguson, the owner of the store where this tea has been bought. She hadn't opened the store yet, so I was able to talk to her for a few minutes. I asked her about the package and she went to the shelf where it's stocked and pulled one off and looked at it. What she said was that the packaging for this brand of tea has always had the sunflower logo on it, as long as she's been stocking and selling it. All she sees are the sealed packages that she sells, and she sees a lot of them."

"Hmmm...so how did I get tea with different packaging? Oh, silly me! Now I get it. Susan had to unwrap the package and then wrap it again after poisoning the tea bags, then give me a package that looked as if it had been bought off a store shelf, so it would look like the tea had just been purchased. Since I never saw a package with the sunflower logo—I can't say that I remember what the very first package she brought to me last December looked like—I wouldn't suspect anything. But wouldn't she need some type of device or machine to rewrap the packages of tea?"

"Spoken like a true detective," Dan said, smiling. "But what if it *wasn't* Susan who unwrapped the tea, put poison in the tea bags, and then rewrapped the package?"

"Then who?"

"That's one of the reasons Jenkins is coming here. In fact, I think he's here now. I hear the sound of a car approaching." Dan looked out of Katherine's kitchen window and saw the police cruiser come to a stop and the state trooper get out of the car.

Dan got up and met the state trooper as he was about to knock on the back door, opened it and let him in.

"Good morning, Officer," Katherine greeted him.

"Good morning to you, Mrs. Kent. You look well and I hope you're feeling better. Dan has told me that you're coming along fine and that you did very well in court."

"I'm a tough old girl," she said, smiling at the two men.

"Mrs. Kent, I have a new search warrant for the Hunters' home and Dan mentioned you had a key to get in."

"Let me go get it."

Dan and Bill walked briskly toward Jerry's house, the trooper holding the key to the front door in his hand. As they stood on the front porch, Dan said, "I'll stay here. Go up the stairs and turn right into the first bedroom. The thing I mentioned to you was in the far left corner of the closet in the back of the bedroom, next to the rear window, and there was a roll of foil or some other wrapping next to it."

Five minutes later, Jenkins walked out of the front door carrying a large heavy-duty plastic bag. In it was a dark brown device with a handle—a foot or so in length and weighing about fifteen pounds—a roll of clear plastic wrap, and a small black object with a shape similar to that of a pistol. After Dan locked the door and they were off the front porch, Jenkins opened the large bag. He nodded at Dan, who nodded back.

"Just as I thought…a shrink wrap machine, with the shrink wrap on the side and a heat gun," Dan said. "That's why Katherine never saw the logo on the herbal tea packaging when she opened it. The original wrapper had been taken off and replaced with the clear stuff you're carrying in that bag. That's the only outer wrapper she ever saw, until I bought a new package and delivered it to her. I think this may be a break-through for the first case, even though I can't yet figure out the fingerprints on the syringe. That's still a mystery. Let's put this bag and its contents in your car. Then I want to take you to where Tony was attacked on the property. I have a hunch about the other case."

The two men walked at the edge of the rocky embankment near the verandah of Katherine's house. The ocean was to their right and the house to their left. Dan put out his hand, signaling Bill to stop.

"Okay, Bill, now I'm standing where Tony was hit. We went over this in detail on Labor Day weekend. If you climb down, or if your eyesight is really good, you can see some blood stains on the rocks where he fell, because the sea water doesn't come up far enough to wash them away. Now, make believe that I'm Tony and you're the attacker with the fireplace shovel in your hand. Get a branch from under the bushes over there."

Dan stood at the edge of the rocky embankment where Tony was the night of the attack while Bill got a broken branch that was lying underneath one of the bushes. "What do you want me to do now, Dan?" the trooper asked, a puzzled look on his face.

"Slowly make a motion like you're going to hit me on the left temple, just like Tony got hit." Dan pointed to the spot on his head as he spoke.

Jenkins raised the branch slowly, with his right hand on the branch to guide it, and then let it descend slowly to where it just touched Dan's left temple."

"OK, Bill, hold it there and turn around and see how close you are to the bushes." Bill looked and nodded. "Now, hit me with a left-handed blow," Dan said.

"That's not easy to do from this angle," the trooper said, as he turned to take a left-handed position, his left hand now on the branch. He grazed the bushes as he took the branch back, causing it to veer off its plane. When he swung his arms down again, the branch missed the spot he had touched before. "OK, so it's hard—almost impossible—to hit you on the left temple from this position if I do it left-handed. I'd probably hit you on the forehead due to the angle that the branch, or shovel, would descend. So, what's the point of all this?"

"The point is that Jerry is left-handed. Further, as a result of surgery he had three years ago, his right arm and shoulder were so weakened that he doesn't have the strength to deliver the type of right-handed blow that must have hit Tony—not with the fireplace shovel, anyway. He didn't even stoke the wood in his fireplace with his right hand, which is why all the fingerprints you found on the shovel were from his left hand."

"How do you know this?"

"I called Jerry's lawyer at home early this morning, just before I phoned you. He got hold of Jerry, who told him what I just said to you. Then I called the hospital and got Dr. Callahan on the phone. He's the one who treated Tony the night he was attacked."

"Of course, I remember. So, what did he tell you?"

"With Jerry's approval, which I got through the attorney, Callahan ran a medical history, which confirmed that Jerry had major rotor cuff surgery in his right shoulder at a Fairfield County hospital. Even after a year of therapy, his upper right side never regained its normal strength, which rendered him virtually left-hand dominant."

"Son-of-a-gun! So, where does this leave us?"

"Well, there is a male member of the Hunter family—a younger one—who's a baseball player with a strong right arm and batting swing, from whose closet you got the shrink wrap machine. This person is also the same size and has a similar facial appearance, except for an age difference, to Jerry."

"I think we better call the defense attorneys, and maybe the district attorneys, also."

"Yeah, I think so. I'm going to call Jon at his college, even if I have to wake him up this morning. I want to get some information on a trip to Rhode Island that Friday night in late June when Tony was attacked."

Bill Jenkins walked to his car as Dan went back to the main house to say good-bye to Katherine. As he entered the kitchen, he saw Miriam sitting at the table. She smiled at him. "Hi," she said affectionately. "Katherine had to powder her nose and said you and the state trooper were in 'the house' searching for something." Miriam used that expression since she could not speak of her former home as hers anymore.

"Yeah, there was something we wanted to take a look at."

"Did you find it?"

"We think so."

"Care to tell me what?"

"Oh, just something in one of the bedroom closets."

"Can you be more specific?"

"I could, but my old cop instincts tell me not to."

"Is this related to the cases?"

"It may be. I'm not sure yet, but Bill is going to do some checking."

"So, what are your plans for today? Any time for me?"

Dan gazed at her. "Maybe tonight. How about dinner at my place?

I have to make a couple of calls and may have to do one or two other things. There's a witness the state is bringing in to Susan's case—some type of expert on poisons I think—that I may want to listen to, so I may make an appearance at the courthouse today. Can we leave it kind of loose on the time? I'll call you later."

"Alright. By the way, I missed you last night. It was lonely, and I enjoy it when we're together."

"Likewise, but I had a very fitful sleep last night which I thought might happen. As I indicated at dinner, I would not have been good company."

"Well, I think you're always good company," Miriam said, smiling at him as Katherine walked back into the kitchen.

Back at his home at Condor's Nest, Dan called a cell phone located at a college in southern New Hampshire. "Jon, this is Dan... You mean you're actually awake? It's not quite ten-thirty and it's the morning. I'm impressed."

"I have morning classes every day except Friday, so I'm always up early—except for Friday and the weekend," Jon responded. "In fact, I just got back to my dorm room from my nine o'clock class."

"I need to ask you to do something," Dan said.

"Yeah, what's that?"

"Do you remember telling me about your girlfriend Nicole being driven to Rhode Island that night back in June when your father was attacked... when we were at the hospital together?"

"Yeah... of course... how could I forget that? Oh shit, I actually did forget that for a moment at the hospital. Jeez, that was probably the worst night in my life. So, what is it you want to know?"

"I'd like you to ask Nicole if she remembers when—that is, what time—she was picked up at her place here at the shore and when she got to wherever it was she was going. Ask her to be as specific as possible."

"Westerly... I know it was Westerly, which is where a good friend of hers has a summer place."

"That's right, I think I remember you saying she had been driven to Westerly."

"Why do you want to know that?"

"I'd like to tell you *why* I want to know this after you tell me *when* she was picked up here at the shore and *when* she arrived at her friend's place in Westerly."

"Is this detective stuff?"

"Maybe."

"Is there anything else you want to know?"

"Yes, but it can wait until you answer the first question," Dan said.

Later that afternoon, Dan, Bill Jenkins, and the four lawyers on the Hunter cases were seated at a conference table in the law offices of Wilcox & Wilcox. The two prosecutors along with Bill Jenkins were on one side of the large oval table, and the two defense attorneys hosting the meeting plus Dan were on the other side.

Joel Stein, the eldest and most senior of the lawyers, spoke first. "So, Officer Jenkins and Mr. Davies, you think you may have evidence for both cases that has a major impact on the guilt or innocence of the accused people?"

Jenkins nodded and then looked at Dan, indicating that he should talk first on their behalf. Dan cleared his throat and began speaking slowly. "As I listened to the testimony in both cases, I started to ask myself if everyone had thought through all the possible scenarios for the commission of these crimes. Last night, I started to piece together bits of a puzzle that's been occupying my mind for the past week or so, as the two trials got underway and as I thought about all that the Kents and Hunters have been through."

Stein, eager to get to something concrete, interrupted. "Excuse me, but you said you may have a breakthrough in each case, which is of keen interest to me…and, I know, to my fellow attorneys."

"I'm sorry," Dan said, "but, we've got some lives at stake here and I want to be sure that, first, I've got something solid to offer and second, that I state it clearly. So, if I go slowly, please forgive me, as I want to get it right."

"Alright…understood," Stein said. "It's just that the quicker we can get to the meat of what you and Officer Jenkins think you have, the better it is for the lawyers who are sitting here and, perhaps, the two people who are on trial."

"Then let me try to get to the 'meat,'" Dan replied. "Regarding the poisoning case in which Susan Hunter has been charged, we've found this shrink wrap machine in Michael Hunter's bedroom closet that is going to be tested for fingerprints, and that we have with us here." As Dan spoke, Jenkins went to the rear of the conference room and, after donning a pair of rubber gloves, took the device from the plastic bag.

"How do you know it was Michael Hunter's bedroom closet and, even if it is, how do you know it wasn't planted there by Susan Hunter?" Stein asked.

"We believe it's Michael's closet because his mother—that is, his birth mother who lived in the house for many years and is now back at Hunter's Point, told me it was his bedroom when she sent me there looking for a sweater to wear one chilly evening," Dan said.

"We don't know for sure that it was *not* planted by Susan, which is why we need to test it for fingerprints," Jenkins interjected.

"When can you get the fingerprint test done?" the D.A. asked.

"Tomorrow," Jenkins answered. "We can put other lab work aside if we have to."

"Anything else?" Stein asked.

"Just some potentially corroborating statements from Katherine Kent and Natalie Ferguson indicating that the tea purchased from the natural food store was unwrapped, poisoned and then rewrapped using the machine sitting on the conference table."

"Alright...so noted," Stein muttered, writing on a pad as he spoke. "What about the other case?"

Jenkins nodded to Dan, indicating that the retired detective should resume talking.

"We've heard testimony from Tony Kent and the doctor who treated him about a blow from a blunt object hitting him on the left temple."

Now, it was the assistant district attorney's turn to interject. "Yes. That testimony was given under my questioning."

Dan resumed speaking. "On Labor Day weekend, I asked Tony to take me to the exact spot where the attack occurred and give me as much detail as he could remember. When I heard the testimony about the fingerprints on the fireplace shovel being from Jerry's left hand, and then learned that Jerry is very much a left-handed person with little strength in his right arm and shoulder, I started thinking about how a left-handed person could deliver the type of blow that struck Tony. So, this morning, I brought Officer Jenkins to the scene to re-enact the attack and get his thoughts. Bill, maybe you want to continue."

The state trooper gave a recount of how they went over the attack on Tony from the perspectives of both a right-handed and left-handed person as the attacker, explaining how the bushes bordering the main house rendered it difficult, if not impossible, for a left-handed person to strike Tony Kent on the left temple. He concluded by saying he now felt it was unlikely that Jerry Hunter could have delivered the blow to Tony.

"So, any thoughts as to who may have done it?"

Dan looked at Bill, then at Allan Bentley, and said, "The same young person whose closet the shrink wrap machine came from...and who knew about the threats that his father made to Tony...and who is the spitting image of his father. He had access to everything in the Hunter house since he lived there, and he had a lot of free time if he was inclined to do bad things there since Jerry—his father—traveled a lot and Susan worked a few days during the week. His real mother is now back at Hunter's Point, much to his delight since he has apparently been carrying a grudge against both his father and Susan after his real mother and Jerry divorced. His whereabouts at the time of the attack on Tony Kent may be in question, and he's an accomplished baseball player with, as his mother stated to me recently, 'a strong right arm and batting swing.'"

"I see," the assistant district attorney mused, now looking into the eyes of his colleague Joel Stein. "One perpetrator for two related crimes and a good frame to get rid of those he despises and get back the one he loves. Not bad, if he could pull it off," he then said softly, shaking his head in disbelief.

Stein leaned forward and looked first at the two defense attorneys, who had been silent so far, and then at Officer Jenkins. "I'd say it's rather amazing that anyone, especially such a young fellow, could hoodwink so many people. Putting that aside, we all want justice to be done, that's for sure. In spite of what some people feel about our office, we're not just trying to get a conviction to put someone away and get the cases resolved. If we're going to convict someone, we want it to be the person who actually *committed* the crime—or crimes, in this instance. While I've been confident all along that we've charged the right people in these crimes, maybe there's a possibility we've overlooked some important evidence and motive. So, having said all this, what do you propose?" Stein looked straight into the eyes of Thad Wilcox as he uttered the question.

The senior of the two young Wilcox brothers leaned back in his chair, stretching out his long legs and folding his hands in front of him. "I think we should subpoena Michael Hunter for questioning and consider him a suspect, confirm what Mr. Davies said regarding Katherine Kent's and Natalie Ferguson's latest statements about the outer packaging on the tea—which we can do with depositions—run the fingerprint test on the shrink wrap machine, retest the fireplace shovel to see if we can pick up any other fingerprints, and ask the judges for a continuance in both cases. With the testimony this morning, I believe that the prosecution has gone through most, if not all, of its witnesses in both cases, subject to calling back one or two, and we're just about to begin. These new revelations obviously affect what we will do and we need some time to change course and prepare a revised defense. Do you agree with this, Jason?"

The younger Wilcox nodded.

Stein also nodded, indicating his agreement with what Thad Wilcox had proposed. "Allan and I will go to the judges and get a continuance. We'll ask for a week. We can tell them we have a suspect who needs to be questioned and who's out of state, and then give them a synopsis of what was said here today without revealing any substantive information. By the way, Allan, you did tell me that Michael Hunter is a college student in the Boston area, didn't you?" Bentley nodded.

The attorneys looked at each other to determine if anyone had anything else to say. Dan noticed this and stated, "There's one ticklish question that I still can't figure out. How did Susan Hunter's fingerprints—and no one else's—get on the syringe, if she wasn't the one who injected the poisoning into the tea bags?"

All the attorneys looked silently at Dan…and then at each other—each of them hoping for someone else to say something insightful and revealing. Sensing their puzzled states of mind, Dan said, "I don't have an answer, but we should all give it some serious thought, since the evidence says that the poison was injected into the tea bags with the syringe. Keep in mind that the match to the paint thinner is too direct to be ignored, even if all the other things we've brought up today implicate someone else."

Dan returned home after the meeting with the attorneys and had just turned on the gas grill to barbecue a steak and grill some potatoes. Picking up the receiver after the fourth ring, he recognized the number on the small caller ID monitor that sat next to his phone in the living room. "Hello? Oh, hey Jon. How are you doing?"

"I think I got the info from Nicole that you're looking for."

"Okay…shoot!"

Jon told Dan that it had taken a while to get hold of her, as she was studying most of the day in the library and had turned off her cell phone. He said she remembered the time because Michael was late picking her up. They were going to leave between nine and nine fifteen, since Nicole wanted to get to her friend's house by ten or so for a party and it's about a forty-five to fifty minute drive to Westerly. When Michael didn't show up by nine-thirty, Nicole called his cell phone and got his voice mail. He called her around nine forty-five and apologized for being late, without giving any real reason…said something like he was tired, wanted to take a quick nap and fell asleep without setting the alarm and slept longer than he had planned to. Dan paced the floor as Jon went on to say that Michael picked Nicole up a little after ten and they got to Westerly just before eleven o'clock. He said that Nicole remembered that time because someone at her friend's place in Westerly was watching the Red Sox game and it was just ending when she got there. Because they were late, Michael walked her into the house in Westerly to make sure she got settled in there alright and to meet her friend. She also remembers that the friend told Michael the final score, since he's a 'Sox' fan, and that he said he was going to watch the eleven o'clock news now that the game was over."

"Thanks, Jon. I appreciate your doing this."

"Now, are you going to tell me *why* you wanted to know this?"

"I need a couple more days before I can say anything or tell you about what we're now investigating," Dan said. "There are lawyers, the ones who took your deposition plus the two working on Susan's case, and the state police—your buddy Jenkins—involved, so I'm not at liberty to discuss everything that's going on. Let me just say that there have been some new developments in the cases."

"Are you saying that it's not just open and shut against Susan and Uncle Jerry?"

"I'm not saying anything at this time, but you can come to that conclusion if you wish. There have been some new leads that need to be tracked down. I *will* let you know when I can speak more freely or when things come to light in court. I can tell you that there's going to be a delay in both trials until these new leads are run down and conclusions are reached about the new developments."

"Does any or all or this involve Michael?"

As Jon had finished asking the question, Dan heard a soft knock at the back door. He knew it was Miriam, since he had confirmed dinner together at his place just before starting the meeting with the lawyers. He also knew he had to end this conversation with Jon, since she wouldn't wait for him, but rather would enter the house herself and soon be next to him in the living room. The gentle knock on the door was her way of signaling that she was present and about to enter.

"No comment. Now I've got to go, so I don't burn all my propane before starting to cook dinner. You stay focused on school and I'll attend to what's going on here. I *will* be back in touch with you."

Dan was just hanging up the phone as Miriam entered the living room. She went over to him and gave him a gentle kiss on the cheek, which he returned.

"So, Mr. Wonderful, what's on the menu?"

"Steak and grilled potatoes, plus a salad if you'd like to make it."

"I'd love to."

Dan grilled outside on his deck while Miriam prepared a salad inside the house. When the food was almost ready, he walked in to get some salt and pepper, but she was not in the kitchen. He looked around. *She probably had to go to the bathroom,* he said to himself. He then glanced out the window of the dining area that looked into the driveway and saw her closing her car door.

She was carrying a cardigan as she walked through the back door and into the kitchen. "I left my sweater in the car and thought I'd need it if we eat outside and then take a walk. The September evenings are starting to get cool."

"Did you forget? You have one here. In fact, I mentioned it when we spoke earlier."

"You're right...I did forget. Please don't tell me I'm getting old and forgetful. Just keep that sweater here. I'm sure I'll need it on another evening."

"I'm almost ready," he said. "Just a little salt and pepper on the steak and we should be all set. The potatoes are just about done."

"The salad is just about done, too. Is vinaigrette dressing okay?"

"Sounds good," Dan replied.

Their conversation was light, with a few comments about the trials, nothing deep. Dan mentioned that Jenkins had called him and told him of a meeting with the attorneys. He said that some new evidence was being discussed, but he didn't know the specifics and Jenkins would not tell him. He didn't like lying, but didn't feel he should let on to her that Michael was now a suspect. He surmised that her reaction would be to call Michael, which neither the attorneys nor the state police wanted, nor would he for that matter. Jenkins knew of their relationship and had asked Dan if he was going to see Miriam during the next couple of days. He cautioned Dan to watch her and see if she acted strange in any way when he made comments about the trials. Dan commented that he had been thinking the same. He was always suspicious when pursuing a lead or trying to establish a trail for clues that arose in a case.

Miriam said she understood and didn't probe. Dan mentioned that the trials would be delayed for a week, which drew a startled response from her. When she asked why, he responded that it had to do with the meeting that afternoon and whatever evidence or findings that had been uncovered. He said that Jenkins had called to inform him of the delay in the court proceedings.

They had wanted to take a walk and stretch their legs after eating, as it was a beautiful September evening, with less than an hour of sunlight left. They soon reached the edge of the beach at Condor's Nest. They embraced and held each other and then walked back to Dan's house. Miriam said she wanted to watch a movie on television that was going to start in about half-an-hour, but Dan had no interest in it. He was standing by her car as she started to back out of his driveway and noticed a slanting streak of sunlight come through her windshield and reflect as light does when it hits a metal object. It blinded him for an instant and he had to turn away. When he turned back, she was waving at him as she drove slowly away from his home.

Chapter 25

Late the following afternoon, Bill Jenkins called Dan Davies.

"Dan, it's Bill. I've got something that's going to be of interest to you."

"Okay…give it to me."

"We ran fingerprint tests today on the shrink wrap machine and ran the fireplace shovel through another battery of tests."

"And?"

"We've got fingerprints from both hands, but mostly from a right hand on the machine, and they're not Susan Hunter's."

"Do you know whose they are?"

"No, they don't match anyone that's on file."

"And, of course, Michael Hunter's prints wouldn't be on file since he's probably never been in trouble," Dan said, snickering.

"You got it. And, one more item: when we ran a retest of the fireplace shovel we found a print from the forefinger of a right hand. It was faint and barely discernible, which is probably why we missed it the first time. And, guess what?"

"It matches the print of the same finger you found on the shrink wrap machine."

"See, I told you that your detective instincts are still there."

"Well, maybe we're getting close to a hunch of mine for the past couple of days," Dan said with a sigh.

"Maybe we are," the state trooper replied. "I have to tell you, I was convinced, just as I think the prosecutors were, that we had all the hard evidence against Jerry and Susan Hunter. I guess it proves you have to follow all the trails. What got you on this track of suspecting Michael Hunter?" Jenkins asked.

"I guess the 'perfect fit' nature of all the accusations and evidence, in both cases. Don't think I just came up with his name out of the blue. It kind of developed over time. As I started to give these cases some serious thought, which I must admit I didn't do until they were close to going to trial, the pieces were just fitting so perfectly and it all seemed so obvious. My experience, though, reminded me that if something seems too good to be true, then maybe it is. Take the fireplace shovel, which Jerry had waved at Tony when he first threatened him and which we now know Michael saw his father do at the first confrontation. If the shovel had been missing from the Hunter home, alarm bells would have been set off. So, if Jerry were going to use the shovel to attack Tony, he'd have to return it, but probably would have wiped it clean of blood from Tony's head if that's possible to do. The trace of Tony's blood on the shovel was a great find for the investigation. But if Jerry really had attacked Tony, maybe he would have used something else and gotten rid of it, so there'd be no DNA evidence. If I had been the attacker, I probably would have used something else. Then there would have been a massive search for the weapon used in the attack. Having the shovel there with Tony's blood on it and Jerry's fingerprints—and no one else's, until now, that is—made this part of the case very tight and straightforward from a prosecution perspective, as Allan Bentley inferred in his opening remarks. I think we all assumed that Jerry was so enraged that he grabbed what was closest to him to get the job done and, when we found a combination of blood and fingerprints, the proof of who committed the crime was right there in front of us, especially since Jerry had no verifiable alibi. But, as we're now starting to believe, maybe it wasn't exactly what we thought it was. Same thing with the comment Jerry presumably yelled at Tony just before he struck him. Heck, anyone who overheard the threats and knew what was going on could have shouted that."

Dan paused for a moment, then continued. "The bugaboo in trying to link Michael to the other case is the fact that Susan's prints are all over the syringe, which has to be the implement that was used to inject the poison into the tea bags. The matches to the holes on the teabags and the poison itself are rock solid. The syringe, and everything linked to it, is one of the reasons I didn't really dispute or challenge the original evidence when it was put together. The only theory I can come up with is that if Michael did, in fact, do the poisoning, then he would have had to get her to grip the syringe when she was either dead drunk—not likely—or sound asleep, which I guess is a possibility if he tried hard and had enough opportunity. If he stayed awake after she went to bed, then it could be possible to do that. Pulling this one off was very clever. It got me believing that Susan was guilty. We should get someone to question Susan as to her sleeping habits and find out if she's a sound sleeper."

"Getting back to Michael," Bill said, "I think you mentioned he goes to college just outside of Boston?"

"Yes, I can give you the name and address of the college."

"Alright, Dan, please do that. I know a couple of people on the Massachusetts force. I'll get him picked up and brought in for fingerprints and questioning. I'm also going home after I make the call. I feel like I'm coming down with something. Feels like the flu, although it's supposedly too early for that."

"Oh, I don't know about that. I've heard that people can get flu-like symptoms almost anytime. I hope you feel better. Keep me posted as to Michael's situation."

"I will, although I'm going to have to send someone else to bring him back here. I've got a full calendar, and if I don't feel better, I may be in bed tomorrow and the next day. Have you met Jim Newhouser? He'll be the one going to Boston to get Michael and bring him back here, if we decide to do that."

"I think you may have introduced me to him once, when I was at the barracks, but I can't say I know him," Dan said. "If anything, we just said hello to each other. One item you don't want to forget is to call Bentley, to see if you need an extradition warrant for Michael or you can bring him back here from Massachusetts without one if, based on the outcome of your questioning, you have justification for an indictment. He's over 18, but under 21, I believe."

"Yeah, you're right. I need to do that. This flu bug, or whatever it is, must be getting to me and dulling my mind. So, Bentley will be my first call and then I'll contact my guy in Massachusetts, unless the prosecutor wants to handle this situation himself. The way I'm feeling, I really don't care who gets it done."

Dan and Katherine were having late afternoon tea on Katherine's verandah on Friday.

"What do you mean 'new development'?" Katherine asked. "I thought all the evidence was in and the cases were moving along. Are you suggesting that someone other than Jerry and Susan could have committed the crimes? Could there be an accomplice? Is there more that one accomplice? What is it you're saying?"

Dan looked into the eyes of the elderly woman he truly liked, admired and considered to be a friend, and said, "Well, the evidence is moving along…sort of. Katherine, I can't get into the details, but sometimes in the type of cases we're dealing with here, the attorneys feel a need to look at the evidence in a different light and, if their argument is compelling enough, they can convince the judge and the other side in the case to grant a delay in the court proceedings. This is what's happened here." He needed to twist the truth and use the attorneys as a decoy, since he didn't want to let on to her that it was *his* challenging of the evidence and looking at the cases in a different light that caused the new development and the continuance of the trials. That would demand an explanation and cause him to shut off communication with her, which he didn't want to do.

"I still don't understand everything you're saying, but I guess that's not surprising for a dumb old girl like me." Katherine had a twinkle in her eye and a wry smile on her face as she spoke.

"Yeah, 'dumb and old' like a fox!" Dan exclaimed. Just then, his cell phone rang. "Excuse me for a moment," he said, looking at the face of the small device and recognizing who was calling.

"Certainly. I'll take the cups to the kitchen while you take your call."

"Hello, this is Dan Davies…yes, Bill, what's up? I've been waiting to hear from you. And, I'm sorry to say that you don't sound too well. How are you feeling?"

The voice at the other end was raspy and sounded fatigued. "I feel terrible and may have to go home after this phone call, but I felt I had to see this thing through today. I've got the weekend to try to recuperate. What an exciting prospect. I was looking forward to teeing it up tomorrow, but it looks like I may be spending this weekend in bed. We got the location of Michael Hunter at his college and made all the arrangements to pick him up and get him to a state police barracks just outside Boston, as we had discussed. It took the entire morning to get all the logistics and paperwork in place, which we had to do because these colleges shut down for the weekend as far as the administration goes. If we hadn't gotten this thing going today, we ran the risk of waiting until Monday. We had Michael's class schedule and figured that we'd pick him up after his two o'clock class this afternoon, outside the classroom building, making the pick-up as non-confrontational as possible. We talked to the administration and they asked us to do it this way, rather than barging into the class and disrupting things for the professor and the other students. The guy I mentioned to you, Newhouser, left here late this morning to be there from our end."

"So, is Michael in custody?"

"No."

"What do you mean, no? I thought you said you had everything in place."

"We did…and still do."

"Then, what's the problem?" Dan queried.

"He's gone," Bill answered. "He apparently took off this morning. His roommate said he got up, had breakfast and then left. He told him he had to go off campus to get something he needed and would be back for a late morning class and the class at two in the afternoon, which the roommate is in. Another guy, who's a mutual friend, told the roommate at lunch that Michael skipped the late morning class, which he thought was unusual, since Michael apparently likes this class and the instructor and always attends. They went to the student parking lot after lunch and noticed that Michael's car was gone. They didn't think much of it, though, and the roommate had to get some information from the library in preparation for the afternoon class, so he went there and then to the class."

"Anything else?"

"Yes, Michael took most of his clothing and shoes with him, along with his shaving kit and a suitcase, which the roommate noticed when he returned to the dorm room after class this afternoon, and was questioned by the college administrator who's our contact."

"So, Michael's gone…after we had our session with the attorneys, but before getting served by the police…and after I had my phone conversation with Jon…and after I had dinner with Miriam at my place. Both asked me about the new developments, and Jon specifically asked me if they involved Michael, since I was getting information on the time line of a trip that his girlfriend took with Michael the night Tony was attacked. Miriam asked me one or two questions, but did no probing at all when I told her the trials had been delayed. If I had told Miriam anything to identify Michael, I'm sure she would have called him, which was why I didn't say anything that connected him to the new developments. Could Jon have called Michael and maybe inadvertently said something that caused him to bolt? They were getting close at the end of the summer and shared a lot about these cases, so that's possible. I'll call him when we get done talking and then I'll stop over at Miriam's on my way home from here. Oh, I didn't tell you…I'm at Hunter's Point, at Katherine's house. We were just finishing afternoon tea when your call came in and she's in the kitchen now, so she can't overhear this conversation. I told her about some new development in the cases, but was evasive with her and blamed it on the attorneys, so she really doesn't know anything about what's going on."

"OK, Dan. Why don't you call me at home if you have anything after you've had a chance to talk to Jon and Miriam. I'm getting sicker by the minute and am going to leave now."

"Will do," Dan replied. After hanging up the phone he thought, *this is puzzling*.

Katherine walked back onto the verandah as Dan was getting up to leave. He walked over to her and gave her a gentle hug. Then, patting his stomach, he said…"That's it for this week. There's only room for one slice of those pies of yours each week…well, maybe two if we make up a special occasion. I've got to go now, so say hello to Anita for me when she gets home tonight, and I hope both of you have a nice weekend. The weather is supposed to be beautiful—a real nice September weekend at the shore. Let's enjoy it, since who knows how many good ones are left? By the way, have you seen Miriam today?"

"No, I haven't. I took an early morning walk to Rocky Bar—I missed not seeing you there—and noticed that her car was gone when I returned. I called her around noon to ask her to join us this afternoon for tea, but there was no answer, so she must have gone somewhere. She sometimes tells me when she's going out, especially if it's a Friday and she's going to a store to pick up something for the weekend, and asks me if there's anything she can get for me on her way back. But she didn't do that today."

Dan walked past his car to Miriam's cottage. Her car wasn't there. He went to the front door and looked in the window on the right side of the door, then on the left side. He couldn't see anyone inside. He turned the latch to open the door. It was locked. *That's strange,* he said to himself. *No one here ever locks the door during the day, even when they go out for a while.*

He walked to his car, got in and closed the door. He pulled out his cell phone to call Jon. As the call went through, he got Jon's voice mail message. After listening to the message and waiting for the tone, he said, "Jon, this is Dan. Please call me at my home phone when you get this message. I need to ask you another question."

As Dan walked into his house, he could hear the phone ringing in the living room. "Hello…Hi there, Jon. Thanks for calling me back."

"What's up, Mr. D.?" came the voice from the cell phone in southern New Hampshire.

"Have you talked to Michael recently…say, in the last day or two?"

"No. I was going to, but had a quiz to study for and a paper to write, so I didn't get around to it. The last time I spoke with him was over a week ago, on either Saturday or Sunday. We try to speak to each other once a week. Either I call him or he calls me. Why do you ask? Is this related to the question about the trip to Rhode Island that Nicole took with him?"

"Sort of…and maybe something else."

"Here we go with the 'maybe' again. Damn it, Dan, what the hell is going on with Michael and all the shit with Dad and Grandma? Is he connected? Can you stop all this 'maybe' crap and talk straight to me?"

"Oh, jeez, I'm probably going to regret this…and, Jon, you need to *promise me* you won't say a word about this to your dad, grandmother or aunt…but, yes…we think that Michael may…and I emphasize the word *may*…be connected to the crimes. We don't have any real hard evidence yet, but we're putting some pieces together that might implicate him. That's why so much is maybe."

"Wait a minute. What are you saying?"

"That Michael could be involved in the crimes against your dad, grandmother and aunt."

Dan could hear a gasping sound from the other phone.

"How could that be? How could Michael be involved with Uncle Jerry and Susan? It's impossible…isn't it?" Jon stammered. "He can't stand either of them after what he feels they did to his mother. He kept telling me over and over that he suspected Susan being behind what had happened."

"Maybe he wasn't involved *with* them. Maybe he was working *against* them, and duping people like you…and me."

"Here comes the God-damn 'maybe' again. Can't you say anything else but 'maybe'? You think he duped me into believing a bunch of lies and that he was responsible for everything that happened? I can't believe it. It's not possible…is it?"

"MAYBE…just kidding. Look, Jon, it's possible that, based on some new evidence we've uncovered and are now investigating, that the wrong people were accused."

"Are you shitting me? How? You're saying that Jerry and Susan didn't commit the crimes and Michael did…both of them?"

"We honestly don't know and are going on hunches and circumstantial evidence."

"So, what are you guys doing? Has Michael said anything? Was he brought in for questioning like Susan and Uncle Jerry were?"

"Well, the state cops were going to do that. They were going to take Michael to a state police barracks in Massachusetts and then, based on the answers he gave to the questions they were going to ask him, perhaps bring him back to Connecticut for further questioning and arrest him—again, depending on a number of things. In fact, they had a warrant and were at his college this afternoon, to pick him up and start to question him, but he took off. He wasn't at class this morning or this afternoon. His car is gone and most of his clothes and his suitcase are gone from his dorm room."

"He wasn't there? He left the campus? His clothes are gone? I don't believe it…that lousy, rotten lying bastard. I'll get his freakin' ass if he did this and tricked me into believing it was Uncle Jerry and Susan when it was him all along. How solid is your evidence?"

"We think it may turn out to be *very* solid, but we can't say for sure just yet. Now, the next question is…do you have any idea where he might have gone?" There was silence at the other end. "Jon, do you know where Michael might have gone?" Dan repeated.

"That lousy, rotten, lying bastard," Jon repeated. "My 'cousin.' The one I confided in and was getting close to. He tricked me. Made me want to go after Uncle Jerry and Susan. I'll get him and beat the living crap out of him. I might just kill him if I get any more pissed off than I already am, which 'maybe' will happen."

"Now, listen, damn it. We've been through this before. Stop talking like this!" Dan growled. "I wasn't going to tell you about this new stuff, because I was afraid you might react this way. I did it for one reason: to see if you know where Michael might have gone. We need to find him. We've got state troopers waiting to move if we have an idea of where he might be." Dan could hear the phone go dead just as he finished this sentence.

Damn it…damn it. Dan was almost shouting at himself as he paced around his living room. He slammed the phone on its receiver. *I'll bet he has an idea of where Michael may have gone. Now what?*

Dan paced around his living room for about another five minutes, and then dialed Bill Jenkins's home number. Janet, his wife, answered. "Oh, hello Dan…Bill told me you might be calling. He's quite sick and has a fever. He just fell asleep and desperately needs some rest. He may need to sleep through the night to break the fever."

"Alright," Dan responded. "We should probably let him sleep. Could you ask him to call me when he awakes?"

"I'd be happy to do that. Can you tell me where you are?"

"Yes. Right now I'm at home, so tell him to call my home number and if I'm not there, then try the cell phone. He has both numbers."

Well, I might as well eat something, Dan thought after pacing the living room for a few more minutes and then turning on the TV set for the early evening news. *I need to figure out what to do, if there's anything I can do. I need to find where Michael might have gone. Who would know besides Jon? Who the hell would know?*

As he was finishing his dinner outside on his deck, he heard the phone in the house ring. He walked quickly into the living room. "Hello? Tony, how are you? And *where* are you?"

"I'm in Hartford. Just got out of a meeting and was debating whether I should stay at my place up here or drive back to Hunter's Point. I was fine until a few minutes ago, when I spoke to Jon, who may be in a car, based on background noise I think I heard."

"Oh, shit," Dan muttered. Then, after a moment's thought, he said, "Have you talked to Allan Bentley? Do you know anything about what's going on with your trial?"

"We talked briefly late yesterday. He said there were new developments in the case and some new leads were being tracked down, and there would be a delay in the trial for about a week. While he wasn't very specific as to what these developments were, he did say it was possible that someone other than Jerry and Susan may have attacked me and poisoned Mom and Anita. I tried to get more information, but he wouldn't tell me any more. He said he was sworn to secrecy."

"He is. And so am I. We all are."

"Who's 'we'?"

"The two defense attorneys, the prosecutors, the state trooper—Jenkins—and me."

When Tony asked about why so much secrecy, Dan told him there were potential breakthroughs in both cases, but he wasn't supposed to say anything specific.

"Well, it seems that you told Jon some specifics, so maybe you can share them with me. In case you forgot, I'm the victim in one of the cases and my son may be traveling by car somewhere based on what you said to him."

"Oh, shit," Dan muttered again. "I knew I was taking a risk by telling him about what we're pursuing, but I didn't think I could do anything else under the circumstances."

When Tony confronted him with some very direct comments, Dan admitted that the new developments involved Michael and that he had apparently left his college campus.

After a brief silence, Tony spoke again. "Jon then gave me a disturbing answer to the next question I asked, which was *why* Michael was being sought for questioning."

"How did he answer that?"

"He said that *you* told him Michael was a suspect…in both cases."

"Great! After I asked him not tell anyone what I had told him, especially you!"

"Why did you tell him anything?"

"I felt I had to, to see if he could help me find Michael. He had been pressing me on why I wanted some information about Michael's whereabouts the night you were attacked, and was getting frustrated at my being evasive. We were at a point where I didn't know how I could ask Jon where Michael might go, assuming he was running away, if he had no idea what Michael was running away from."

"So, what did he tell you…about where Michael might go?"

"Nothing. He made threatening remarks about 'getting' Michael. Then, he hung up. Did he tell you anything?"

"Just about the same thing—that's he going to 'get' Michael." After another expletive exclamation from Dan and a query about where Jon might go to "get" his cousin, Tony said he had started to think about a place, after Jon mentioned he had an idea as to where Michael might go just before they hung up.

"So, what's your thinking about a place?" Dan asked.

"Well, at Jon's graduation party, Michael and I were talking for a while, and I mentioned to him that when we were driving back to Hunter's Point from his prep school in Rhode Island, Jon had pointed out a place off Route 1—a hideaway the boys call a 'love nest.' It's an abandoned cottage in the Charlestown area near Wappinger Pond, which is either near or part of Burlingame State Park. Michael seemed to enjoy the brief chat we had had about it and also seemed to know why it's abandoned."

"Why do you think Michael might go there?"

"I'm guessing that's where Jon thinks he may go. Neither of them has ever mentioned any other place like this. It's the only place I can think of that's a possibility. I'm thinking about this place because Jon seemed fairly confident when he spoke. Look, Dan, if there's another place that these two know about and haven't told me, then we could be barking up the wrong tree and off on a wild search that takes us nowhere. But, this is the only place that seems possible to me. Except for a couple of trips to places you can only get to by flying, Jon has really never been anywhere except Connecticut and Rhode Island, and he did spend his high school years in Rhode Island. Oh, and one other thing. Michael made another comment about this place that I remembered."

"What was that?"

"He said that before Memorial Day and after Labor Day you can really have privacy. That tells me the cottages around there must be seasonal and the people who own or rent them do so during the summer, which makes sense. Since it's now almost two weeks after Labor Day, maybe it's private again."

"Maybe you've got something. What does your gut tell you?"

"That my son is on his way there. As you know, he gets crazy when someone attacks his family. I think he feels that Michael has gone there, perhaps to hide for a while, which means he must believe that Michael's involved in these crimes. My only question is how will he get there, since he doesn't have a car?"

"You said it sounded like he was in a car. Do you think he stole one?"

"No, I don't think so…certainly hope not…but he definitely may have borrowed one. Don't ask me from whom, because I don't really know any of the kids he hangs around with at the university since he just got there. He is resourceful, though, and I think we should assume he's in a car and on his way to the hideaway."

"Well, then, I guess we don't have any other choice, do we?" Dan said with a sigh.

"What do you mean?"

"We've got to go to this place and see for ourselves if Michael has gone there…and if Jon is going there…even if we run the risk of going on a wild goose chase. If both of them have gone there and they come into contact, we could have a real donnybrook."

"Are you saying we need to go there tonight?"

"Yes, Tony, tonight! Unless you want your son to deal with this situation all by himself."

"Alright…alright," Tony said. He then gave Dan directions to Burlingame State Park and where he thought the abandoned cottage was. "I think Prosser Trail is the road that leads to Wappinger Pond and the YMCA camp that is apparently very close to the abandoned cottage. Once you find the YMCA camp, look for a group of cottages adjacent to the camp. I think it's close to the water, because Jon mentioned once that they always walk along the edge of the water and sometimes go in when they're at the place. Sorry, this is the best I can do."

"For someone who's never been to a place we're trying to find, that's not bad," Dan said. "I'll get my map out and try to verify what you've told me and trace a route. Now, how are we going to do this—logistically, that is?"

"I'll drive from here," Tony replied. "I'm probably close to an hour and a half away and you're about an hour or so from the beach. I'll stop home first, which is on the way and only takes five or ten minutes off my trip, to pick up something just in case there's a confrontation and then drive there. What about you?"

Dan said he wanted to take a quick shower and would then leave. He told Tony that he would also get something and call Bill Jenkins, to let him know what they were doing and see if he could join them. Then, remembering that Bill was sick with the flu, he told Tony that he would probably be traveling there alone.

"Anything else?"

"Remember to bring your cell phone and have it on. This scenario is so speculative, I don't think I can call another state trooper if Jenkins is too ill to make the trip, especially since we're crossing the state line. You and I are going to have to do this by ourselves. Besides, we're only dealing with Michael. It's not as though we're trying to catch an armed and dangerous criminal…at least I hope not. I can't imagine he has an accomplice. Jenkins didn't mention anything about any other kid taking off with him. I'll call you when I get into Rhode Island to see where you are."

Fresh from a shower, Dan donned a polo shirt, jeans, socks and sneakers, and grabbed a sweatshirt and cap. *Do I really need "Smitty"?* he asked himself. *I would hope not, but I probably should take it. You never know, especially if Michael and Jon wind up going to this place and these kids get out of hand—especially Jon.* He went to the bottom drawer of his dresser to get his long-time companion on the police force, which he had not used since he retired: a five-shot, 38-caliber Smith and Wesson revolver. He reached around but felt nothing. Dropping to his knees, he took out about ten pairs of socks and looked at the bottom of the drawer. It was bare, except for a piece of paper with writing on it. He took the paper out and started to read a handwritten note.

Dan,

By now, you've probably figured things out. Without you, we might have succeeded. After getting to know you, I guessed that you would eventually put the pieces together. I had hoped, however, it might take longer and I could have left in less of a rush. Michael is all I have and I need to protect him and be near him at all costs. I planned it all and guided Michael as he helped me execute the plot.

I hate Jerry for what he did to me and wanted to get back at him and Susan, but I feel terrible about Katherine and Tony. We never intended to harm them so badly. Things got out of control, which I regret, and I'll have to live with hurting people I care for.

We'll be going far away where no one can find us, so I need to say good-bye to you, and tell you that I was getting strong feelings for you—perhaps too strong. I'm sorry I had to take your gun, because I've heard how cops get attached to their weapons, but I felt I needed it for security. I hope I don't ever have to use it, and that I'll be able to return it to you some day.

Affectionately,
Miriam

Dan, still on his knees as he read the note, gasped. He sank to a sitting position on the floor of his bedroom. *Miriam...God almighty, Miriam! This whole scenario and series of terrible events is about her—not Michael—getting revenge. He's just her pawn—the boy who would do just about anything for his mother—in a deceitful plot she concocted and that I didn't see. She's good...very cunning. She was the only woman I had any feelings for at all since Sarah. I wonder if she means what she wrote or if her taking to me was just a ploy to keep me off track and away from the path to what really happened. Was it all a charade? A setup? Shit, I can't believe it!*

Dan then thought about the blinding light sensation through the windshield of Miriam's car last night. *That had to be the slanting rays of the sun shining on "Smitty" and reflecting back to me.* He reasoned that the gun must have been on the floor of her car, and that when the sunlight hit the metal barrel it came back at him. The revolver was sending a signal to him. *Damn it, I should have realized that!* Then it became clear to him. Miriam must have slipped in to the bedroom while he was barbecuing and thought she was making the salad. Returning from her car with a sweater was a ruse, after she had taken the pistol. He then surmised that she must have written the note at her place before coming to his home. He cringed a bit at the thought that Dan Davies—the experienced and supposedly smart detective from the big city—had been outsmarted by a jilted woman.

Getting back to the situation at hand, he knew that he had to forget about his pride and emotions for now, and deal with the reality of traveling to Rhode Island without his trusted weapon to a place that he had never been to and had only a rough idea as to its location. He began to wonder if Miriam and Michael were there together—perhaps rendezvousing on their way to wherever it was they might be going.

What if they are meeting there and Jon arrives before I do? he thought. He shook his head and said to silently himself, *Friday nights are getting a bit too exciting on the sleepy Connecticut shoreline...too much like New York!*

Chapter 26

They walked hand-in-hand along the water's eastern edge, as the sun was beginning to set over the forest on the opposite side of Wappinger Pond. They were alone in a secluded area. Miriam had met Michael earlier in the afternoon and they had gone to purchase a number of items at a local hardware store, storing them in the trunks of their cars along with their luggage. Then, they had gone for an early dinner, since neither of them had eaten all day and they were hungry. Miriam took a few steps away from the edge of the water and motioned for Michael to sit on the sand next to her.

"I need to tell you about where we're going," she said to him. "First, though, do you realize that our lives around here are over, that we're fugitives and can never go back to Hunter's Point, and that you can never go back to the college you left this morning? It's what I told you could be the outcome when we planned all the things that you did for me…for *us*…throughout the early part of this year and the summer."

"I don't want to face up to that, Mom, but I know it's true. Your phone call last night was pretty explicit. That damn shrink-wrap machine …I can't believe I left it in my bedroom closet at the house when we moved into the cottage. It was in the far corner and it's dark there. We were done with the tea poisoning and had Susan indicted. I just forgot about it. Damn, my only mistake! But I guess it only takes one to get caught."

"Maybe yes…maybe no. These plots carry risks and unknowns, which I certainly realized could occur," Miriam said. "I didn't figure that because your father is so left-handed and you're so right-handed, the blow to Tony's head had to come from a right-handed person and would be almost impossible for your father to deliver, with the bushes so close to where you hit Tony. And, neither of us wanted to bring Katherine or Tony to the point of being near death. Maybe that batting swing of yours is a little too strong and you put too much poison in the tea bags. If the injury to Tony and the illness that Katherine suffered hadn't been so severe, then perhaps challenging the evidence and revisiting the investigation, especially by Dan—and I'm sure he has put the pieces of the puzzle together by now—might not have been so intense and we could have gotten Susan and your father convicted of lesser crimes, which would have satisfied the goals we laid out when we conceived this whole thing."

"Yeah, maybe you're right. So, now that we're cooked, where are we going, Mom?"

"Well, my love, it's going to be a lot different from Hunter's Point and Boston, and far away. The one thing that will be similar is that we'll be near the ocean. That was very important to me, and I thought it would also be important to you."

"So, does this place have a name?"

"Yes, it does. Like most locations, it has three names. The first is the country—Canada."

"Canada? Are you kidding?" Michael asked incredulously.

"We're fugitives, Michael...don't forget that. You may have actually committed the crimes, but I'm your accomplice, so I'm as guilty as you are. We're in this together, as I've told you all along. I've got forged papers that make us Canadian citizens. Thank your father for providing the money to pay for them."

"So, where in Canada are we going?"

"To a remote place in the province of New Brunswick."

"New Brunswick? I'm not sure I know exactly where that is."

"You will soon enough. We're going to a spot on the far eastern side of Canada, next to the northern and eastern borders of Maine. The place I found is beautiful. It's near the Bay of Fundy."

"This is like a geography lesson...New Brunswick...Bay of Fundy ...places I barely know exist. So, back to my first question. Does this place you found for us have a name?"

"Yes, it does, and it's the same as a well-known area of Boston."

"Are you going to tell me or do you want me to guess?"

"You've been in the Boston area for a couple of years, so let's see how well you know your local geography. This should be easy for you. What's the area between Fenway Park and Harvard Bridge—the one that crosses over the Charles River?"

Michael smiled at his mother. "You're right, this is easy. That's the Back Bay area. Is that it, Back Bay?"

"Bingo."

"Really? Back Bay in the province of New Brunswick in the country of Canada. That's the spot we're going to?" Michael's head was shaking as he spoke.

"That's it, Son…our new home. I have a map in my car. I'll show you where it is when we go back to the cottage and get ready to leave." She moved closer to him as she spoke. "I bought a nice little house for us."

"How did you get the money to buy this place?" he asked.

"Money is not going to be a problem. I paid cash for our new home with money from the settlement with your father. It was fairly inexpensive, at least by standards we're used to in Connecticut. Your dad was generous, I have to say. He hurt me emotionally, but did take care of me financially. I had to plan for an outcome in which we would have to get away, and I wasn't just going to leave my home in Fairfield County and a million dollars behind. So, one thing I hadn't told you—or anyone else, for that matter—is that I put my house on the market in the beginning of the summer and it sold just before I returned to Hunter's Point. I had a condo rental lined up in case our scheme to get me back there didn't work out. I've now completed shifting my funds into a savings account at a Canadian bank with a branch where we'll be living, and an investment account at a brokerage firm in Toronto, all under my new name, Mary Holmes."

"So, you're now going to be Mary Holmes?"

"As soon as we arrive at the Canadian border I will be, and maybe when we check into a hotel somewhere later tonight. I wanted to keep my initials the same. Oh, by the way, you've got to put new license plates on our cars before we leave. I have them with me, and the registrations, too. You should bury the old plates that are now on the cars in the woods and I'll burn the existing registrations."

"Okay, I can do that. So, what's my new name?"

"It's still Michael. I didn't think you'd want to change that, but you're also going to be Holmes. As far as the Canadian government is concerned, your father is unknown. I'm an unwed, single parent, and you're my only child."

"Pretty slick, Mom. Sounds like you've thought of just about everything."

"I hope so, although be prepared for anything that might happen when we get there. That's it, Son—new lives on the run with new identities in a new land. We tried our best to get back together at Hunter's Point and did so for a short while, but maybe it wasn't meant to be for the long term. We'll have to figure out a way to survive with this new life that's in front of us, and I'm confident we will."

"Well, if we're going to be fugitives, shouldn't we get ready to leave now and be on our way to our new homeland?"

"Not just yet, but very shortly. There's something I want to do. I'm tired and a bit sweaty from all we've done today and I'd like to get refreshed before we start out on our journey away from here."

Michael had a puzzled look on his face as his mother smiled lovingly at him. His look became one of shock as Miriam quickly took off her clothes and ran naked, diving head first after she had taken two or three steps into the body of fresh water. Swimming under water for several yards, she stood up in water that was now almost up to her neck. She motioned for him to join her. He took a few steps toward the water and then stopped in his tracks—staring out at her. After she motioned for a second time, he stripped off his clothes and ran headlong into the water. When he reached her, she put her arms around his neck and kissed him tenderly. As they embraced, she exclaimed, "That's the first time I've seen you nude since you were a little boy. You're quite a hunk! I can see why the girls like you."

"Come on, Mom, you're embarrassing me. And, Jesus, as for being in the nude, I've *never* seen *you* naked. This is really kind of strange."

"I know that, but I'm not embarrassed if you're not. And don't be surprised if you see me approach you without clothes on some winter evening when we're in our new house in Canada."

Michael was silent—totally dumfounded and speechless by what his mother had just said.

She then loosened her embrace and said, "We're going to be alone for a while in a desolate place with a very cold winter and many long nights ahead of us. We may both be lonely before we find new companions, so please try to understand the longings of a woman who was cast aside, and then found someone who satisfied her needs but had to leave because of our circumstances."

Michael trembled, trying to comprehend what she was saying, but still unable to respond verbally.

Miriam then dove back into the water and swam underwater most of the way back to shore. Standing up and facing her son, she said, "Let's go back to the cottage, dry off and put our clothes back on, put the new plates on the cars, and get out of here. It'll be dark when we're ready to leave. We'll travel as far as we can tonight. We should be able to drive through most of Massachusetts...perhaps to southern Maine if we're lucky and don't get too tired."

"Hey there...so where are you?" Dan asked Tony Kent, who was on the other end of a cell phone call.

"I went past the Mohegan Sun Casino exit on Route 395 a few minutes ago and am almost on I-95."

"Great...I'm glad to know you didn't take the exit by mistake and go gambling tonight," Dan cracked into his phone. "Well, then again, maybe you should have, since we're already taking a big gamble with this crazy trip."

"And where are you, Dan?"

"I'm just getting off I-95, not far from the Rhode Island border, and should be on Route 1 in a few minutes. So far, your directions are good, and I've got my map next to me if I need any further assistance. I should be there in about fifteen to twenty minutes, and I'm guessing you're five, maybe ten, minutes behind me. I got delayed a bit at my place. You may not believe this scenario."

"What's that?"

"The entire series of events with you, your mother and your sister was, I think, set up and planned by Miriam. Michael was apparently acting at her direction and guidance, which means this plot had to be in the works for a long time, maybe since soon after the divorce last year."

"Why do you say that?"

"She left a note in my dresser drawer, from which she took my revolver."

"What? She took your freakin' gun? I didn't know you had one, although I guess I shouldn't be surprised. How did she know you had a pistol and where it was?"

"Well, I sure as hell am not kidding about this. The note is on the front passenger seat of my car, underneath the map. As for how she got the weapon, I now recall we were talking one night about my days as a detective and then my retirement. I remember discussing firearms. In the course of the conversation, I must have said that I hung on to my revolver, a 38-calibre Smith and Wesson, even though I haven't used it since I retired, and kept it loaded and out of sight under my socks in my dresser. Don't ask me why I may have said that, but it must have been part of a casual conversation that evening when we were sitting on my deck sipping brandy."

"So, Miriam is armed. Maybe it was good that I stopped at home."

"Huh?" Dan replied.

"I'll explain when I meet up with you. Dan, if Miriam took your gun, that means she's on the run. Jeez…I wonder if she's going to the same place we are?"

"I don't know about that, but I do know she's meeting up with Michael somewhere and taking him away…far away…based on what she wrote. They must be driving two cars. The question is, where are they now and where the hell are they going? This is a big country. If they're not at the place we're driving to, then I'll call the state police barracks where Jenkins is stationed and get an all-points bulletin out for them. I know one of the cars they have—Miriam's. I'm not so sure about Michael's, though."

"I know Michael's car, so we're covered," Tony replied.

"Okay, good. I'm going to sign off now. I'll set flares when I get to the place."

Michael stopped to look around as he emerged from the woods, a shovel in his hands. He headed back to the abandoned cottage, where he saw his mother burning papers outside in the gravel driveway, registration forms from the Connecticut DMV and auto carrier insurance cards. "I buried the plates in separate locations in deep holes, so I don't think anyone will ever find them. It was nice of whoever used to own this cottage to leave a shovel under the back porch. The new plates are on the bumpers and the new registrations are in the glove compartments."

Miriam smiled at him. "If you can toss dirt on top of my little fire when the papers have been burned into ashes, that should take care of it."

She walked over to him and gave him a gentle kiss on the cheek.

Looking at the fire, Michael said, "That should only take a few minutes."

Dan stopped his car in front of the drive leading to the YMCA camp. He had seen the sign for the camp just as he approached the entrance drive. He got out two flares. Darkness was beginning to descend, and he wanted to make sure that Tony knew he had arrived there. He placed the first flare in the ground just off the pavement and lit it. He then started walking to a spot about seventy-five feet closer to the entrance drive where he would place the second flare, to give Tony a good signal.

Miriam was climbing the steps to the front porch of the cottage as Michael tossed dirt on the fire—the papers now completely burned. "I'll get my things and then we can get out of here and be on our way," she called back at him. "Do you have everything of yours, Son? We don't want to leave any traces that we were here."

"Everything but the clothes I had on before. I decided to change for the trip. I'll get them, lock the front door from the inside, and then climb out the back bedroom window and close it, so the next guy can get in, whenever that may be. Hopefully, not before we leave here tonight."

"You boys…so mischievous…but, I must say, this is quite a place for nighttime trysts."

As Miriam opened the door to the cottage and went in, Michael stood over the burnt papers. He held the shovel and was about to dig up and toss some more dirt to extinguish the remains of the small fire. Suddenly, Jon leaped out of the trees bordering the property and ran toward him. Before Michael knew what was happening, Jon had reached him and, with all the force he could muster, buried his right shoulder into Michael's chest with a perfect hockey check. Michael was stunned as he fell hard to the ground, letting out a shriek as he fell. Miriam heard him and came out on the deck.

"What's going on?" she screamed.

Jon then turned to her and said, "It's me, coming to get the liar who almost killed off my family." He then jumped on top of Michael, who was still stunned by the vicious hit that Jon had laid on him and the impact of hitting the ground so hard.

"Damn you," she yelled at Jon, as he started pummeling Michael. Miriam ran into the cottage and came out in less than twenty seconds brandishing Dan's revolver. "Get off of him or I'll shoot you," she screamed, starting to walk down the steps.

Michael had regained his senses and his wind and was able to give Jon, distracted momentarily by Miriam's screaming, a hard kick in the mid-section that knocked him backward and allowed Michael to extricate himself from Jon's grip. Miriam aimed the pistol toward Jon and pulled the trigger. Miriam had never fired a gun and the bullet went wildly over Jon's head. She lowered the revolver, aiming at Jon's legs, and fired again. This time the bullet hit the ground just in front of him, ricocheted and struck Jon in the right ankle, shattering his outside bone.

"You bitch," he screamed out in pain at her. He tried to get up, but he was immobilized. He writhed on the ground in excruciating pain. He reached down and tried to grab his injured ankle as Michael rose and brushed the dirt off his clothes.

"I didn't mean for it to end this way, Jon," Michael stammered. "We just wanted to get Dad and Susan out of Hunter's Point, not seriously injure your dad or make Katherine get so sick. I wish you hadn't come here. This complicates things."

Grimacing in pain, Jon retorted, "Well, that's tough shit, you bastard. I'll get your rotten ass if it's the last thing I ever do."

"You're not going to do anything, boy," Michael shot back. "We're going far away and in your condition, you're not in any shape to come after us—at least for a while. And, by that time, we'll be long gone."

"Come on, Michael, we've got to get out of here," Miriam then said forcefully.

"What are we going to do with him?" Michael asked.

Miriam shrugged. "We've got to leave him here. He's not bleeding, and maybe he can crawl back to his car, wherever that is, and call someone for help. Come on. We've got to leave. I'll go back in the cottage and get my purse and clothes. Get the stuff you need out of the cottage and lock up the place the way you do it."

Dan almost burned himself as the gunfire went off just as he was about to light the second flare. Shaking his hand, he lit the flare, and then ran back to his car. *Those two "cracks"...they sound just like Smitty,* he said to himself. *Is this possible? Can Miriam be here? And, if so, who would she be shooting at? Oh, no...please...not Jon! Well, I guess this tells me which side of the camp I go to—at least to get started.* He got into the car, drove past the entrance to the YMCA camp, and took a left turn into the first road past the camp, a dirt road with no name. He went about a hundred yards and saw a light in a cottage. He brought the car to a stop and pulled it to the left side of the dirt road. He walked quickly to an opening in a grove of trees. There were a number of cottages in front of him. He guessed there were four or five, and that the water was just in front of the one farthest from him. A light was coming from the third cottage. All the others were in total darkness. Then, the light went out. *That's got to be the one,* he thought. *They must have turned on a light and then turned it out. Or, if it's abandoned and the electricity is turned off, maybe there are candles inside. That would make sense...the boys who come here to "do their thing" by candlelight! If they turned off a light or put out a candle, they must be getting ready to leave. I can't wait for Tony!*

Dan raced toward the cottage. As he got within forty or so feet, he could hear someone groaning, as if in severe pain. As he approached the front of the cottage, he recognized a familiar figure, who also recognized him. "Dan, get out of here. Miriam has a gun," Jon shouted at him.

Suddenly, there was a noise from the cottage, the sound of a creaking door. Dan hovered over Jon as Miriam opened the front door and stepped out onto the deck.

Recognizing each other instantly, they stared at each other in the twilight. "You've got something that belongs to me," Dan yelled at her as he saw Smitty in her right hand. "And it looks like you've used it, which you said you didn't want to do."

"I didn't want to use it," she retorted, "but I had no choice. Jon got in the way."

Dan, who believed in surprise when in certain confrontations, decided not to respond with words but rather with action. He ran toward her, keeping his body low. He was at the bottom of the steps when the revolver went off again. Dan was turned around as the bullet ripped through his left shoulder. He fell backward onto the ground. "I don't believe it!" he cried out. "I've been shot with my own weapon."

"You shouldn't have come here," she yelled. "It would have been a lot easier if you had stayed home. Then we could have gotten away without a confrontation."

"My many years in law enforcement wouldn't allow me to do that."

"Then I'm afraid you'll have to live with the consequences." Turning back to the cottage, Miriam shouted, "Michael, we've got to get out of here…now. Forget about shutting the place down. Let's just get out of here! Get my purse and clothes, along with yours. I'll keep an eye on our two intruders." She turned back to face Dan, who was now on the ground holding his injured shoulder and looking at Jon's shattered ankle.

There was a look of anger on her face as she spoke to him. "Don't move, Dan. I'll shoot you or Jon again if I have to."

Michael was groping around, since it was now dark inside the cottage. "I can't see anything in here. I need to light another candle."

"Alright, do it…but, hurry up. There's a box of matches on the kitchen counter."

"I found them," came Michael's voice from the inside the cottage. A moment later, there was light inside the cottage. Then in another minute, it was dark, as Michael emerged from the cottage carrying Miriam's purse and their clothes.

Dan got up and started walking toward the open front porch where Miriam and Michael were now both standing.

"Don't come any closer," Miriam said sternly to Dan. "I meant what I said in my note. I'll protect him at all costs—even your life. And Jon's if necessary." She pointed the revolver at Dan and then at Jon as she spoke.

Dan stopped in his tracks, and then retreated to where Jon was sitting on the ground.

Miriam started walking slowly down the steps, holding the gun in front of her and pointed at Dan, as Michael walked closely behind her. As she reached the step just above the ground, Michael was a step behind her. Suddenly, from the left side of the cottage and hidden because of the darkness, Tony bolted toward them, raising a dark object as he ran. In one quick motion, he raised and then swung a shotgun downward and hit Michael in the back of the head with the barrel, just as he was about to take the last step. Michael fell forward from the force of the blow, crashing into Miriam from the back and forcing her into a forward free-fall toward the ground. As Michael landed on top of his mother, there was the loud blast of a single gunshot. The two fallen bodies lay in a heap. Neither moved.

Dan, looking in bewilderment at Tony, walked over to the two bodies. Michael was unconscious. Dan felt a lump on the back of his head where he guessed the shotgun barrel had struck. Even though it was getting dark, he could make out dirt marks, a bruise and bleeding on the front of Michael's face from the headfirst fall onto the ground. With his left shoulder bleeding and experiencing great pain from the bullet wound, Dan then motioned with his right hand for Tony to roll Michael off of Miriam, who they almost could not see because of the darkness and Michael's body acting as a cover.

Tony rolled Michael's body off of Miriam's. She was motionless. With his left hand, Tony grabbed her by the waist and rolled her onto her back. The revolver was smoking and still in the grip of her right forefinger, now pointed upward as her right arm lay on the ground. Looking closer, Tony could see blood oozing from the region of her heart and starting to cover the front of her light-colored short sleeve blouse. Tony looked at Dan and spoke. "She must have landed on the gun."

Dan nodded, his mind quickly processing the fall and what must have happened. He looked at Tony and Jon and then said, "Miriam definitely landed on the weapon. Her right forefinger must have accidentally pulled the trigger, which had to be the result of her instinctively folding her arms in front of her to try to break the fall. Her left arm must have gotten below the right, struck the ground first and jolted her right hand. Her forefinger, which you can see is curved and locked in a shooting position, must have pulled the trigger and discharged a bullet into her heart. The barrel of the gun probably moved from the jolt of her right hand, directing the bullet toward her heart."

Tony and Jon nodded but said nothing.

As she lay on her back, Miriam opened her eyes and looked up at Dan and Tony standing over her. Her lips started to move and, barely audible, she whispered, "Tony, you were not part of the original plan, but we couldn't resist taking advantage of the opportunity you gave us by having the affair with Susan. Please believe that we never meant to hurt you so badly, and tell Katherine that I never thought the poison in the tea bags would almost kill her. Dan, I've grown to love and hate you, which I trust you will understand. Please say good-bye to Michael for me. Much of what was done was for him, as well as for me. I'll take my unending love for him with me as I go away." Her eyes closed.

Dan knelt on the ground and put the first three fingers of his right hand on the left side of her neck. He then stood up and turned to face Tony. Shaking his head, as a single tear started to trickle down the right side of his face, he said, "She's gone. And now the nightmare that's been inflicted on an entire family at Hunter's Point should be over." Noticing the shotgun still in Tony's right hand, now hanging limply and almost touching the ground, he said. "I guess that's what you stopped at your home on the way here to pick up. I'm glad that at least one of us was armed with a weapon. This situation got a lot more ugly and violent than I ever thought was possible."

Tony looked sheepishly at Dan and said softly, "I may have had a weapon, but it was a good thing I didn't need to fire it."

"Why do you say that?" Dan asked, a puzzled look appearing on his face.

"Because it's not loaded. I forgot that I used up all the shells while hunting last fall. It's the only time I ever use it. I left my house in such a rush that I didn't realize I had an unloaded shotgun until I arrived here. If I had remembered, I may have grabbed something else. I got scared and felt kind of stupid when I heard the blast from your gun and saw you get shot. Luckily, my shoulder has healed so that I could swing the damn thing, sort of like how someone swung a fireplace shovel at me a while ago."

Dan smiled. "Weren't you the guy that said 'what goes around comes around'?"

Tony cast a wry smile back at Dan, and then looked toward Jon, who winked and smiled at his father as he fought the pain in his ankle. Turning back to look at Dan, Tony said, "Let me go to my car and get my cell phone. I'll call an ambulance to get you, Jon and Michael to the hospital for treatment, and Miriam to the morgue, and will bring back some rope to tie Michael's hands, just in case he comes to. Perhaps, Dan, everything has come around, since it seems to be my turn to take care of you guys tonight...a Friday night, no less."

"Yeah," Dan groaned, wincing in pain. "Another delightful one at the shoreline."

Chapter 27

On the following Wednesday morning, the courtroom was quiet as Judge Julian Frisk, having taken his seat, nodded at District Attorney Joel Stein. "Mr. Stein, I believe you wish to make a statement."

"Thank you, Your Honor, I do. In the matter of the people of Connecticut versus Susan Hunter, the state is dropping the charge of Attempted Murder against Mrs. Hunter, and asking for her immediate release. We would also like to express our regret to Mrs. Hunter for the accusations made against her and the difficult situation she has endured. We can only hope that Mrs. Hunter will find satisfaction in knowing that justice has prevailed and that she was not falsely convicted for a crime that she did not commit. In approximately thirty minutes, in the courtroom that adjoins this one, my colleague, Assistant District Attorney Allan Bentley, will be making a similar statement regarding the charge of Criminal Assault against Jerald Hunter and reading to the judge the same confession from Michael Hunter, the son of Jerald Hunter, that I am about to read."

Susan Hunter breathed a sigh of relief and, grasping the left arm of Thad Wilcox with her right hand, sank slightly into her chair as the district attorney looked over at her, a faint smile appearing on his face.

"Your Honor, I would now like to read a written confession from Michael Hunter that covers both cases involving the Hunters who are being tried by this court."

"Proceed, Counselor."

"Your Honor, ladies and gentlemen of the jury, and Counsel for the defense. The following are the written words of Michael Hunter, who was arrested in a hospital located in Charlestown, Rhode Island this past Saturday, after regaining consciousness from a head wound suffered in an altercation Friday evening in the Charlestown area, and brought back to Connecticut on Monday of this week, when the confession was taken."

Returning to his table near the front of the courtroom, Stein placed a typed paper in front of him and began to read.

> "I, Michael Hunter, acting on my own free will and, having been advised of my legal rights, confess to poisoning, with methanol, herbal tea that was consumed by my relatives Anita and Katherine Kent over several months this year. Further, I confess to striking Tony Kent, another relative, on Friday night of the fourth week of June, with a fireplace shovel that was in our house at Hunter's Point. The plot to poison the Kent ladies was conceived and planned at the end of last year and carried out in the winter and spring of this year. The attack on Tony Kent was decided on the spur of the moment, early this summer, after I discovered that Uncle Tony and my step-mother were having an affair and called my mother to inform her.
>
> The motive my mother and I had was to get my father and Susan convicted of crimes that would take them away from Hunter's Point and allow my mother to return and be with me. That is all we wanted—to be back together and rid of Susan. Since my mother could not reconcile with my father due to the divorce and his banishing her from Hunter's Point, we felt that my father also had to go, and the situation with Uncle Tony gave us the means to achieve our goal. My mother guided me and instructed me in what to do and when to do it. My mother and I loved each other deeply, were devoted to each other, and acted as a team.
>
> The plot to frame Susan involved poisoning tea that she was buying for Katherine Kent and that we knew Katherine and Aunt Anita were consuming. I got Susan's fingerprints on a syringe on two occasions when she was sound asleep in the early hours of the morning, and then—wearing thin rubber gloves and using the syringe—injected paint thinner from our tool shed into the tea bags. Mom told me to place the syringe behind the towels in the downstairs guest room bathroom, where she knew Susan and my father would not

go, since they never use that bathroom, but where the police might look. I used a shrink wrap machine to rewrap the outer plastic packaging to make the tea packs appear that they were from the natural food store where they were purchased. We always had an extra package ready to replace what Susan was buying, and I would come home to Hunter's Point from college every four weeks, which was the time cycle for the tea being purchased and delivered to Katherine, based on their consumption pattern. A mistake I made was leaving the shrink wrap machine in my closet when Mom returned after Susan and Dad were indicted, and I moved from our house into the cottage with her.

Regarding the attack on Uncle Tony, we thought that, because of the animosity that my father was feeling toward him—displayed in front of two witnesses besides myself—pinning a criminal assault charge on my father would be fairly easy to do. This opportunity arose because of the affair that Uncle Tony was having with Susan. I planted one of Susan's panties at Tony's cottage and one of Tony's lighters at our house, to get my father suspicious that maybe something irregular was taking place, which Susan subsequently admitted to. When Dad found out and threatened Uncle Tony, we planned the attack—using the fireplace shovel that Dad had brandished at Uncle Tony. After using it to strike him, I noticed a blood stain from Tony's head on the fireplace shovel when I replaced it. This turned out to be convincing evidence to the police that my father had committed the crime—especially since I used rubber gloves and knew that my father's fingerprints would be all over the shovel due to the many fires that he made at our house. The words I shouted at Uncle Tony just before I hit him with the shovel were those that Mom and I felt would be attributable solely to Dad. The fact that we are the same size and look almost the same in a dark place added to our belief that my father would be accused. Finally, driving Jon's girlfriend Nicole to a friend's place in Westerly, on my way to Charlestown, Rhode Island, gave me an alibi for the night of the attack."

Joel Stein then looked up and faced the judge. "That concludes our statement and reading of the confession by Michael Hunter, Your Honor. We move for dismissal of the charge against Mrs. Susan Hunter."

"So granted," Judge Frisk thundered, pounding his gavel. "Case dismissed. The defendant is free to go."

Susan, on her way out, noticed Dan sitting in the middle of the courtroom. "Thank you," she whispered at him. This time, Dan could read her lips clearly.

Forty-five minutes later, Susan and Jerry embraced outside the adjoining courtroom, after Jerry's case was dismissed and he was released.

Dan and Bill Jenkins, who had attended the two closing court proceedings, shook hands near where Jerry and Susan were embracing. Dan's left arm was in a sling.

"The state of Connecticut and its law enforcement agencies are indebted to you, Dan, for everything you did. We missed a lot that you picked up."

"Thanks for those thoughtful words. Now, Officer Jenkins, I'm going off to resume my retirement, and want to get away completely from the life of a detective that I thought I'd left once before. So, let's make our next get-together a social one—say, a barbecue with you and your wife at my place."

Epilogue

The following Friday night, they were gathered around Katherine's dining room table—Jerry, Susan, Anita, Dan and the host, Katherine. Tony was conspicuously absent and Jon was at school, having returned there on Monday with his injured ankle in a cast.

Katherine raised her glass of champagne and motioned for the others to do the same. Then she said, "Well, this has certainly been quite an experience. I hope we all have learned something from this. We've encountered anger, revenge, violence, illness and injury—physical and emotional. But, as I've grown to appreciate more and more as I've aged, what really matters is how we react to crisis and challenge. Let us remember what my father envisioned when he purchased this property and divided it between my brother David and me. We are a family and we need to come together and act like one. Tony will be staying away for a while, visiting Anita and me occasionally, and will certainly be here for holidays and other special occasions. Susan has assured me that anything between her and Tony is over, so we don't have to worry about any indiscretions among family members. Jerry has said that his jealousy and rage about the affair between Tony and Susan has subsided, and he's prepared to reconcile with Tony, so we shouldn't have to deal with this nasty and thorny issue any more. Jerry is also going to drop the assault charge against Jon. I didn't ask for what has happened here, and could complain about not deserving it, since I was a victim. However, I'm not going to do that. What I am going to do is ask that all of you do your part to make this family a loving and caring one that will stay together for the future. That's what my father and brother would want. Therefore, in spite of what they did to me personally and to this family, I mourn for Miriam and forgive her and Michael—who I hope will return to us someday. Finally, I want especially to thank Dan for everything he has done, because without his efforts we probably wouldn't be sitting here tonight as a family."

Smiles were exchanged, glasses were clinked and champagne was consumed, in a toast to more peaceful and pleasant times at Hunter's Point.